A Lot Like
FOREVER

A Lot Like
FOREVER

FROM THE AUTHOR OF *UNDER AN ALASKAN SKY*

JENNIFER

USA TODAY BESTSELLING AUTHOR

SNOW

Entangled Publishing, LLC
644 Shrewsbury Commons Ave., STE 181
Shrewsbury, PA 17361
Visit our website at www.entangledpublishing.com.

Amara is an imprint of Entangled Publishing, LLC.

Edited by Lydia Sharp
Cover design by Bree Archer
Cover art by massonforstock/Depositphotos,
franckreporter/Gettyimages, and
sunnychicka/Gettyimages

Interior design by Toni Kerr

Print ISBN 978-1-64937-213-0
ebook ISBN 978-1-64937-228-4

Manufactured in the United States of America

First Edition September 2022

AMARA

ALSO BY JENNIFER SNOW

BLUE MOON BAY SERIES

A Lot Like Love
A Lot Like Christmas
A Lot Like Forever

WILD RIVER SERIES

An Alaskan Christmas
Under an Alaskan Sky
A Sweet Alaskan Fall
Stars Over Alaska
Alaska Reunion
Alaska Dreams

COLORADO ICE SERIES

Maybe This Time
Maybe This Love
Maybe This Christmas

*"The strongest people are not those who
show strength in front of us,
but those who win battles we
know nothing about."*
~ Unknown

At Entangled, we want our readers to be well-informed. If you would like to know if this book contains any elements that might be of concern for you, please check the back of the book for details.

PROLOGUE

Ten Months Ago...

Rain pounded on the soft top of Whitney Carlisle's convertible Miata as she pulled out of the empty parking lot of the mayor's office. The storm raging outside, combined with her blurring vision, made driving along the coast toward Rejuvenation a hazard, but Whitney didn't have much choice. Her mom had taken a turn for the worse, contracting a severe lung infection that had her confined to her bed.

Intense crashing waves breaking against the shoreline was normally a breathtaking view on days like this, but today, they looked dangerous and uninviting. An involuntary shiver ran along her spine as she peered through the swishing windshield wipers.

Her vision had been terrible all day, slowing her progress at work. After several hours staring at the computer screen, her line of sight would narrow, and waves of dizziness had been tougher and tougher to fight. If Trent were in town, he'd be driving that evening, but he was away at a conference and wouldn't be back until the following week.

Cliffs to her right were jagged and deep, and large rock formations jutted from the ocean waves. Whitney's grip tightened on the steering wheel. She blinked several times to refocus on the lines of the road separating her lane from oncoming traffic. The asphalt felt slick under her tires, and heavy rain beat against the windshield, the wipers on full speed barely able to keep it clear.

A storm warning had been issued for that evening, and on the local radio station, officials continued to caution people to stay off the roads.

Maybe she should turn around at the next exit and head home.

She could call Rejuvenation and let them know she wasn't going to make it that evening.

But three days with no visit was too long. Her mother was sick, and she was refusing her meds again. Whitney knew the time clock was running out on her days at Rejuvenation. Moving her to a new, stricter facility farther away would break Whitney's heart, but she needed to do what was best for her mom.

Her gaze drifted through the window at the steep, winding curve ahead, and she swallowed hard, her knuckles white as she approached the turn, slowing her speed a little just in time to make the bend safely.

To her right, several small rocks tumbled down the mountainside and bounced across the road in front of the car. One hit the windshield, and she jumped. Then swore under her breath as the tiny rock chip spiderwebbed across the windshield.

Her eyesight narrowed, and she blinked several times, then squinted when it didn't work.

This shitty week could end anytime now.

Her mother always said that troubles always looked darker and more insurmountable at night.

Daybreak brought with it a new perspective, a new hope…

Whitney clung to that sentiment now just as a larger boulder appeared out of nowhere, cascading down the mountainside. Her blocky vision hadn't noticed it until it was too late. She gripped the wheel and hit the brake. Colliding with the boulder was sure death, but now the car swerved on the flooded road and started to spin.

Whitney held on tight as she lost control of the vehicle. Panic rising in the back of her throat prevented her ability to scream as the car crossed the yellow line, hit the shoulder, and flew over the short guardrail.

Airborne for seconds that felt like an eternity, Whitney closed her eyes and braced for impact.

The shriek of crushing metal.

Intense, searing pain.

And everything went black.

CHAPTER ONE

Now...

"Do you think the severed arm is too gory?"

Whitney glanced up from her laptop at the plastic Halloween decoration her friend Sarah was holding. With bruised-looking skin, a fractured bone protruding, and dark-red blood, the fake limb was eerily realistic, and she had to force aside her aversion to the upcoming spooky season as she contemplated critically.

"I think it will be fine for the adult tours. Maybe twelve and over?"

Sarah nodded and placed it in the "yes" pile, then continued sorting through the stack of decorations she'd bought in L.A. the day before—as soon as the Halloween pop-up shops opened in the city. Unlike Whitney, Sarah lived for anything Halloween. As kids, she always had the most elaborate, homemade costumes and won the prize for "most school spirit" more than anyone else. She spent her own money decorating the family home with tombstones, ghosts, witches, and goblins and had been featured on the local news for her extreme efforts.

This year, Sarah's recently renovated inheritance, Dove's Nest B&B event venue, would be transformed into a spooky haunted house for the whole month of October and host various

Halloween events in their small coastal town of Blue Moon Bay. Sarah's fiancé and business partner, Wes, had already started on the exterior decor of a decrepit, crumbling facade. Though he had voiced the irony that they could have left the inn in its former condemned state and saved themselves a lot of work restoring the place.

As head of marketing and tourism in Blue Moon Bay, working out of the mayor's office, Whitney was designing the haunted house announcement and marketing materials that would be distributed throughout Southern California the following week to announce the upcoming events. Small towns loved their holidays, and Blue Moon Bay was no exception. Tourist numbers being low in recent years, they needed anything they could get to draw people back to the community.

Seated next to Whitney on the comfy outdoor furniture on the B&B's deck, her best friend, Jessica, was scrolling through gory desserts on her cell phone. "Ohhhh, these frozen eyeballs would be perfect for the drinks."

Jessica owned the bakery in town, Delicious Delicacies, and had taken on the responsibility of providing desserts for the B&B's haunted house. And like Sarah, Jessica was all in.

Whitney shuddered as she glanced at the image of the realistic-looking eyeballs floating on top of bloodred martinis. "That's disgusting."

"You should see the zombie-themed cake I'm making," Jessica said, her eyes lighting up.

Whitney shook her head as she laughed. "It's so hard to reconcile my bubbly, sweet friend with this horror fanatic you turn into this time of year." As delicious as Jessica's baking was, Whitney would not be eating the desserts at the event.

She wished she could get into the spirit the way her friends did, but she was mentally already on to Christmas...and by Christmas, she'd be moved on to planning for spring. Working in the marketing industry, she was constantly a season or two ahead of reality, never really having time to stop and enjoy the one she was in. By the time she hit Submit on these materials and they were on their way to the printer, she'd be lucky to even notice the pumpkins popping up on porches all over town in the coming weeks, as she buried herself in festive images on stock photo sites and prepped all the brochures and posters for the local holiday schedule.

A cry sounded on the baby monitor next to her, and she jumped.

Sarah laughed, her face instantly taking on that love-crazed look only a new mom would have. "It's Henry. I'll be right back."

Jess jumped up and said, "I can get him."

But Sarah shook her head. "He'll need to be changed first."

"Okay." Jess sat back down with a grin. "You can get him."

Jess would have no trouble changing the baby, but they both knew Sarah was still in that protective new-mom stage where she liked to do everything the baby needed herself. She and Wes hadn't even had a real date night since the baby was born, but they didn't seem to be in a rush to leave baby Henry and his older sister, Marissa, with a sitter. They loved their family time, and it was endearing to see the four of them together.

A moment later, Sarah returned with the adorable four-month-old bundled in a soft, knitted blue blanket, his little foot sticking out one end. Jessica instantly reached for him.

Sarah pouted. "I just got him."

"He's yours. You can have him anytime. Auntie Jess only gets to cuddle him a few times a week. Don't be selfish," Jess teased.

Coupled up since Christmas with the local doctor, Jess was likely to be starting a family anytime now, too. Her best friends would probably race her to the altar as well. Though Whitney was already engaged, her wedding plans hadn't been firmed up. And sometimes it felt like they never would be.

Sarah reluctantly handed the baby boy to Jess, but instead of going back to her chair, she sat on the edge of theirs. Being two feet away from the baby would be too far. She gently touched his cheek. "Isn't he the most perfect thing you've ever seen?" she asked, staring lovingly at the tiny face poking out of the blanket.

Jessica agreed. "So perfect it hurts."

"He's smiling now, too," Sarah said. "Real smiles. Not the gas grimaces we thought were smiles a few weeks ago."

Jessica cooed and cawed at the child, trying to draw out one of those smiles, but the baby wasn't having it. Sarah tickled his chin, but still nothing.

"He's selective," Sarah said with a laugh.

Jessica cuddled the baby and begrudgingly

glanced at Whitney. "Want to hold him?"

Whitney shook her head, checking her watch. "I actually have to get back to the office." She closed her laptop, stood, and collected her things. "Sarah, I'll finalize these event promo brochures and send you the digitals for the website and social media this afternoon."

Sarah nodded, still distracted by the baby. "Sounds great. No rush."

What didn't sound so great was Whitney's abrupt refusal to hold the baby. She knew her friend was a little hurt by Whitney's standoffish way when it came to her child...but it was just difficult for a lot of reasons she wasn't quite ready to share with her friends yet.

But she bent to look at baby Henry and gently touched his toes peeking out from under the blanket. "Such a cutie," she said sincerely.

And the baby blessed her with a smile that had her chest knotting.

Sarah's shoulders relaxed a little. "See? He likes you," she said, and Whitney heard the slight note in her friend's voice that secretly pleaded for her to show more instances of affectionate Auntie Whitney.

"Talk to you both later," Whitney said, descending the stairs and heading toward her new car. It wasn't the banana-yellow two-seater convertible that had once been *her* baby, before she'd totaled it in a car accident the Christmas before. This one was a basic black SUV. Safe, dependable, better handling on slippery roads. And plenty of seats for the family her fiancé Trent envisioned in the not-so-distant future.

Whitney waved to her friends, and her hand shook slightly as she reached for the door handle.

Be cool in front of them.

Her friends tried to pretend that they weren't, but she knew they were constantly watching her lately. Since the accident, they all worried about her, and she was desperate not to show any sign of fear around them.

But her heart raced as she climbed in behind the wheel and started the engine. The memory of that night going off the road on the curvy, winding stretch of coastal highway was never too far from her mind.

It's only eight blocks and four minutes to the office.

Eight blocks and four minutes later, Whitney breathed a sigh of relief as she pulled into the parking lot in front of the tourism office and slid her sunglasses to the top of her head. Opening her purse, she retrieved her concealer and lowered the mirrored visor. The darkness under her eyes was getting harder to hide. She dabbed the light concealer onto her finger and reapplied it beneath her lower lashes, blending it in with her slightly darker tanned skin.

She grabbed her coffee from that morning from the console and got out of the car, forcing her legs forward.

What she really wanted was a nap, but if she gave in to that craving and fell asleep, she wasn't sure she'd ever wake up.

Seeing Scott Rodale's Escalade in the parking

lot, she picked up her pace. The mayor's son was back in Blue Moon Bay after finishing his master's degree in business at UCLA. He was currently working as her assistant, but Whitney knew he'd specialized in communications. Scott was smart, a real go-getter, and he was a fast learner. The nagging sensation that her job could be on the line only fueled Whitney to work harder.

"How was lunch?" Kim Digby, the office receptionist, asked as Whitney entered the office. Fall-colored, leaf-shaped garland entwined with orange lights hung from the desk, and a plastic pumpkin sat on top. The distinct smell of pumpkin spice lingered on the air from Kim's scented candles she liked to burn when no one was around.

"Lunch was good, thanks." If her lukewarm third coffee of the day and half a muffin counted as lunch. She couldn't remember the last time she'd eaten anything substantial. The night before? No, she'd been at the office past nine, and she refused to eat after eight. Lunch the day before? Nope.

But who had time to eat when there was always work to do, emails to respond to, calls to make?

Her workload was a challenge when tourism was steady. Lack of it in recent months made it even more so, as she was constantly striving to find new ideas to bring people to town.

Down the hall, through the open blinds in the office window, she saw Scott in his mother's office. Door closed.

They could just be having lunch. Discussing family stuff. Not executing Scott's plan to steal my job out from under me.

Still, instead of rushing off into her own office, she lingered a beat at the reception desk. "Did you finish that episode of *Love in the Books*?" she asked Kim. The latest reality show that had everyone talking was about a group of romance authors battling it out for a publishing contract. Who knew watching people write would be so fascinating?

Kim looked slightly surprised at the attempt at chitchat as she pointed to Netflix paused on her computer screen. "I'm addicted. I'm going to lose my job. Thank you for telling me about this show," she said.

Whitney forced a laugh. "You're the mayor's niece—I think you're safe."

Unlike me.

Whitney was a graduate of an online marketing course she'd taken part-time while holding down three jobs, a non–family member of the mayor's who could and would be replaced if she didn't continue to give 110 percent every day. She was lucky that Mayor Rodale had taken a chance on her, and in the last seven years, she'd refused to allow her boss any opportunity to second-guess that decision. She swallowed her unease. "Any calls?"

"Messages are on your desk."

"Thanks." Whitney walked into her office and closed the door.

Brilliant rays of midday sun shone through the large ceiling-to-floor window, warming the space. She adjusted her air-conditioning before sitting at her desk. Removing her shoes, she wiggled her toes, trying to regain circulation in her swollen feet. The usual icing hadn't been helping the last few days. By tomorrow, she'd be wearing flats.

She forced a breath. It could be worse. So much worse.

But anything that slowed her down annoyed her. She needed this job now more than ever. The cost of Rejuvenation, her mother's living facility, was a large expense every month, and there was no way Whitney would consider moving her to a more affordable home. No other job in town would pay her as much without a degree.

Like Scott's.

She flicked through the messages on her desk— two from local photographers following up on the quotes they'd provided to contract next year's Blue Moon Bay tourism calendar, one from a local artist hoping to showcase their work in the Winter Art Walk... She stopped at one from Rejuvenation. Her mother was refusing her Alzheimer's meds again.

Her mother could be so stubborn about it sometimes. Just the day before, Whitney had explained to her how important they were to take. And in her lucid state, her mother agreed. But during her more confusing times, she was more difficult to reason with.

Though forcing medication on her mother made Whitney feel like a hypocrite.

She continued going through the messages, seeing one from Trent. She knew why he was calling. He'd texted her as well. He wanted to confirm their appointment at the jeweler's that evening to pick out their wedding bands. At five o'clock, she'd be sending a "Sorry, got stuck at the office" text. He was pushing for a wedding date, hoping these trips to the jeweler's, bridal shops, and flower shops would get her in the planning mood faster.

She stared at the picture of the two of them on her desk. Their first date, taken at the local pumpkin patch. It had been a favorite tradition of hers every year as a child with her parents, but it had been Trent's first time there. It had quickly become their new tradition. They'd gone every year the last seven years...except last year when she'd been too busy to take the time off to go.

Seven years together.

If she could go back to that day a lifetime ago, knowing what she did now, would she have said yes to that first date?

• • •

THEN...

Whitney parked her brand-new banana-yellow convertible in Jessica's driveway and climbed out. She stood back to admire her very first car. She'd fallen in love with it the moment she'd seen it on the lot. Was it practical? No. But it was fun, fast, and sexy, and she was twenty-three years old. She had a whole lifetime to buy practical.

And besides, she was riding a high, and the car suited her current state of mind. Things were looking up. New job, new car, and new place...

Two days ago, she'd signed the lease on her own house and had officially moved out of the place she'd been sharing with Jess. It was an exciting time, yet she felt a tug at her chest as she walked up the front steps. They'd been roommates since high school graduation. They'd had some great memories together in the house, but it was time for Whitney to get her own place. A few months into her job at the mayor's office as head of marketing and tourism and a small down payment, she was feeling financially secure enough to make the move.

And as much as she loved living with Jess, they both needed their own space. It wasn't as though she'd moved far—she was four blocks away. They'd still see each other all the time. They may even be closer now when she didn't have to deal with Jess's messiness and Jess didn't have to put up with Whitney's late-night working, the sound of typing echoing off the walls in the small bungalow, keeping her awake.

This was the right thing. For everyone involved.

Whitney unlocked the door and entered. "Jess?" she called as she walked down the hall toward the living room, following the sound of someone getting up from the couch. Those damn creaking springs. She grinned. They'd furnished the place on a budget, and the secondhand couch had always been noisy. They kept saying they should buy a new one, but there was something sentimental about this one that neither of them had wanted to part with.

But now they were both doing well enough with Jess's bakery, Delicious Delicacies, a huge success in its first year and Whitney's new job—they planned on going furniture shopping together that weekend. No more creaky couch for either of them.

"Bet you'll be happy to get rid of—" Whitney stopped short at the living room entrance, seeing a six-foot-five, two-hundred-pound man standing there. A six-foot-five, two-hundred-pound *naked* man. "Shit, sorry. I didn't know Jess had company," Whitney said, covering her eyes with her hand. Then, because she was only human, she snuck another quick peek at the godlike, magnificent creature standing in her best friend's living room.

Where had he come from?

She'd only moved out two days ago. Why the hell hadn't her friend mentioned she was dating someone? They told each other everything. Had it been a one-night-stand situation? Had Whitney walked in on the guy before his walk of shame? Not that he had anything to be ashamed of. Nope. Nothing, another quick peek confirmed.

"It's okay," the guy said. "All clear."

Whitney removed her hand.

Hell no it wasn't!

He'd put on his jeans. *Only* his jeans. He was still standing there shirtless, and the muscles upon muscles in his chest, stomach, and shoulders were making her slightly dizzy. How did a person achieve a body like that? Perfectly sculpted yet smooth and almost soft-looking...

Betrayal immediately hit her. She was lusting after Jess's new guy. A sense of disappointment quickly followed. This guy was dating her friend, or at least had spent the night with Jess, which made him permanently off-limits if this was just a casual thing. Not that Jess really did casual. So even worse, Whitney was going to have a front-row seat to Jess's happily-ever-after with this man.

She was a terrible friend.

"Is Jess here?" she asked, trying to avoid looking at the amazing body, which was difficult when he took up so much space in the tiny room.

"She left an hour ago for the bakery," he said. "Can I help you with something?"

Huh, that was awfully forward. *She* was Jess's best friend. She'd been her roommate for four years. He was the newcomer to this situation, and he was acting like he and Jess were already an item?

Hold up, buddy! Don't go buying those his-and-hers towels just yet.

Although Jess would probably be thrilled to hear the guy was acting like a boyfriend already. Jess fell hard and fast for most of the men she dated. A hopeless romantic, she was already looking for "the one" and couldn't wait to settle down and start a family. Whitney would tell her all about it. It would help after the confession that she'd seen her boyfriend's junk.

"I just stopped in on my way to work to drop off my house key," she said. One that would now probably belong to this guy.

"You must be Whitney." He had a warm smile, and the most incredible set of dimples appearing on an otherwise very manly face.

"I am Whitney," she said, almost robotically, still captivated by the smile.

"I am Legend," he said, echoing her tone with a laugh.

She frowned. "Your name's *Legend*?" Not a typical name, but it was actually fitting. He didn't look like any real man she'd known in her everyday life.

But the guy shook his head. "No. It was a joke… like the movie." He shoved his hands into his pockets. "You know what, never mind. I'm Trent." He walked toward her, hand extended, and she took a step back out into the hall. No way was she making physical contact with the guy.

He dropped his hand awkwardly.

"I'm late for work, so I'll just leave this key here," she said, placing it on the table near the door. Another secondhand treasure that had an old telephone book propping up one of the legs to keep it steady.

"Sure. Okay. I'll let her know it's there," he said.

"Great. Thanks." She headed for the door. Quickly. The space inside the small house seeming a lot smaller with this guy in it, and she needed the fresh fall air to clear the image of his naked body from her mind.

"Hey, Jess was actually planning on introducing us later tonight at some pumpkin patch thing," he said behind her, "so maybe we could pretend this didn't happen."

Jess had invited this guy to their annual fall tradition? Without even asking her? She wasn't sure how she felt about suddenly being the third wheel on one of her favorite fall activities. Or having to hide her attraction to her best friend's date all evening. And she couldn't help the sudden territorial feeling she was struggling with.

She turned and frowned. "Jess and I are best friends. We don't keep stuff from each other. I'll have to tell her that I saw…" She pointed to his lower region, her cheeks feeling slightly flushed.

"Her cousin's penis? Maybe save her the gory details. That may just gross her out," he said with a grin.

Whitney's mouth dropped. "Cousin…" She racked her mind. Jessica only had one aunt. Another one of Frankie's kids? Whitney thought she only had girls. She couldn't remember ever meeting this guy…but he did seem a bit older. Thirty at least. "Why haven't I met you, then?"

"I moved to the city straight out of high school and just moved back. I bought the old tavern on Main Street. Jess is letting me crash here for a few days until I find a place."

Cousin, *not* boyfriend. Staying in Blue Moon Bay, *not* just visiting. An obvious setup for Whitney later that evening, *not* an awkward third-wheel situation.

This meeting had certainly changed course for the better.

"Well, welcome home," Whitney said.

The dimples were back, and this time she felt zero guilt for enjoying the sight of them.

"Thank you. It's great to be back," he said. "And when we officially meet later, I'll be sure to have clothes on."

"That's a shame, but probably for the best," she said with her own teasing wink.

CHAPTER TWO

Now...

A two-hundred-and-sixty-pound, six-foot-three bouncer sobbing like a baby was an unexpected sight.

Trent sighed as he *beep-beeped* his Jeep in his reserved parking stall and walked toward the entrance to his bar, Trent's Tavern, that evening.

"I told you, you can't work here if you're using," he told Max, his former bodybuilder competitor turned friend and employee, as the man stood outside, waiting for Trent to unlock the door. Weepiness could be an unfortunate and unpleasant side effect of steroid use.

Max wiped his eyes with the back of his tattooed arm and sniffed. "Nah, man. I'm clean. My sister in New York just sent a video of my niece playing with her new rescue kitten. Wanna see?" Max extended the phone toward him.

Trent shook his head. "And have two burly men sobbing like babies in front of the club? No." He laughed as he unlocked the door, and then they entered the bar.

"I thought Angel was opening tonight. Didn't you and Whitney have plans to look at wedding rings?" Max asked, tucking his cell phone into a pocket on his military-looking black cargo pants.

Trent's jaw twitched as he tried to make light of

his fiancée canceling on him again. "She had to work late." And wedding ring shopping could wait. Just like decisions on wedding dates, venues, flowers, cake…

"I thought *you* were ambitious, but that beauty of yours never seems to stop," Max said.

It was true, and while Trent knew Max meant it as a compliment, Whitney's demanding work schedule was putting a strain on her health *and* their relationship. But he'd never admit that to his friend. Any issues he and Whitney may be having were private, and they'd work through them together. As a team. He was confident that they'd just hit a bit of a rough patch this year. Things would get better.

He flicked on the interior lights, and his eyes widened as he scanned the place.

Angel, his club manager, had been busy, too.

Overnight, his tavern had completely transformed. Lacy, gauzelike black fabric draped across the open wood beams. Orange pumpkin-shaped string lights hung from every corner of the ceiling. Old-fashioned-looking black-and-white photos hung on the walls, the creepy, hollow eyes following him as he moved, the faces turning into skulls based on the angle at which he stood. A large animatronic vampire butler moved as he approached, bending to "offer" him a drink that looked like blood. Near the pool tables, a jumping spider sat waiting to terrorize unsuspecting victims. Everywhere he looked, there was a Halloween decoration to be discovered. "The place looks amazing."

"All Angel." Max confirmed he'd had nothing to do with the decorating.

"Where did she get all this stuff?" he asked Max. He hadn't noticed any large, unapproved charges on the company credit card he'd given her for ordering supplies and inventory.

"Said she had it all in storage from her move. Apparently, she used to decorate her house in L.A. every year for an annual Halloween party her husband would throw for industry VIPs. Her apartment is too small to use any of it, so she brought it here."

Angel had recently moved to Blue Moon Bay with her two teenage boys after a messy divorce with some famous director Trent had never heard of. And didn't want to know. Angel hadn't exactly opened up about the relationship, but he could read between the lines. Just the fact that the guy had left Angel and the kids high and dry, refusing to pay alimony and child support unless she took him to court, was enough for Trent to know.

But Angel was landing on her feet, and she was the best manager he'd ever had. Made even more obvious by the decor inside the club. Left to him, there might have been a pumpkin or two outside. She definitely deserved a raise.

Trent headed toward the bar and checked the supplies. They opened in an hour, and he suspected the place would be busy. This time of year, as the weather turned cooler along the coast, indoor dining and entertainment schedules resumed. His bar was known for good food and local entertainment. With two locations currently doing well, he hoped to expand even farther along the coast.

Of course, everything was refilled, restocked, and ready to go. He could always count on Angel.

"Hey, aren't you headed to the Bartenders Convention tomorrow morning in Las Vegas?" Max asked, removing his jacket and hanging it on a hook in the back room. Underneath, he wore the Trent's Tavern logo T-shirt staff were required to wear, but the logo was barely readable as it was stretched unrecognizable in the too-small, tight-fitting shirt. In Max's defense, getting one to actually fit the man would be a challenge. Trent would have to place a custom order, like he did for his own shirts.

"I canceled the trip," he said. "I have a lot going on here…" The last time he was away, just before Christmas the year before, Whitney had had a car accident. It was silly, but he couldn't help but feel nervous about leaving her alone. That somehow, he could keep her safe if he was there. She worked too much, too hard, and had apparently fallen asleep at the wheel. It was a miracle she'd survived the crash in her tiny two-seater soft-top convertible. Trent shivered just remembering the pictures of the crunched yellow metal at the scene of the accident.

Of course, Whitney would never admit to the stress she was still under, despite doctors' orders to slow the pace a little, but he could see it in her tired eyes and sudden weight loss from lack of eating. Confronting her about it only made her withdrawn and even more stressed, so he'd learned not to nag her, despite his major concerns. At least when he was there, he could make sure she got *some* sleep at night and force-feed her while she worked if necessary.

Unfortunately, lately, it almost seemed like she preferred when he was away. As though she could breathe easier when he wasn't around to keep an eye on her. He knew part of it was that she knew he was always on the verge of a relationship chat. He didn't want to put pressure on her about the wedding she refused to plan, but they'd been engaged for three years, together for seven, and he wanted to move on to other future plans.

That was his main motivation to expand. Maybe if his bar chain was financially lucrative enough, Whitney wouldn't feel like she had to work so much. He could help take the pressure off her. She worried about finances and being able to take care of her mother in the seniors' medical facility, but Trent was more than willing to take on that financial responsibility. If she'd stop being so stubborn and let him. Since moving her mother into Rejuvenation, Whitney wouldn't even entertain the conversation of him helping with those costs.

Seven years together and they still had separate bank accounts.

It was something he'd like to change. Something he'd hoped would change once they were married. Maybe she'd feel more comfortable blending that aspect of their lives then. At least he hoped.

"I could go to the conference," Max said, surprising him.

"Really?" He hadn't thought of sending someone in his place. Max had only been working there a few months. He hadn't thought the guy was actually going to stick around when he'd first approached Trent about the bouncer job. He'd thought Max was just passing through and needed a few shifts for gas money, but it had been two months now, and Max hadn't expressed any plans to leave just yet.

"Sure. Why not?" he said as he poured a glass of diet soda and took a sip. "I can attend all the seminars and sessions and report back."

"You're interested in bartending?"

Max shrugged. "Honestly, I'm not sure what I'm interested in, besides bodybuilding, but you know that lifestyle has a time limit."

He did. Always athletic from a young age and becoming addicted to working out as a teen, Trent had competed in bodybuilding competitions into his late twenties, but he knew it was too much of a strain on his health to go beyond that. He'd spent his competition money on this first Trent's Tavern location seven years ago and had worked his butt off to open the other location. The first two years in business had been the hardest. Never one to be book smart, he'd struggled to complete a business management course online, an accounting course after that, and then bartending and bar management courses whenever he could. He could now run every aspect of his business himself, and that gave him peace of mind and confidence.

But having other staff who were also knowledgeable made sense. If he planned to keep expanding, he'd need help and people he could rely on. Angel was a great addition to the team, but if

Max was serious about sticking around and becoming a bartender, he'd do his best to encourage and facilitate his buddy's transition into a different career as well.

Trent nodded. "Yeah, you know, that's actually a good idea." The conference tickets he'd bought a year in advance before the popular event sold out were nonrefundable. Now they wouldn't go to waste.

Max cleared his throat. "Maybe Angel should come, too..."

Ah, so the guy *did* have his eye on the single mom. Trent had suspected there was more to Max's eagerness for extra shifts, and he saw the two of them laughing and flirting sometimes as they worked. But Trent knew Angel was still processing and adjusting to her new life, and she had her hands full with her teens. She didn't strike him as being quite ready for a new relationship yet, and there had certainly been enough male attention focused her way.

Trent felt a protectiveness over her, as if she were one of his sisters, so he pointed a finger at Max. "Be careful there. She's not ready for you yet," he said with a grin but also a warning tone.

Max held his hands up. "Don't worry about me, man. I'm just saying if she needs a rebound, I'm up for being used."

Trent laughed. He'd once thought of himself as just the rebound guy, the casual fling guy, the no-strings-attached guy, too. But that was before he'd met Whitney...

• • •

THEN...

Not only had Jess introduced him to the most beautiful, smart, funny, and caring woman Trent had ever met, but she'd also helped him make a valuable business connection. As head of marketing and tourism for Blue Moon Bay, Whitney was the perfect person to ask for help with the promo for the tavern's grand opening event.

Having the excuse to spend time with her again had taken the pressure off actually inviting her out on a real date after the pumpkin patch group outing the week before.

But he was doing a miserable job trying to hide his intentions—he couldn't even take his eyes off her as she toured the newly renovated bar. Dressed in a slim-fitting, professional business suit, her long blond hair pulled away from her face in a low ponytail, three-inch heels echoing on the wooden bar floor, she was absolutely intimidating.

She was so far out of his league, but the week before at the pumpkin patch, they'd seemed to hit it off. He hadn't exactly made the best of impressions earlier that day when she'd walked in on him naked, but he thought he'd redeemed himself by carrying the heaviest pumpkin she could find and had to have all around the farm the entire evening, so that no one else could steal it. His arms still ached, but seeing her laugh whenever she'd look at him, trying to seem unfazed by the eighty-pound, awkwardly shaped gourd in his arms had been worth it.

He'd yet to debrief with Jess to see if Whitney had said anything about him, but he was dying to know if he even had a shot. She was one of those women who would make a man give anything for just another minute of her time. Right now, he had her attention, and he hoped she liked the renovations and changes he'd made to the old bar.

He waited, watching her expression as she scanned the interior. When she smiled, he released a sigh of relief.

"Good?"

She nodded. "More than good. It's amazing. Hard to believe it's the same bar."

Her praise meant so much, and he barely knew her. He sensed she was the type who would give it to him straight, so her opinion mattered. His mom and sisters were just so happy and proud that he was back in town and on this new life path that it was hard to discern if they were being completely honest when they claimed the bar looked great, or if their judgment was clouded by love. Either way, he valued their support.

"I can't believe you left the old jukebox," Whitney said. Clipboard in hand, she made notes of the things she wanted to mention in the grand opening event flyer and added the jukebox to the list.

"Are you kidding? It was the best part. I don't think the previous owners knew what they had in this old classic beauty. I certainly didn't tell them," he said with a laugh. The Rock-Ola 1414 President was from the 1940s and valued at $50,000. Trent couldn't believe the previous owners had included it with the sale price.

Whitney gently touched the machine, her hand stroking the smooth finish, and Trent had never been so jealous of an inanimate object. "Does it still work?"

He reached into his jeans pocket for a coin and handed it to her. "Give it a try."

She popped the money in the slot, and the machine lit up. So did her expression in the neon glow, and the tug he felt in his chest told him he was a goner. Before meeting her, he would definitely have classified himself as a one-date-per-woman type of guy. He liked to have fun and spend time with the guys. In his twenties, he'd had no desire to settle down or be in a committed relationship. He hadn't really felt the shift, but since meeting Whitney, he knew he wasn't interested in just a casual thing with her. His mother had always warned him that one day he'd meet someone who would completely captivate him heart and soul. She'd been right. And he was utterly terrified that this woman he'd just met held the power to destroy him.

Whitney peered through the glass at the song selections and, settling on one, she keyed in the numbers. The first few beats of an old twangy country song started, and he grinned.

Could the woman be any more perfect?

He started to hum the melody, and she turned to him in surprise. "You like country music?"

"I even know how to two-step."

Her eyes narrowed. "You're kidding."

He extended a hand to her.

She glanced at it, and he held his breath in her momentary hesitation. Did she feel the same connection to him as he did to her? Had the night at the pumpkin patch been something she'd been thinking about all week as well? Was he someone she might be able to see a future with? He hoped so, because all of a sudden, he saw the new future he wanted for himself. In that bar, there with her… everything suddenly fell into place, and everything made sense. He wasn't freaked out or worried. He had zero doubt in his mind that she was the one for him.

As soon as her hand touched his and he was drawing her closer into his arms, he knew he wanted to hold that hand and hold her in his arms forever.

"I actually don't know how to two-step," he confessed. "But maybe we could sway?"

She moved closer and rested her head against his chest. And they swayed.

CHAPTER THREE

Now...

"How's the haunted house looking?" Trent asked above the sound of the wind whipping through the open windows of the Jeep as they drove along Riverside Drive toward Rejuvenation Assisted Living the next day.

"Creepy," Whitney said distractedly, typing furiously on her iPhone. She needed to get to Rejuvenation to convince her mother to take her pills, but shit was hitting the fan back at the office. The latest fall events promotion brochures had arrived that morning with a huge, glaring typo right on the front page.

Of course, Scott had been the one to discover it.

Arguing with the designers that she hadn't approved a proof before they were sent to the printers was sapping her energy. And on top of that mess, a press release had gone out the day before with the wrong date for the Fall Carnival.

That one *may* have been her fault, but the damn font they'd used made it very hard to tell the difference between a 1 and a 7. Once again, Scott had been the one to call attention to the mistake. He did have a good eye, she'd give him that.

Trent placed a hand over the phone screen.

She shot him a look. "Did you say something?" she asked, swiping his hand away.

"I said, I hope you're not taking on any of the work to make sure that the B&B is ready."

"Of course I am."

"Of course you are," Trent said on a deep breath as he pulled into an empty space in the living facility parking lot.

Whitney glanced up from the email she was typing. "What's that tone supposed to mean?" She turned in the passenger seat to face him.

Behind his dark sunglasses, she could see his disapproval. He thought she was a workaholic, and maybe she was. But that hadn't bothered him when they first met. Back then, he'd admired her strong work ethic. And he worked long hours at the bar, ensuring its success, expanding quickly over the last few years. It was okay for him to be ambitious, but not her?

"It means that I think you're overcommitting again."

Whitney blinked. "Excuse me?"

Trent held up a hand. "Nope. You're not getting an argument. I just meant that you do this—you take on way too much, and you wear yourself out."

One time. The one time she'd shown any sort of weakness, passing out behind the wheel after several long projects, and he used it against her. Last time she showed any weakness, if she could help it. "I'm fine."

Somedays, keeping her illness a secret, even from Trent, was the hardest part, but she had too much going on right now to have everything crumble around her. Pretending things were fine was the only way she could survive her heavy workload, and the latest bill from Rejuvenation reminded her how important it was to keep her employment.

These recent mistakes had her anxious enough. Scott lurking in the wings, ready to pounce on her position the moment she messed something up, had her suffering from nightmares whenever she did try to sleep. Being self-employed, his own boss, Trent couldn't possibly understand the pressure she was under. If she told him, he'd only insist she take time off and start to take better care of herself. She knew she should, but that would mean relying on him more, and her independence streak was deep-rooted.

Being adopted at a young age, she'd never quite shaken the feeling of needing to be self-reliant, despite amazing, supportive parents and wonderful friends. She trusted Trent more than anything, but there was still a small part of her that kept a guard up in self-preservation.

Trent touched her shoulder. "You're amazing. But that doesn't mean you have to do everything for everyone all the time. You have your own career, your mom to take care of..." He paused. "And a wedding to plan."

Her eyes narrowed. "So that's what you're worried about—the wedding. You think I'll put off making decisions because I have all of this Halloween and fall stuff on my plate for the next few weeks." Work was hardly the reason she refused to commit to wedding plans. Planning things was what she did for a living. She could bang out the details for the entire event in less than an hour with her extensive local contact list and hard-earned relationships in town with vendors. The time commitment wasn't a factor in her delaying.

"Won't you?" Trent challenged, obviously not willing to drop the issue.

"No. As a matter of fact, I decided on wedding colors yesterday." Or right this second. She had to give him something. Get him off her back for now. She was too busy to keep having the same discussions.

"Wedding colors?" he asked slowly, as though it wasn't quite a huge step forward.

She held her chin high. "A lot of other decisions depend on the wedding colors." At least that's what she'd heard Jessica and Sarah say. Or caught wind of it when she tuned out as they discussed wedding plans. Which seemed to be all the time…when they weren't talking about the baby, of course.

"Okay. What are they?"

"The colors?"

Trent nodded. "Yes, the colors. What have you decided?"

Whitney fought to control the tightening in her chest. So much pressure. It was just freaking wedding colors. "Um…blue and silver." There. Decision made.

"What shade of blue?" Trent asked.

Did it freaking matter? "A light blue…like sky blue."

"Silver and sky blue. You mean like the Rejuvenation logo over there?" he said, pointing to the sign she was desperately trying not to stare at directly.

Damn. "Yes. Exactly like that." She grabbed her purse and reached for the door handle.

"Whitney."

His voice made her pause, and the feel of his hand on her cheek melted her annoyance. He'd make things so much easier if he were an asshole. If the passion between them had faded in the years they were together, she'd have a reason to postpone their future together. If their friendship wasn't so strong, it would be easier to hide her hesitancy. If he didn't know her better than anyone, she could fake how she was feeling.

"I'm happy with any color you choose, and I'm okay with your indecisiveness. What worries me is *why* you're struggling with this," he said, brushing a thumb along her jaw.

She swallowed the lump in her throat. He was such a good man. Caring, loving, supportive… He deserved so much more than what she could give him. The words—the truth—were always just there on the tip of her tongue. But, as usual, she swallowed them back. "It's nothing. I'll make a decision soon. Lots of decisions." Including the biggest one she hated to make.

She got out of the car, and Trent took her hand as they entered Rejuvenation. Right now, she had other things to worry about.

Inside, it was a relief to see that the seniors' home looked the same as always. No fall or Halloween decorations in sight. They didn't decorate for the seasons or the holidays. They kept the rooms and common areas the same so as not to confuse or hurt the patients who may not be aware of the passing time or seasons.

"Hi, Marla," she said, approaching the reception desk. The attendant was one of her mother's regular nurses and had been working with her for the more than two years since she'd moved her mom into the facility. Prior to that, her mother had been living with Whitney and Trent, but when the Alzheimer's had gotten so severe that her mother had been afraid of them, they'd had no other choice but to do what was best for her. "How are things today?"

Please let one thing go right this week.

The nurse's expression wasn't promising. "She's not having a good day."

Whitney's chest tightened. "Did she take her meds?"

Marla shook her head. "She keeps refusing. Whitney, I know you know what that means."

Her mother would need to be moved to a stricter facility with doctors who had the authority to force her mom to take her medication. Or have an additional nurse assigned just to her mom's care. Rejuvenation was for seniors with mild illnesses, those that needed a little extra help sometimes. Her mother's illness was getting worse, and her time at Rejuvenation was limited, unless Whitney could afford the additional costs of individualized care. "I'll try to talk to her," she said. She took a deep breath, steadying her emotions, pushing everything else aside.

Days like today were the hardest.

Marla led the way down the hall toward her mother's room. The sound of a seniors' fitness class to their left and a bingo game being called in the dining room to their right had Whitney struggling with the sadness desperate to strangle her. This was such a great place for her mother. But trying to get her mom to participate in the activities here was a challenge. Her doctor believed that if she exercised and interacted more with the other seniors, her memory might improve a little, or at least it would slow down the progression of the aggressive disease.

But her mother preferred to be alone. She missed Whitney's father, and the void in the woman's heart was upsetting. Whitney missed her dad, too. With him gone five years now and her mother slowly slipping away, she would be alone soon.

She glanced at Trent and squeezed his hand tight, drawing strength from him.

"It will be okay," he said.

She wished that were true.

Marla knocked on the partially open door. "Lydia, you have visitors."

"I'm tired," her mother said. "No visitors today." Her back was turned to them, her gaze lost somewhere outside her window, at the ocean in the distance. Her hair was matted, and she was wearing the same nightgown and housecoat she'd been wearing when Whitney had visited two days before.

She needed to get here every day.

The staff did their best, but they couldn't force residents to do things they didn't want to do. Her mother needed *her*, and she couldn't give in to exhaustion at the end of the day or use her own illness as an excuse. Her mom came first.

"These people are really nice. You'll like them," Marla said. She turned off the television and the radio and closed the curtains. Eliminating distractions made it easier to communicate and hold her mother's attention. "Stay as long as you like," she told them before closing the door.

"Thank you," Trent said, sitting in the armchair next to the bed.

Whitney approached her mother. "Hi, Lydia. I'm Whitney." Keeping her voice steady and eyes free of tears was the hardest part. Keeping the mood positive and light was essential not to upset her mom, and it was often the most exhausting part. Seeing her mother like this was torture. She used to be so strong and independent. She'd been a marriage therapist with a successful practice until she'd gotten sick. She'd done yoga every day and had been otherwise healthy. Now, she looked so weak and frail. Lost and alone.

Whitney choked on the lump rising in her throat and swallowed it down. She could break down later. In private.

Her mother looked at her.

Please come back. Please recognize me.

"Whitney. What a lovely name. My husband and I couldn't have children, but I'd always liked that name."

She nodded. "Thank you. You and your husband did have a child—you adopted a little girl late in life." How many times had she said those words? It was important to be honest with her mother, remind her of things, but some days she thought it would be easier on everyone if they pretended to be visitors like Marla said.

A look of confusion appeared in her mom's dark eyes as she shook her head. "I think you have me confused for someone else, dear," she said.

Chest aching, Whitney smiled. "Did you want some help getting changed?"

"No, thank you. I just finished organizing my clothes."

Whitney glanced at the dresser in the corner. Clothes spilled out over the overstuffed drawers. The closet was empty. Tomorrow, her mother would take everything from the drawers and hang it all in the closet. She did this on the days Whitney didn't make it in for a visit. The doctor said it was her way of staying busy, feeling like she'd accomplished something.

Whitney went to the drawer and took out her mother's favorite blue-and-white-striped T-shirt. "I like this. Can we put this one on?"

"I don't think it will fit you, dear. You're so tiny," she said.

Whitney set the shirt aside. She'd try again later.

Her mother sent a sidelong glance toward Trent. *"Psst."* She nodded Whitney closer. "Is he a cop?"

"No. He owns a bar in town. Trent's Tavern."

"Damn. I thought he might be able to help me."

"I can still try to help," Trent said, standing and approaching. "What do you need?"

Lydia waved him closer. He bent at the knees to listen and meet her gaze.

"The staff here are stealing from me," she whispered.

"What are they taking?" he asked.

"My wedding ring," she whispered, her forefinger and thumb circling her ring finger of her left hand. "I can't find it. And now my husband thinks I don't love him. That's why he hasn't been by to see me in a few days."

Whitney turned away, needing a second.

Hallucinations were a side effect of the medication, but they gave her mom comfort. Without the meds the last few days, the visions of her father had stopped. Meaning other effects—the important ones that helped with these episodes of forgetting—had, too.

"Well, then we need to find it," Trent said.

"Do you know where the nurses might be keeping it?" Lydia's eyes widened.

"You know, you could be right that the nurses took it, but my guess is they put it somewhere safe for you," Trent said, standing and scanning the room.

"Maybe…" Lydia said, not convinced.

Whitney watched as Trent opened a jewelry box on the dresser and retrieved the antique wedding band. "Is this it?" he asked.

Her mother's face lit up.

God, she loved this man so much.

He handed her mother her ring, and she slid it on effortlessly. She'd lost a lot of weight since moving into assisted living. Refusing her meds often went hand in hand with refusing to eat or bathe or participate in activities. The ring dangled from her thin finger, and Whitney knew the nurses kept it in the box so she wouldn't lose it for real.

"Thank you, young man," her mother said.

"My pleasure," Trent said. "But hey, could you do something for me?"

Lydia eyed him suspiciously. "Like what?"

He picked up her pills and a glass of water. "The nurses here really ride my ass when you don't take these, so you think you could help a guy out?"

Lydia's laugh made tears spring to Whitney's eyes, and she wiped them fast before anyone saw.

"Fine. Hand them over," Lydia said, taking them and washing them down with the water.

"Thanks," Trent said, winking at her above her mother's head. "Now, how about you change into that shirt and I'll kick your ass at Gin."

"You're on," her mother said before turning to her. "Can you help me?"

"My pleasure," Whitney said, and she sent a grateful look to Trent.

What would she ever do without him?

• • •

After every visit to see Whitney's mom, Trent always felt the tug of guilt at not seeing his own mother often enough. As the only male child out of five, he always teased that he was his mother's favorite. And she always retorted that he would lose that place of honor if he didn't start visiting more. He was the only one living in Blue Moon Bay, so there were no excuses.

After grabbing two pumpkin spice lattes from Delicious Delicacies, he headed next door to his mother's shop, Frankie's Fabrics. She'd owned the fabric store on Main Street since before he was born. As a kid, Halloween had always been a favorite of his. His mother would bring him and his sisters into the store as soon as the festive prints arrived before putting them out on shelves, and they'd each pick out their costume pattern and fabric. And she'd also make them Halloween pajamas for after trick-or-treating.

"Hello, hello!" he called as he entered the shop. He saw several women perusing the patterns and a few others matching colors to wall paint samples.

His mother's head was barely visible above a tall stack of Halloween fabrics on the cutting table. "You better have caffeine," she said.

He laughed as he carefully handed her a cup over the fabric pile. "Would I dare visit without it?" From September until January, his mother's shop was hectic. Other times during the year, things were steady, but it was the last quarter sales that essentially kept the small shop in business.

His mother took a big gulp and shot him a grateful look. "Thank you! I was about to text Jess for a delivery." Trent loved that two of his favorite people had shops side by side. He knew Jess was like another daughter to his mom, as his cousin had spent a lot of time at their home while her antique-dealer parents traveled the world, looking for treasures to sell in their own local shop. It also made him feel better knowing Jess was nearby in case his mother needed anything. She was in good health in her early sixties, but after watching Lydia's health decline so quickly, he knew how fast things could change.

He scanned the fabrics. "Need some help?"

"Grab those scissors to your right," his mother said, repositioning her glasses on the edge of her nose.

Trent grabbed them, set his own coffee down away from the material, and got to work. Each stack of fabric had the order pinned to it. Customer name and amount they needed. He knew his mother always cut 10 percent more, because she claimed everyone always underestimated how much they really needed. Of course, she charged them for what they'd initially ordered and they were none the wiser.

She took a secret pleasure whenever they'd come in and report they'd had "just enough," never revealing her secret.

Trent knew how to cut fabric, having helped her in the shop over the years.

"So, good news," he said. "We have colors."

His mother's eyes predictably lit up as she turned her attention toward him. She pulled out a stool and sat, allowing him to work while she watched. "Really? That's progress."

He nodded. He wouldn't tell his mother that he called bullshit on it being progress and more that Whitney had felt trapped into giving him an answer about something. His mother loved Whitney and was so excited about the wedding. His mom was concerned about Whitney lately, just like everyone else, and he wanted to try to ease her mind a little. And a part of him was grasping at the hope that this one decision might lead to others.

"What are they?" Frankie asked, sipping the latte.

"Light blue and silver."

His mother immediately shook her head, disappointment in her expression. "Those are Sarah's colors. She's already selected the bridesmaid dress fabric and is planning on a winter wedding. She and Wes already have a date."

Damn. He knew it. He forced a laugh. "Well, then scratch that. We don't have colors." He cut along the length of fabric with a friendly ghost pattern on it and avoided his mother's thoughtful gaze. "Sarah and Wes already have a date, huh?"

He was happy for his friends, and with the pregnancy the year before, they'd pushed off their wedding date, but it made sense they'd get to the altar first. They were so much in love. Sarah was an amazing mom to Wes's daughter from a previous marriage, and the new family was picture-perfect, running an event center out of the B&B together and Wes's construction company thriving.

"January first," Frankie said. "I'm surprised Whitney didn't tell you."

"I'm sure she just forgot. She's got a lot happening at work." More likely she hadn't wanted to tell him for fear of it spiking a new conversation about a wedding date of their own.

He could tell his mother was biting her tongue, holding back a similar comment. He appreciated her ability to know when he didn't need any more doubt added to his own thoughts. "Hey, so I found a possible location for the third bar," he said, tying a piece of string around the cut fabric and reattaching the order slip.

"Already? Wow. The Game Room location just opened a couple of years ago." He heard a note of caution in her voice. He knew she was worried about him expanding too much too quickly, but truth was, his bar was the only thing besides his relationship that he'd been truly passionate about since he gave up weight lifting. Working out, competing had been an addiction, and giving it up had been difficult. It had left a huge gap in his life. The bar—and Whitney—had filled that gap.

He feared losing both…and the impact that would have on him.

"But it's doing great."

"That's wonderful, honey," his mother said supportively. "I can't wait to see it." Break over, she jumped off the stool and got back to work beside him. "I was thinking family dinner next Sunday? We haven't all gotten together in a while. Kara will be back from college on break, and I'm inviting your other sisters and their families, as the kids are on some school holiday on Monday. They won't have to rush back to the city. You and Whitney free?"

He nodded. "I am, and I'm sure Whitney won't turn down the chance to see everyone," he said, forcing more confidence than he felt into his tone. She hadn't gone with him to his mother's house the last several times he'd visited, and he knew his mother was desperately trying to be supportive and not show how upset Whitney's absence made her. The two had always been really close, especially with Lydia's failing health. He hoped to somehow help them get that closeness back.

"Wonderful," his mother said with a smile. He knew that smile was hiding her own skepticism that she'd be seeing her future daughter-in-law next Sunday.

• • •

THEN...

Trent had never introduced a woman to his family before. There had never been anyone else in his life who he'd wanted to take home. Family was the most important thing to him, and allowing someone close enough to join that tight circle had never happened before. Until now. With Whitney.

And luckily, in this case, his mother knew Whitney probably better than he did, being Jess's best friend, yet Trent still felt nervous as the two of them walked hand in hand up the front steps to his family home on Christmas. Dating for more than two months, they'd really connected, and it was time to bring her home to "meet" the rest of his family.

Not as Jess's best friend. But as his girlfriend.

Of course, he hadn't exactly asked her to be his girlfriend yet. They hadn't really put a label on what was happening between them. But they weren't dating other people, and they spent practically every evening together... They still hadn't had sex. A lot of kissing, touching, and intense make-out sessions, but they were taking their time.

But Trent knew he wanted her to be his girlfriend. He wanted her to be much more than that.

He was definitely in love with her, but he was worried about saying the words too soon and scaring her off. Whitney was so strong and independent, he was nervous that maybe she didn't want anything more serious than what they had. She was younger than him by almost eight years—he might be ready for the next chapter of his life, but she may not be on the same page yet.

His arms stacked high with Christmas presents, he allowed her to go ahead of him to open the front door.

The noise and chaos that greeted them from inside warmed him. He loved his big family and when they were all together like this. It didn't happen often enough with his older sisters married and living in other parts of California and his younger sister, Kara, an annoying teenager who would prefer to be with friends than hang out with family.

But that day, everyone he loved was in the same room.

As they entered the living room, where his family had gathered to open presents, Trent's nervousness grew. How did he introduce her to his older sisters, who may not really know her all that well?

"Hey! There he is," his sister Rachel said, taking the stack of gifts from him. She eyed Whitney with unconcealed interest. "And who is this?" Her tone suggested his mother had filled them all in already on the fact that he was dating someone and was bringing that someone to Christmas for the first time ever.

His sister was setting him up.

"Um, Whitney, this is my sister Rachel. That's her husband, Grant, over there and their son, Dawson. Sitting under the tree is Michelle, and that's her husband, Craig, on his phone near the window…" Starting with the family was easier. It gave him a moment of reprieve before he had to decide how he was going to introduce her. "Those little troublemakers are my nieces Joy and Bethany. And you know my sister Kara." He pointed to the teen, wearing her headphones and watching YouTube videos on her phone. He paused. Hesitated. "And everyone, this i-is…"

Whitney turned to look at him as he continued to hesitate and stammer. "Who am I, Trent?" she asked with a look of teasing challenge in her pretty eyes.

A room full of expectant faces waited for his answer. Sweat pooled on his lower back, and his mouth was dry.

He swallowed hard. "This is Whitney. My girlfriend," he added, staring into her eyes. He held his breath as he waited for her reaction. He could sense the approval and acceptance from his family around them already, catching grins from the corner of his eye.

And when Whitney smiled, all the tension eased from his shoulders.

"Damn right I am," she whispered to him as they joined the others.

Seated next to her under his family Christmas tree, surrounded by the sights and sounds of love and happiness, Trent knew he wanted to spend every Christmas, every Easter, every family event and every Sunday dinner with her there with him.

"This okay?" he asked her.

"This is perfect," she said sincerely, squeezing his hand. "This feels like home."

Trent couldn't remember having made the holiday wish, but somehow he'd gotten exactly what he wanted.

CHAPTER FOUR

Now...

Whitney checked the time on the clock hanging on the boardroom wall. Three minutes after nine. She cleared her throat. "I wonder where Scott is. He did say nine o'clock, right?"

Mayor Rodale nodded, glancing up from her phone. "I'm sure he's just running a little late. He hasn't found a new place in town yet, so he's still commuting."

From San Diego. Three months into the job and he still made the long trek through a traffic nightmare to get to work every day. Made Whitney wonder if he was as committed to moving back to Blue Moon Bay as his mother thought he was. If so, wouldn't he have found a place by now?

Still, she wouldn't get her hopes up or let her guard down anytime soon.

"Hey, sorry I'm late," he said a second later, entering the boardroom with a stack of vision boards under his arm.

He may be late, but he came prepared. She sat straighter as he moved to the front of the room.

"Thanks for meeting with me," he said, setting the boards on the display easel and picking an imaginary piece of lint from his suit.

He'd dressed the part today as well.

Business casual was the typical dress code in the

office, and she was used to his dress pants and short-sleeve dress shirts. Today, his charcoal pinstripe suit, purple shirt, and silver tie meant he wasn't messing around. Whatever this was about was important to him.

"Absolutely. What do you have for us?" Mayor Rodale's full attention was directed at her son now, and Whitney shifted in her seat. Maybe she needed to put together a formal presentation of her own about some of her new ideas, like creating a new town website. Her boss hadn't seemed as optimistic that an updated site, featuring local businesses, would impact tourism as Whitney was, but maybe she just needed to deliver the idea in a more concrete way with projected numbers and stats... and vision boards.

Scott smiled as he flipped over the first board on the easel.

Television viewer graphics. Sitcoms, documentaries, TV dramas, and reality television were presented by age and income demographics.

"Television is one of the leading advertising venues—the average American spends six hours a day in front of a screen. However, it's an opportunity that Blue Moon Bay tourism hasn't been able to take advantage of...yet." He glanced at Whitney.

She sat forward. "Television ads are also expensive on our smalltown budget, and research shows that an ad needs to be seen an average of seven times before a consumer responds to it. Our highway billboard advertising has made the most sense in that daily commuters, such as yourself, get that repeat imagery." Whitney looked at Mayor

Rodale for her agreement, but the woman was unreadable, just nodded for her son to continue.

"Right. I totally agree. The billboards are fantastic," Scott said. "I'm just talking about additional exposure. Exploring avenues we've yet to break into."

"It's not that we haven't thought of other avenues…" She paused and changed her tone. She didn't want to sound like she was on the defensive, but Scott had to realize that she'd considered this option before. "But unfortunately, our budgets are tight, and between the road signs and the tourism video and yearly calendar, there's not much wiggle room to experiment." She'd love to run television ads, too, if their small-town budget could accommodate them.

He smiled, undeterred. "Okay. But what if I had a way to spotlight Blue Moon Bay during prime-time viewing to the younger, high-income-bracket demographic we are trying to target…without it costing us a cent?"

She scoffed. "Nothing is ever free, Scott."

"What opportunity are you presenting?" Mayor Rodale's interest was certainly piqued.

Oh, come on. There was no way Scott could deliver what he was suggesting.

He replaced his vision board with a new one. "*Race Across America* is one of the leading reality television programs as far as repeat viewers…in the twenty-four to forty-eight age bracket."

"Yes, but an ad slot during those episodes would cost thousands." Their limited funding couldn't even secure a twenty-second promo ad during late-night infomercials.

He nodded. "I'm not talking ads. I'm talking about this." He slid a media release across the table toward her.

Mayor Rodale leaned closer to read over her shoulder.

"The show is filming its sixth season starting in March, and they are looking for new challenge destinations. Key checkpoint towns for contestants to visit to advance in the race. See, each leg of the race, teams have to perform certain tasks—"

Whitney held up a hand. "I've seen the show."

"Great. So I say we pitch them Blue Moon Bay as a location for this season."

Mayor Rodale nodded, her smile wide. "Yes. This is a great idea…"

"Okay, but can we accommodate the show's requests? We don't want filming to interfere with our regular tourists… What about liability insurance?" Had Scott done all his research on this? Where was that vision board—the one with the risks and possible issues with this idea?

"These shows carry insane liability coverage, and contestants sign waivers for their participation. And March is one of the slowest months for tourist season, so this will give us a little boost."

"I agree with Scott," Mayor Rodale said.

Whitney's stomach twisted as she nodded. "Yeah, of course. I do, too."

"So, Scott, what are the next steps? How do we apply?" Mayor Rodale asked.

She was already on board with this? It had taken Whitney six months of providing research stats on the effectiveness of the billboard advertising to get the funding approved.

But if Scott was right about this not costing anything, it was less of a risk financially.

"We pitch Blue Moon Bay as a challenge location to the show's executives."

"That sounds like an easy meeting to secure," she mumbled under her breath and immediately regretted her sarcasm when her boss shot her an odd look. She needed to be a team player. And if Mayor Rodalc liked this idea, she needed to be in support of it, too.

And it would be a great opportunity for the town if they could secure a spot on the show. Damn it, why hadn't she ever thought of this? Reaching out to production companies with a press release, highlighting the beauty and filming potential in Blue Moon Bay would have been so simple. And shit, she was practically addicted to *Race Across America*—she'd watched every season so far.

"I have a friend who works on the filming crew," Scott was saying. "I'm sure I can get us a pitch meeting if we submit an application." He stopped and turned to her. "That's if you're good with this, Whitney."

They both stared at her.

She forced a smile. "Of course I am. It's a wonderful idea." Her jaw clenched. "Great job, Scott."

Mayor Rodale sat back in her chair and nodded. "Good. This is really good. Scott, if you can arrange that meeting, I have no doubt the two of you can put together a fantastic pitch."

The two of them.

Whitney pressed her lips together. What could she say? After all, this was Scott's idea.

"Of course, Whitney will take lead on this. I'll assist when and where needed," Scott said, surprising her.

Mayor Rodale looked hesitant, and Whitney felt nauseous. But her boss nodded her agreement as she stood. "Okay, let me know if I can help in any way. I trust you both to make this happen."

She could trust Whitney to make it happen. Scott may have gotten the ball rolling, but she needed to be the one to secure this win for them. Scott had just given her another opportunity to prove why she was the best one to do her job, and she couldn't fail.

• • •

"Another round for lane eight," Marsha called to Trent from where she collected several beer mugs and her tip from a recently vacated table.

"Coming right up," he said as another group sat at the table.

Tuesday nights were always the same at the Game Room that hosted the bowling alley, ax-throwing room, and theater in town. It was one of the busier nights of the week with leagues and half-off pints offered from his bar. His tavern on Main Street was popular on weekends, but this location was arguably his most lucrative and regular week-night activities kept the place hopping without the really late hours.

He poured the pints of beer and placed them on a tray for Marsha as Jess approached the bar in her Bay's Singles bowling team shirt. She'd stayed on the team, despite not being single anymore. No one seemed to mind, though, since the team consisted of another on-again/off-again couple and several divorcées. The league's purpose was for singles to mingle, but in a small town, where everyone knew practically everyone, anyone could join as long as they didn't have a wedding ring.

His cousin liked to tease her boyfriend, Mitch, and remind him that there was only one way to get her to quit…

Trent suspected that proposal was coming any day now. He'd seen Mitch and his mother whispering a few times when they were all together. Definitely scheming something.

"Hey, Jess, the usual?" he asked.

"Yes please," she said, climbing onto a barstool. "Whitney working tonight?"

"Yep, apparently Scott pitched an idea to try to land a spot on that reality TV show, *Race Around the World*."

Jess's eyes widened. "You mean *Race Across America*?"

He shrugged. "Sure." He wasn't a reality TV fan. The shows always felt contrived and scripted for drama and conflict.

"I love that show! That would be so fun to have them filming here."

Trent didn't share his cousin's enthusiasm. This new project on top of Whitney's already full schedule meant more stress, more overtime, more pressure. But of course, he'd only shown support when she'd told him about it earlier that day. He'd learned his lesson about showing concern about her workload. "I guess," he mumbled.

Jess frowned. "You're still really worried about her, aren't you?"

He nodded, allowing his frustration to show. He could be honest with Jess. She cared about Whitney the same as he did. She'd often broached the subject with her best friend about slowing the pace a little, too. But nothing good had come of it. "She acts like she needs to do everything for everyone and that she can't take her foot off the gas for even a second."

"I know she's worried about Scott," Jess said. "She feels her job is threatened."

"How could Mayor Rodale *not* recognize what an asset she has in Whitney? She's been a fantastic and loyal employee for years."

"I agree, but I can understand why she's concerned. Scott is family, and sometimes things aren't fair."

Trent finished pouring the beers and placed them on a tray for Jess. "I just wish she'd take a day for herself just to relax. Maybe you and Sarah could invite her to a spa day or something?"

"Sure. Who can say no to massages and pedicures, right?" she said as positively as possible, but they both knew the answer to that.

Whitney could.

"Hey, are you both going to the Keller-Marshall wedding this weekend?" Jess asked.

Trent raised an eyebrow. "We were…but I'm

guessing I'll be flying solo now that Whitney has this new pitch to work on." He didn't even need to ask if she'd be working that weekend, and he suspected she would be relieved to have a valid excuse to miss another wedding. She'd been avoiding them as much as possible.

"Well, you're welcome to come with Mitch and me," Jess said, placing cash on the bar and picking up the tray.

"Thanks," he mumbled. He was tired of being the third wheel whenever Whitney bailed. Regular date nights used to be a thing with them, and she never used to miss important events in the lives of their family and friends. In the last two years, things had changed. He couldn't remember the last real date they'd had. Just the two of them without cell phones, emails, or interruptions. He missed the time together.

"Hey! Quit it, man!"

"You quit it, asshole!"

A commotion near the arcade caught his attention, and he turned to see what the yelling was about. Two teenage boys were pushing and shoving each other near the antique PacMan game. He squinted in the neon lights to see who the trouble-makers were.

Damn, one of Angel's boys.

He dropped his dishtowel onto the bar and hopped over it to hurry toward them. A group had now gathered around to watch the action. He pushed his way through the sea of teenagers. "Hey!" He got there just in time to see Angel's son Eddie throw a punch that landed squarely on the jaw of a smaller, younger teen.

Shit.

"Hey, break it up," he growled, stepping between the two boys before the other kid could
retaliate. His cheek was red and already swelling
fast. They struggled to move past Trent to continue
the battle, angry glares flashing in their expressions.
"Both of you calm down."

Realizing they wouldn't get past him—being a
human wall of muscle had its perks—they
retreated, but only slightly.

"What's going on?" he asked.

"This jerk just pushed me out of the way to take
over the game," the other kid said, jutting his chin
at Eddie.

"He was playing for an hour. There are other
people waiting," Eddie said, folding his arms across
his chest.

"That's not how it works here, *city boy*," the
other kid spat, moving closer. "You play till you
lose."

Eddie's nostrils flared, and he took a step closer,
too.

Trent held the two of them apart. He suspected
this wasn't the first encounter between them. They
most likely attended the same school. Angel had
said her sons were having a tough time adjusting to
the smaller school, and the other kids hadn't been
as welcoming as she'd hoped.

"Look, you two, it's just a video game." It
looked like it was more than that, but neither of
them would comment.

The boy's cheek was now bruising, and he

touched it and winced.

"Let's get you some ice for your cheek," he told the kid. "And you, Rocky Balboa, have a seat," he told Eddie. "I'm not done with you."

Eddie looked ready to refuse but then slumped into a chair, arms still folded, a deep scowl on his face.

Trent led the way to the bar. "He's new to town. You and your friends should try cutting him some slack. Maybe include him so he doesn't feel like an outsider."

The teen scoffed. "We did. He said he didn't need friends, 'cause he wouldn't be slumming it here for long."

So the teen hoped to move back to the city. That didn't surprise Trent.

"Well, maybe try again," he said.

The boy just shrugged.

After getting the injured teen settled with a bag of ice, leaving him with his group of friends, Trent approached Eddie. His angry expression was focused on the group across the arcade. Trent sat next to him. "Care to tell me what that was really about?"

Eddie didn't look at him. "No."

"You sure?"

"Look, I know you're my mom's boss, so go ahead and rat me out."

Trent sighed. "I don't want to get you in trouble with your mom. But I also can't allow violence in this place. And that kid and his friends are not likely to let this go."

He shrugged. "I don't care. Let him come at me again."

"By the sounds of things, you started this," Trent said.

The boy's jaw clenched as he stood. "I don't have to take a lecture from you."

Trent stood, and the boy cowered slightly, only reaching Trent's chest. "No, you don't and I'm not giving one." He sighed. "Look, I know it's tough moving to a new place, starting a new school and all that, but you'd have an easier time if you made an effort."

His expression changed slightly from anger to sadness, but then it was gone again in a flash. "Whatever, man," he said, turning and leaving the arcade.

Trent watched him go and waited to make sure the others didn't follow him out. They'd gone back to having fun, the incident forgotten except for the shiner already appearing on the boy's face.

He couldn't quite explain the protective instinct he felt, but he wished there were a better way he could help the kid.

CHAPTER FIVE

Now…

You are missed…

The video text messages from Jess were killing her.

Sitting on the edge of her bed that Saturday evening, Whitney watched Trent on the dance floor at a friend's wedding with a dozen kids ranging from toddler to teenagers. An up-tempo hip-hop song played, and her fiancé was busting out all his best moves. The kids were laughing as he attempted a break-dance maneuver and fell on his butt.

He was amazing with kids. He loved children. Being from a big family, with three siblings, he wanted lots of kids of his own. Two of his siblings were married already, with big families, and Trent visited them all in San Diego every chance he got. He was by far the cool, favorite uncle. On their first date, he'd mentioned wanting six children, a big, noisy house like the one he'd grown up in, and Whitney had since talked him down to three, secretly hoping once the babies started arriving, he'd settle for two.

You have to stop letting him go stag. Lots of single women here are ready to pounce, the caption from Jess read.

She knew her friend was kidding, but Whitney didn't doubt it. If things ended between them, Trent wouldn't be lonely long. The thought made her chest tighten, and she forced several deep breaths.

Grabbing a stack of marketing brochures for the town, needing artwork approval, she sat back against the pillows, refocusing her thoughts on work, and Trent entered only moments later.

"Hey, what are you doing still awake?" he asked, kicking off his shoes.

"Just waiting up for you." The last few weeks had been tense, and she longed to feel close to him again. It was selfish, but the headaches and blurry vision, spontaneous pains in her chest and legs, were happening more and more frequently, and he was the only thing that made it all better. Even if only temporarily.

He removed the shirt and tossed it in the general vicinity of the hamper. It missed and dangled from the edge.

It was hard to care about Trent's messy ways when he was built like The Rock. Muscles as far as the eyes could see dipped below the waistband of his jeans. Until Trent, she hadn't known an eight-pack was possible, and the layers of muscle in his forearms made every steroid popper at the gym envious.

He removed his dress pants and socks and climbed into the bed next to her. Immediately, his big arms were around her, pulling her on top of him. "I assume this is why you waited up?" he said, his hands sliding up her exposed thighs beneath his college T-shirt. She always wore his shirts to bed.

Her body ached with longing as she leaned lower to kiss him. "You assumed right." She needed to talk to him. She needed to tell him everything. But right now, she just needed *him*.

He seemed pleasantly surprised, as though he'd expected her to push him away to get back to work. How many nights had she done that? How many evenings had she been too tired, too busy, too distracted to give him the love and attention he deserved?

"You know how much I love you, right?" Trent asked, serious as he brushed her blond waves away from her face.

She swallowed hard. Those crystal-blue eyes so full of affection, she could see his love. Feel it in every part of her being. His gorgeous face was the one she wanted to wake up to every morning for the rest of her life. Seven years together, they'd been building toward forever... "Is that the problem?" he asked when she didn't answer. "I haven't been making it clear how much I adore you?" In one quick motion, he'd reversed them. Supporting his weight on his insanely sexy biceps, he lowered his face to her neck, leaving a trail of hungry kisses along her collarbone.

Desire for him eased her guilt over letting him believe her distant coolness was a result of lack of attention. She wasn't the clingy, demanding type. She was independent and strong. She didn't need Trent—she *wanted* him.

But it was unfair to him to let him marry her when she could never give him everything *he* wanted.

He lifted the edge of the T-shirt, sliding his strong hands along her stomach, inching higher to cup her breasts.

She closed her eyes as her body awakened.

How could she walk away from him? His love and devotion rivaled his passion for her. He was everything she'd ever wanted.

If only she could be that for him.

She clutched his shoulders as he leaned closer and captured her mouth with his. Desperate, searching kisses had her gasping.

"I want you, Whitney," he murmured against her ear, his warm breath against her neck making her shiver.

"You can have me."

At least for now.

• • •

THEN…

Spending the holidays with Trent's family had only solidified Whitney's feelings for him, and being accepted into the warm, caring family meant so much to her. Her own family consisted of her adoptive parents, who were a lot older. Their home was safe, secure, and loving, but it had never been the laughter- and fun-filled environment she'd experienced with the Connollys.

It had only made her fall harder and faster for him.

And that evening, sitting inside his apartment with a raging thunder-and-lightning storm outside that had cut the power, reducing them to battery-operated tea lights and board games for entertainment, Whitney knew it was time to take things to the next level.

"And I win again," Trent said, raking in the pile of Hershey's Kisses—their poker chips—in the middle of the coffee table as he won yet another hand.

"Where are you getting all the aces? And how are you so good at these games?" Monopoly, Clue, Scattergories, trivia…he'd won them all.

He laughed. "Family board game nights gave me lots of practice, I guess." He unwrapped a Hershey's Kiss, extended it toward her lips. She opened her mouth, but instead, he popped it into his own.

"Hey! Not nice."

"If you want chocolate, you're going to have to actually beat me at something," he said with a grin.

Whitney got up off the floor. "I can kick your ass." Maybe it was the whiskey talking or the false confidence she had in her two years of karate lessons. Either way, she was bouncing on the balls of her feet, fists clenched in front of her face and challenging the man who had 130 pounds on her to rumble.

Trent nearly choked on the chocolate as he laughed. He slowly set his own whiskey glass on the table and then got to his feet. "Remember, you asked for this."

"Bring it," she said, throwing a quick, light jab in his direction. It connected with his upper abs, and it didn't escape her notice how solid they were.

Damn, dude was smokin' hot.

How on earth had she managed to keep from having sex with him this long? Three months.

Ninety days. That was her general rule. If a man could make it past the "probationary period" of their relationship, then she'd entertain the thought of physical intimacy. Very few guys made it. And she'd be lying if she said she hadn't been tempted to break her own rule and waive the waiting period this time with Trent. Their make-out sessions had gotten hot and heavy lately, and there were a few nights…

But no more waiting.

Trent moved around her slowly, as though calculating, stalking, waiting for the perfect opportunity to make a move in.

She rotated, adrenaline coursing through her as heat rose in her body. She threw several more punches toward him, which he blocked with ease.

"That all you got?" he asked.

When she went for the sidekick, he saw his advantage and took it. Grabbing the extended leg before it could make contact with his hip, he moved in close and dropped her until she was hovering just inches from the floor.

Caught unaware and slightly out of breath, she stared up at him. His face was so close to hers. Her breathing was labored as she clung to the front of his shirt.

"What was that about kicking my ass?" he asked.

"I went easy on you," she murmured.

"I seriously doubt that," he said, his gaze landing on her lips.

She licked hers, inviting the kiss she so desperately wanted. Passion flashed in his expression when his gaze met hers again.

He lowered his head, and his mouth captured hers.

They fell the rest of the way to the floor, his hand gently placing her head against the soft carpet. His body pressed against hers, and she wrapped her arms around his neck, drawing him closer. Never wanting to let go.

Desire fueled through her as she deepened the kiss, savoring the taste of the whiskey on his lips. His hands rested on her hips and slid upward slowly. His fingers toyed with the base of her shirt, and she moaned her approval against his mouth.

His hands slipped inside, smoothing over her stomach and up higher over her rib cage. Her body trembled as she reached for the base of his shirt. This was it. This was the moment she'd torturously made them both wait for.

Trent broke contact with her mouth and sat them both up to remove the articles of clothing. Then he slowly laid her back down and buried his head in the crook of her exposed neck, placing kisses along her skin, her collarbone, her chest…his caress moving lower.

Whitney swallowed hard, her hands tracing the contours of the muscles on his back as his kisses left her wanting so much more. He was by far the hottest man she'd ever dated, and their time together was everything.

They'd only been together three months. Could these strong, overwhelming feelings be real? As much as she was lusting for him right now, they definitely felt like more. She was falling in love with him.

He seemed to sense a hesitation as he broke away slowly and stared down at her. "This doesn't need to happen right now," he said. "I can wait. However long you need."

But he wanted it, too. She could feel just how badly pressed against her leg. She swallowed hard as she stared up at him. Only they could know when was the right time. For them.

And right now, her body and her heart were saying she was ready. "Make love to me, Trent," she said.

His gaze was loving as he lowered his head back toward hers. His hands slid lower, unbuttoning her jeans and tugging the fabric. She lifted her hips to allow him to slide them down over her ass, hips, and thighs. He followed the fabric down the length of her body, removing them and tossing them aside before removing his own jeans.

His cock strained against the front of his underwear, and a mild panic took hold. While she'd obviously thought about this moment with Trent, fantasized about it, she hadn't really contemplated what it meant to be with a man as large as he was.

He was large everywhere.

His gaze took in the direction of hers, and he laughed gently. "It's not as big as it looks," he said with a teasing grin as he lay back between her legs.

She wasn't so sure about that.

What she was feeling pressed against her body certainly wasn't small.

"And don't worry, I plan to make sure your body is perfectly ready for me," he whispered against her mouth.

Damn, she was practically there already. She could feel the wetness on the inside of her underwear and tingling between her legs.

Trent lowered his mouth to her neck and kissed and sucked gently, making her entire body come alive. He removed her bra and placed a trail of kisses along her chest, over her breasts…down her stomach.

Whitney closed her eyes, enjoying the feel of his mouth on her body. His kisses were intoxicating. She wanted to wrap her entire body around him and hold tight. She craved to be as close to him as possible.

He reached for the waistband of her underwear and slid them off over her legs, his fingers gently caressing her flesh. A prickling sensation flowed over her skin, and she shivered slightly.

"Cold?" he asked.

"Just the opposite," she said as she lay there completely naked and exposed, but without any feeling of vulnerability. She was safe with Trent in this intimate space. She already knew she could completely trust this man. That she could rely on him and give herself to him without fear of getting hurt.

He removed his own underwear, and, reaching for a condom from his jeans pocket, she watched as he rolled it on over the large shaft before rejoining her. When he did, he repositioned them to put her on top.

"This way, it's all at your pace. You're in control," he said, his hands gripping her thighs as she slowly positioned herself over him.

She pressed her hands down onto his chest as she felt the tip of his cock at her wet opening. She wanted him inside her so badly, it was hard not to hurry. But she slowly lowered herself down farther, taking him inside her carefully, gently.

Trent's grip on her tightened, and he moaned at the pleasurable sensation. It felt so amazing to have him filling her so completely. So thick, so hard, so long. Every inch of him hitting all the right spots inside her.

His gaze took her in as she moved slowly up and down, riding him.

"I could stare at you all day," he said when his gaze met hers.

"You're not too bad on the eyes, either," she said, quickening her pace a little.

Weeks of foreplay, flirting, kissing, and touching had her desperate for a release. Whenever they were together, she couldn't stop touching him, kissing him, just wanting to be near him.

He was all-consuming, and she hadn't realized just how intense the attraction between them was until that moment, when their bodies were connecting and it felt as though their hearts and souls were also one.

Trent grabbed her waist and lifted her up and down. "I know I said you're in control, but I'm going out of my mind."

She smiled as she lowered her upper body toward him and kissed him. She continued to ride him, now harder and faster, grinding her hips into him, pushing her pelvis as close as possible while deepening the kiss. They were both panting and desperate for air, but neither broke the contact between their lips.

"Whitney, I'm close," Trent murmured.

She was, too. Dangerously close. Close to orgasm...and more incredibly, close to falling in love. She held tight to him as she brought them over the edge.

And seconds later, she let herself go...

Surrounded by the romantic flickering tea lights and the sound of the storm raging outside, Whitney free-fell into complete ecstasy and love.

CHAPTER SIX

Now...

Trent hummed as he stacked clean beer mugs behind the bar on Main Street the next day.

"Someone's in a good mood today," Angel said, entering the bar twenty minutes before her shift was scheduled to start.

He shrugged casually as he turned to greet her. Truth was, the night before with Whitney had him riding a high. Their sex life had always been amazing, but in recent months, the frequency had reduced. When they were first together, they had sex almost every night. Sometimes multiple times in the same night. Her energy and fiery passion for life had unsurprisingly extended to the bedroom.

The past year, though, things had...not fizzled out exactly, just became a tamer, more controlled flame, and the fire wasn't lit as often. But that happened in all relationships. It was natural. Over time, things changed, evolved. He was prepared for that. It didn't mean their connection wasn't as strong or that their love was starting to fade.

But last night, that original, new relationship passion had returned, and it was more of a relief than he'd expected. He'd missed her in a lot of different ways lately, including their physical connection.

"It's a good day to be in a good mood," he said.

"Tell that to my boys," Angel mumbled as she removed her jacket to reveal the tight, V-neck Trent's Tavern logo T-shirt that was part of her uniform. Stylish, form-fitting jeans and low-heeled boots completed her look. She'd turned a lot of heads since moving to town, and he suspected she was the reason his male clientele had increased by 10 percent in recent months. But he worried about her. She looked thinner, and the dark circles under her eyes seemed to be getting increasingly darker.

He wished there was something he could do to help. Maybe if by some miracle Whitney agreed to a spa day with Jess and Sarah, he could suggest Angel tag along. She hadn't really made a lot of friends in town yet, and he'd been meaning to try to make that connection. She and Whitney had the same hardworking, independent spirit. He knew they'd get along great.

"Still struggling, huh?"

"*Struggling* is an understatement. Eddie won't talk to me unless it's completely necessary, and Liam won't come out of his bedroom." She slumped onto the barstool across from him, and he poured an iced tea and slid it toward her. "I know they miss the city and their old rooms and their father...lord knows why," she said under her breath. "But I just wish they'd give this place and this new life a chance."

He nodded. He wasn't sure if Eddie had confessed about the fight at the Game Room, and it wasn't Trent's place to say anything. The family needed to figure things out, and he still wasn't entirely convinced that the fight had been entirely

Eddie's fault. Sure, he'd thrown the punch, but the other teen hadn't been completely innocent in the whole thing.

"Do you want advice, or are you just looking to vent?" Growing up with three sisters had been very educational. Women didn't need saving when they were expressing feelings. Sometimes they just needed someone to listen.

Angel sighed, her thin shoulders sagging slightly. "Mostly venting. But if you do have any ideas on how to get them to like me again, I'm all ears."

He wasn't sure if teenagers ever saw eye to eye all the time with their parents, but he had an idea for helping the boys integrate better into the community that couldn't hurt. "What about the football team? Wes Sharrun and I coach the local team, and we could use a few new players." He didn't tell her that Eddie's anger might be better channeled with the physical-contact sport.

She considered it. "I'm not sure it's really Liam's thing, but Eddie could definitely use an extracurricular activity that would help him channel some of his...negative energy."

So she did see her older boy's anger. He should have known. Angel seemed to be very intuitive with her children. She was just hands-on enough but tried to give them their space.

"Thanks, Trent."

"Absolutely. Practice is Tuesdays at seven p.m." He wasn't completely convinced that he'd see Eddie there, but the best he could do was offer. Anything further would be overstepping.

Angel glanced around. "Where's Max?"

"He went to the bartenders' convention in Las Vegas last week and then decided to stay a few extra days to visit friends." Trent hoped Max wouldn't reconsider the idea of becoming part of his team. The notes he'd sent by email he'd taken at the conference had been impressive. He really had gone to learn, and Trent was happy that he'd been serious about the opportunity.

"Really?" Angel said. "He wants to become a bartender?"

"It surprised me at first, too. I wasn't sure how long he was sticking around, but he says he's considering it for Life: Act Two."

"Well, that's good," Angel said, and Trent detected a note in her tone.

"You think so?" he asked teasingly.

She scoffed and swiped at him. "I feel safe with him manning the place, that's all."

He sobered slightly. He knew Angel had been through a lot, and he wanted her to always feel safe here. He reached out and quickly touched her hand.

"Hey, you and the boys are going to be okay. Things will get better."

She stared at him searchingly, as though wanting to take those words to the bank. Her light-blue eyes reflected a glimmer of repressed tears. "Promise?"

Unfortunately, he couldn't. All he could do was be there and offer any support the family might need. "Can they get worse?" he asked gently.

"Good point," she said with a laugh. She climbed down from the stool and rotated her shoulders. "Shaking it off," she said, before regaining her tough facade and getting to work.

• • •

Traffic was stopped on Route 1 heading south. Of all days for her GPS not to warn her about a major collision on the highway.

Whitney drummed her fingers along the steering wheel, willing the cars ahead to move faster. The car two spaces in front crept forward, but the one directly in front of her didn't move. Whitney peered through the windshield, her gaze drilling a hole into the back of the driver's head.

She was texting.

Whitney waited.

Now she was shuffling through songs on her iPhone.

The car two ahead of her inched forward several more feet, and it took everything Whitney had not to wail on the horn.

Patience was something she had very little of today.

Burning hot ninety-degree weather outside made sweat collect on her back beneath her white blouse despite the air-conditioning blasting through the ventilation.

Squinting, she read the time on the dash. Twenty minutes until her specialist's appointment in San Francisco.

Despite how close it was, the license plate in front of her was impossible to read, and the exit sign in the distance…she wouldn't even attempt.

She was more of a hazard on the highway than the texting, music-searching girl in front of her. But she needed to get to the appointment, and it wasn't something she wanted to reveal to her friends or Trent just yet. Once she spoke to the doctor and got more clarity and hopefully a plan to fix her ailing health, then she'd tell everyone what was going on. She didn't need them worrying about her any more than they already did.

Once there was a real solution, she'd confess the problem.

Whitney followed the GPS directions to the specialist's office, but twenty minutes later, she wished she was back in the traffic jam. The clinic waiting room was standing room only, and she paced near the door, answering emails, checking her social media profiles…making a grocery shopping list… She looked up and glanced around. It didn't seem like anyone had been called in yet. The reception staff were chatting among themselves, and she could see several doctors in the lunchroom—a half-eaten birthday cake on the table.

What on earth was taking so long? What was the point of making an appointment if they still made you wait? She checked the time.

Six minutes? That was it? That's how long she'd been there? It felt more like six hours.

"Whitney Carlisle?" a nurse called, appearing in the waiting room with her file.

She nodded. "That's me." Grumbles and annoyed looks followed her as she crossed the waiting room, and then the nurse led her down the hall to an examination room.

"Dr. Kyle will be right with you," the nurse said, sliding her file in a plastic holder near the door.

"Thank you."

The door had barely closed before it opened again.

"Whitney!"

She jumped, startled by the doctor's booming, cheerful voice that hardly fit the setting of the clinic. The place was full of patients with incurable diseases. Maybe she'd selected the wrong specialist.

"Hi, Dr. Kyle." She crossed her legs, but seeing her swollen ankle protruding over her heel, she unfolded her legs and shoved them back under the seat. It was silly, but maybe if she didn't appear to be sick, he'd tell her she was okay.

"Nice to meet you. Dr. Forester told me you were his favorite patient," he said, taking a seat behind his desk.

Whitney blinked. Her family doctor had said that?

"Kidding," Dr. Kyle said, opening her file. "Jennifer Aniston is his favorite patient." He paused, glancing up at her. "Kidding again."

Whitney forced a smile. "Funny." Not exactly what she looked for in a specialist.

"You're nervous," he said, removing his glasses from his lab coat pocket and putting them on. His eyes immediately became tiny and faraway through the inch-thick prescription.

Were they joke glasses? Another attempt at humor to put her at ease? She cleared her throat. Best to just jump into the reason she was even there. "The symptoms have been getting harder to live with lately. I'm exhausted all the time, my joints are swollen, especially my ankles, and my eyesight..." She hated to admit all of this, but she was there hoping for answers, desperate for a way to fix herself. Without it, she would need major life changes. None that she wanted to make.

After her car accident the previous year, the attending physicians had discovered something in her blood work even more serious. Dr. Forester had said that sickle cell anemia had no cure, and a year ago, she'd barely felt sick. If it hadn't been for the accident, she may have gone on for years not knowing. She'd made it to twenty-nine not knowing she had the hereditary disease. She'd thought the headaches and poor vision were from stress and working too much. Long hours staring at a computer screen. But tests at the hospital had revealed a blocked artery in her chest, and further testing had revealed she had the disease.

Being adopted and moving states as an infant, not all of her medical files from birth had transferred with her. From her own research about her disease, both her birth parents had had to be carrying the sickle cell trait in their DNA to pass it along to her. She'd been one of the "lucky ones" to live without symptoms up until the year before.

Thank God she'd found out before she'd gone through with marrying Trent, having children. And that their pregnancy scare early in their relationship had been a false alarm. Not that she wouldn't have been thrilled to start a family with him, but she refused to knowingly pass along this gene to a child, and it shattered her to know that children may not be in her future. Or Trent's…

"I'm going to send you for more tests," Dr. Kyle said, filling out a medical requisition form. "And then we can go from there."

Whitney fought to control her annoyance. "I've already had tests done. The results are in the file." All this sneaking off to see doctors was stressing her out more than anything. She wasn't ready to tell anyone about her illness. She just wanted a fix. Or at least for something to make the symptoms less debilitating. She'd gone through all the tests already, and she'd had to wait several months for this appointment. She felt like she was running out of time…

"These are from a year ago," he said, taking the test results out of her file. "When you weren't having any other symptoms except the blocked artery in your chest and mild vision problems. I want a full, complete evaluation of your blood cells, your sight, everything… I'm also sending you for an MRI."

Suddenly she missed the not-so-funny funny guy who had walked in. This new serious tone was making her stomach twist. Air struggled to make it all the way to her lungs. "Okay," she said tightly.

There really wasn't a choice. She suspected he was right to assume that things had gotten worse in ten months. Maybe they shouldn't make people wait so long for appointments.

Annoyance toward the health care system helped to refocus her emotions away from the intense fear that threatened to take hold when she stopped too long to think about her illness or all the things in her life it could affect. Ignoring it, or at least trying to, made it a little less real. Made it feel a little less like she was teetering on the edge of a cliff.

"As you know, there's no cure for sickle cell anemia, but we can certainly try to make the symptoms less severe." He handed her the requisition. "Don't put off these tests."

The urgency in his tone wrapped around her, cinching tighter until her next words were barely more than a whisper. "I won't."

• • •

THEN…

They'd had sex twice and they'd used protection both times. There was absolutely nothing to worry about.

Unfortunately, common sense and rational thinking were doing nothing to ease Whitney's anxiety as she scanned her monthly menstrual calendar and realized she was six days late. She was always on schedule. Living with Jess, the two of them had synced up, and Jess used to tease her that Whitney was her monthly reminder.

But she was definitely late this time.

Standing, she closed her office door and squeezed her breasts. They felt fine. Maybe a little sore… But that happened at the start of her period, too. She'd been irritable and slightly more emotional the last few days—even crying over a touching life insurance commercial—but again, she was often more sensitive the days leading up to her flow.

Damn, if only the signs were a little more obvious.

She'd barely even noticed the missed start date. If it hadn't been for Jess asking to borrow a tampon earlier that day and Whitney not carrying one, she may not have even realized. So busy with work and late nights seeing Trent, getting the bar ready for the grand opening event had preoccupied her time and thoughts.

But women missed periods all the time because of stress or other reasons. Didn't mean for sure that she was pregnant, right?

She sighed as she checked her watch. Only one way to find out.

Fifteen minutes later, she was standing in the family planning section of the local pharmacy, hoping no one she knew saw her as she scanned the various options for pregnancy tests.

Two lines. Plus signs. One that said "yes" or "no." That was the one. Couldn't get that message confused. She reached for it with a shaky hand and quickly made her way out of the aisle.

"Hey, pretty lady." Trent's voice behind her as she headed toward the cashier made her freeze in her tracks.

Oh no. What the hell should she do? She hadn't wanted him to know until she knew for sure…

She quickly hid the test behind her back as she turned to face him. Her smile felt forced as she met his gaze. "Hi…" She noticed the pack of condoms in his hand and almost winced at the irony. May not be needing those...

"Taking a lunch break?" he asked as he approached and leaned in to kiss her cheek.

"Yeah, just a quick one." She'd planned on taking the test in the office bathroom, then figure out what to do before seeing him that evening at the bar.

"Want to grab a bite?" he asked, taking her free hand and leading the rest of the way toward the cashier.

"Oh, I should get back," she said, her heart pounding as he placed the condoms on the counter. He gestured for her to place her item on the counter as well, and she shook her head. "That's okay, I got it."

"I insist," he said. "Least I can do if you won't let me buy you lunch."

She sighed as she reluctantly took the test from behind her back and placed it onto the counter. She sucked in her bottom lip and winced as she stared at his reaction.

Don't freak out... Please don't freak out.

He looked slightly confused and more than a little surprised as he turned to face her. They'd agreed to be exclusive, so there was no question that if she were pregnant, then the baby was his, therefore Whitney tried to read his conflicted expression as the cashier rang in their items, with her own expression one of unconcealed amusement at the irony. "Twenty-two sixty," she said. "Unless you'd like to put the condoms back."

Trent ignored her. "Are you...?" he asked Whitney.

"I don't know for sure," she said, handing the cashier several bills and taking the test. This wasn't exactly a conversation she wanted to have in front of an audience. She hadn't been expecting to have this conversation with Trent so soon. She'd been hoping to know for sure, hoping to have time to decide what to say, decide how she felt about it, decide what she wanted to do...

But here they were.

She picked up his condoms and handed them to him, then led the way outside for privacy. Immediately, she turned to him and started to speak. "Look, it's probably nothing, but I'm late."

The bright winter sun made it almost impossible to see his expression as he said, "How late?"

"Almost a week. Which is unusual for me, so I thought I should check." She swallowed hard, and her hands shook slightly in the silence that followed. Of course, he was freaking out. Why wouldn't he? She should be freaking out, too. They barely knew each other. The relationship was new. "I should get going. I'll call you later."

She turned to leave, desperate to escape the thick, awkward tension in the air around them.

"Whitney, wait!"

She turned back, and he instantly reached for her. "Sorry about my reaction," he said. "I'm just surprised."

She nodded.

"But I'd like to be with you when you take the test...if that's okay?"

He wanted to be there? It shouldn't surprise her. Trent was a great guy—kind, caring, supportive.

No matter the outcome, she knew he'd be there for her…and a baby. Air trapped in her chest, and she fought the anxiety threatening to overwhelm her.

He pulled back and bent at the knees to look her in the eyes. "Will you wait for me? Tonight, after work, we'll take the test together?"

Relief flowed through her as she nodded. "I'd like that." For better or worse, "yes" or "no" on that tiny little display screen, she knew they were in it together.

And even in her panic, the thought gave her a sense of peace.

• • •

"I can't do it," Whitney yelled from the other side of the bathroom door in her house later that evening.

Trent stopped pacing the hallway and leaned against it. "What do you mean?"

"I mean I can't pee," she said.

"Try running the water," he suggested. He waited and heard the sound of the water running in the sink, but a moment later, still nothing. "I'll grab you a glass of water," he said.

In the kitchen, he poured a glass with a trembling hand.

Whitney might be pregnant. In just a few minutes, he could learn that he was going to be a father. He knew most men would be freaking out after only a few months of dating, but Trent felt nothing but excitement at the possibility. His only source of nervousness was for Whitney. He knew she was career-focused and wasn't ready to have a family just yet, so he worried she might not share his excitement if the test was positive.

But he knew he loved her and he was ready for whatever happened. He was back home, starting a new life, with a new business, and he'd found a woman he wanted to spend his life with. A baby might be accelerating the pace a little, but he wasn't afraid. He had faith in them.

He carried the glass of water to the bathroom door and tapped on it. She opened it a crack, and he handed her the glass. "Thank you," she said, sounding nervous.

She closed the door and, an excruciatingly long time later, he heard the toilet flush.

He held his breath as she exited the bathroom with the stick. "Now we wait," she said.

Now they waited.

Sitting side by side on the floor in the hallway, the stick between them, holding hands and taking turns sneaking a peek at the test, they waited together.

Trent's heart raced, and he could hear Whitney's pounding just as hard in the silence as time ticked on. If only he could read her thoughts. He suspected she was contemplating the options, the next steps, possible new futures just as he was. So much hung in the balance.

"That's time," she said softly a moment later. "I can't look."

He squeezed her hand and held tight as he took a deep breath and picked up the test stick.

The word "no" in the display window had his

heart sinking deep into his stomach. He hadn't realized how badly he'd wanted the outcome to be different until that very second.

Whitney studied him, reading his disappointment wrong. "Oh no, I'm pregnant, aren't I?"

He cleared his throat, shook his head, and put on a brave face as he said, "Nope. False alarm. All good." Truthfully, this probably was for the best. They hadn't been together long. She wasn't ready. Still...

"Oh, thank God." Her shoulders sagged in relief, and Trent fought his own conflicted emotions as he put an arm around her and pretended he was just as relieved as she was.

CHAPTER SEVEN

Now...

Scouting locations was one of the hardest parts of expanding. There were countless bars and clubs for sale along the coast and in the city, but finding one that he could transform into a Trent's Tavern without too many costly renovations was the real challenge. He only had two locations so far, but he hoped to eventually get to ten, and with the exception of the Game Room location, he wanted them all to have a similar and familiar aesthetic.

Whenever someone entered a Trent's Tavern along the sunny coast of California, he wanted them to be met with the same charm and comfort that they received from the O.G. location in Blue Moon Bay.

Trent pulled his Jeep into the lot of a run-down, old, country saloon-looking building an hour outside Blue Moon Bay and cut the engine. Climbing out, he met his real estate agent, Meredith Blau, at the front door. She was dressed in a bright teal suit, coral blouse, and matching heels, her big blond hair reaching an impressive height. He almost needed sunglasses, looking at her, and her interior matched her sunny exterior.

"Hey, Meredith. Nice to see you again. Thanks for meeting with me," he said, shaking her hand.

"I'm glad you reached out, darlin'," she said, her

thick Southern accent on display. "This place has been sitting on the market for a while now…" She lowered her voice. "Between you and me, it's because it's overpriced. The owners were about to do another price drop, so if you're interested, let's hang tight for a few weeks before making any offers."

This was why he'd hired Meredith Blau—she was fantastic in making sure her clients got a fair deal. He nodded. "Thanks for the tip."

He scanned the exterior as she unlocked the door. The place had some decaying wood along the windows and doors, but the rest of the building looked structurally sound. He knew from the listing that the roof had recently been replaced, after a bad storm along the coast had ripped part of it off. He wasn't worried about another occurrence of that. That storm had broken records and was unlikely to happen again. New windows and doors would be necessary as well as a new awning, paint, and some cosmetic work.

Landscaping would be easy enough, as the place was only steps from the beach. The outdoor wrap-around deck extended almost all the way to the sand, without a lot of greenery to be maintained. The view would be spectacular any time of year, and he could build an enclosure for the cooler, wetter months. There was plenty of parking and easy access to the highway.

So far, not bad.

He followed Meredith inside, and his optimism faded slightly as she flicked on the interior lights. The place was a bit of a nightmare. Country saloon from the wild, wild west vibe, the interior seemed it hadn't been updated since the early 1900s. Might have been part of the charm the owners had been going for, but it wasn't Trent's style, and based on the lack of business in recent years, it didn't seem to be a draw for the Gen Z crowd, either.

But...the place had good bones.

"Don't judge it for what it is. Judge it for what it could be," Meredith said.

This was where her other skill set kicked in. Talking *him* into making a decision.

The location on Main Street had been an easy acquisition—the timing and price had been perfect—and the bar at the Game Room had made sense...but this one was a little riskier. Being an hour away from Blue Moon Bay, he'd oversee operations, but he wouldn't be there on a regular basis, running the show. He'd have to trust that someone else could handle the day-to-day operations.

"The seating capacity is two hundred and fifty," Meredith said, checking the listing information on her cell phone. "Including the outside deck space, it can accommodate up to three hundred."

"I assume you have access to the numbers they were bringing in before they shut down?"

She nodded slowly. "I'll be honest—they aren't great," she said, confirming his suspicions. "But look at this place. You can see why. No one under seventy-five would walk in here."

He sighed as he looked around. She was right about that. The deer heads on the wall alone would turn away the vegan crowd that populated this area, and the musty, lingering smell of cigarettes wouldn't appeal to anyone, especially health fanatics.

"But with the right improvements and the right marketing, this place could be the next hot spot along the coast," Meredith said.

Right marketing... There was only one person he'd trust with that job, but she was already so busy. Could he really put that extra pressure on Whitney when he was always saying that she took on too much already? But he couldn't hire someone else to do it without completely pissing her off or making her feel like she wasn't absolutely the right person to do it.

Stuck between a rock and a hard place on that one.

He sighed as he shoved his hands into his jeans' pockets. "How much lower do you think the owners would be willing to go?" He anticipated at least a $30,000 reno budget, and the start-up costs would cut into profits from the other locations for at least the first year.

But it took money to make money, and he was smart in his risk-taking.

Meredith smiled. "I'm confident we can get them under two hundred thousand."

Still a little higher than he'd wanted, but the location was perfect, so it was worth the extra investment.

"Okay," he told Meredith. "If you can work your magic, then let's do it."

She hesitated despite her own best interests. "Do you want to discuss it with Whitney first? It's a big decision."

He did. He absolutely did. But if he had to wait on his fiancée's availability to have this conversation and have her take time to come see the place, he'd lose the opportunity. He didn't doubt that there would be other offers on the place once the owners posted the price drop. He suspected Meredith had other clients interested already as well. He couldn't wait on Whitney.

And while that thought unsettled him, he refused to let it bother him too much. He knew it wasn't that Whitney wasn't interested in what he had going on, she just had her own career, her own life...and lately that gap had seemed even more expansive. Meredith was right. These decisions should be made together when they impacted both their futures, but he wasn't sure his fiancée needed this extra burden right now, and Whitney trusted his instincts anyway.

"I'll be sure to run it past her before I sign on a dotted line," he said.

Meredith's bright, pearly white smile returned. "Great, darlin'! Well, let me start haggling."

Trent laughed as she immediately jumped on a call to the sellers, and he continued his tour around the place alone, but he couldn't deny the uneasiness in the pit of his stomach. This was a huge decision.

And he wished he had his future wife here to talk it through with.

CHAPTER EIGHT

Now...

"Isn't that your sister Rachel's car?" Whitney asked as she and Trent pulled into his family's home that Sunday.

She'd been successful in dodging Jess's calls and texts about getting together at the B&B with Sarah all week, her workload at the office only part of the reason she was steering clear of her friends: the rest of it the secret she was keeping and the fact that she knew their perceptiveness would catch her recent weight loss and the ever-increasing dark circles her concealer was no longer effectively hiding. For now, everyone assumed it was work stress and, as usual, her inability to slow down.

But after missing the previous few Sunday family get-togethers at the Connollys', she couldn't skip this one, too, and besides, she missed Frankie. Not seeing her as often as before was tough when she'd been a second mother to Whitney for years and, most recently, the only one she could still truly connect with and get advice from.

She may not have that much longer, and the thought of everything she'd be losing if she lost Trent made it hard to breathe.

Whitney scanned the street in front of the large bungalow, and panic settled in its familiar comfort zone deep in her chest, seeing other family members' cars as well. "What's everyone doing here?"

Trent put the Jeep in park and turned to her. "Mom's planning a little extra-special dinner, that's all." He reached across and brushed her curls from her shoulder, letting his hand rest there.

It didn't provide the intended comfort. Her heart raced. Had she been set up? What was she walking into? An intervention where they all demanded she set a wedding date and pick colors and a cake design and—

She forced a breath. "Why?"

Trent took her hand and squeezed it. "Don't worry. It's nothing extravagant. Just dinner with our family."

Our family. The *whole* family. Those words burned a hole in her chest.

"Come on." Getting out of the Jeep, he walked around the front while she gathered her things, and he opened her door for her. He took her hand as they made their way up the front steps, the railings decorated with fake cobwebs and several menacing-looking spiders on them.

The urge to jump back into the Jeep and drive away was overwhelming. Inside would be a chaos of love, laughter, and fun, and she was void of all those feelings right now. How was she supposed to pretend in front of everyone that everything was okay? But until she told Trent the truth, what other choice did she have but to keep going along with this?

She'd barely had the strength to keep her eyes open all day. These random bouts of exhaustion irritated her. She had so much to do, and when she did take an afternoon off, it would be nice to be able to actually enjoy it, instead of just wanting to spend the time sleeping. Three cups of coffee today were the only things propelling her body forward.

Opening the door, the familiar sounds and the scent of homemade baked pumpkin pie hit her like the crashing wave she'd been expecting, but not fully prepared for, leaving her with a helpless sensation of drowning. Spending time here with all of them would only make things that much harder if she was forced to end the relationship with Trent.

"Whitney!" Trent's sister Kara was the first to notice them, and Whitney braced herself for the hug as she came toward them, a mojito in hand.

"Hi, Kara. Great to see you," she said, hugging her quickly. She needed to start distancing herself. Just in case her test results proved that there was nothing the doctors could do to fix her.

"You too!" Kara said, pulling back to eye her. "Where've you been?"

"Work's been crazy." It was her go-to excuse. Everyone had to be tired of hearing it by now, even though it was true.

"I get it. This semester's courses are kicking my ass." Kara was a premed student at UCLA.

"You'll get through them. You always do," Whitney said. Kara bordered on genius, graduating high school at sixteen and completing her first-year university courses by correspondence, since she was still too young to leave home and go live on campus in L.A. She had a consistently perfect GPA, and her empathetic nature left no doubt that she'd make a fantastic doctor someday.

She'd be the best person to have on her side through her illness…if only Whitney could talk to her about it.

Trent cleared his throat next to her. "Hello? Your brother's here, too."

Kara ignored him, her question directed at Whitney. "Like my hair? I took your advice and added the blue," she said, lowering her head to show off the blue streak down the center of the shaved mohawk style she'd sported since before it was cool.

"It looks great." If anyone could pull off the edgy, short hairstyle, it was Kara with her petite, pretty features and small frame. Unlike Trent, all his sisters were short and petite. And the hairstyle suited Kara's personal style of ripped denim and full-sleeve tattoos.

"You look even more like a parrot now," Trent said, finally getting her attention.

"Jerk."

"Hey, you guys! Kara, let them come in," Rachel said, appearing in the foyer. She was radiant, from her long, dark hair to her manicured pink toes… her six-month baby bump visible in the flattering maternity dress she wore.

The sight nearly killed Whitney. She'd forgotten that Rachel was pregnant again.

"Yes, come in. I actually brought someone for you both to meet," Kara whispered. "Mom's showing her embarrassing baby photos right now." She turned to Trent. "And you—no more stealing my girlfriends."

"That was one time before I was happily betrothed to this fantastic lady," Trent said, wrapping his arm around Whitney and kissing her head.

Whitney tried to laugh at the story she'd heard before, but their playful banter just increased the feeling of anxiety weighing on her.

Soon, Trent could be on the market again. God, what if she saw him around town with someone else? Blue Moon Bay was going to become a lot smaller, and reminders of him and them together would be everywhere. Hell, she was best friends with his cousin.

How would this ever be okay? Would she have to move?

Inside the living room, they were greeted by the rest of the family.

"Uncle Trent!" Aaron, Trent's oldest nephew, called out as a Nerf football sailed past Whitney's head.

Trent caught it effortlessly, but Rachel scolded him. "Hey, that could have hit Whitney. No playing ball in the house."

"Nah, Uncle Trent never misses a pass," Aaron said. "And I'm just getting warmed up for today's game, Mom."

The family's traditional game of football after dinner. Whenever they were all together, they could make two teams of six, and the competitive spirit among the siblings was high. Something Whitney used to enjoy as well, but with her swollen ankles and spotty vision today, she'd be sitting this one out.

"Think fast," Trent said, tossing it back.

"Trent! You are a bad influence on him," Rachel said, but she laughed.

"That's why I'm the favorite uncle," he said.

"Yeah, well, just wait until you have your own," she said, intercepting another pass from her son with ease. "Whoa! Look at that—pregnant and all."

"You're a superstar, sis," Kara told her. "Come into the kitchen," she said to Whitney, leading the way. "And be honest, okay…my last two relationships haven't exactly gone well, so I'm not trusting my own judgment anymore. From now on, I'm polling the family opinion."

"We'll give it to you straight," Trent said, following close behind.

"I wasn't talking to you. I meant I want *Whitney's* opinion," Kara said as they entered the kitchen.

Unfortunately, Whitney wasn't sure hers should be considered in a family poll anymore, but she nodded.

"Hi, you two," Frankie said, putting Kara's baby album away and standing to hug them.

Whitney breathed in the familiar soft floral scent that she'd come to associate with Frankie. Warm, inviting, like the woman herself. "Great to see you, Frankie."

Relief washed over the woman's face. "Oh, good."

Frankie hugged Trent, then gestured another woman forward. "Trent, Whitney, this is Arielle, Kara's new girlfriend."

The young woman looked around the same age as Kara, about twenty-two, if Whitney had to guess, but she was only about four foot nine and maybe a hundred pounds. Even smaller than Kara, and Whitney hadn't thought it was possible.

"You are *not* on my team for football," Trent said, extending a hand to her.

The girl laughed. "You may regret that. I played rugby in high school. Division champs."

Trent put an arm around her shoulder. "On second thought…"

"Your brothers-in-law are outside, pretending to check the rain gutters but really trying to avoid any actual work in the kitchen… Why don't you join them?" Frankie said to Trent, giving him a slight shove toward the kitchen door.

He glanced at her. "You good?"

So far from good, but she nodded. She wouldn't ruin today for him or Frankie. Or the rest of the family who'd made the drive in. "Of course."

He kissed her cheek, then grabbed a beer from the cooler and headed outside.

From the window, Whitney could see him shake hands with his brothers-in-law and then set his drink aside to chase after the little ones playing tag in the yard. Squeals of delight and laughter drifted in through the open windows. A sound that used to give her so much hope about their future together.

"Man, the kids adore him," Kara said, standing next to her, her arm draped around Arielle's shoulders.

"The feeling's mutual," Whitney said.

"Hey, now that the men are gone, Whitney, could I steal you for just a second?" Frankie asked.

"Sure."

She followed the woman down the hall, scanning the row of family photos she'd seen a thousand times. School pictures from kindergarten to graduation. She loved seeing Trent grow from a shy, small kid to the confident star quarterback. A large family photo was on the far wall, a picture of all of them on the beach three years before, while Trent's father was still alive.

"In here," she said, stopping outside her bedroom. "I have something for you."

"Frankie, you shouldn't have."

"Well, it's not really from me," she said, going to the closet and reaching for a small garment bag. She unzipped it and took out a beautiful antique white wedding veil. A tiara of pearls and small diamonds made up the headpiece, and soft, delicate lace hung down from it.

Whitney's breath caught in her throat, recognizing it. "My mom's veil."

"It's so beautiful. She gave it to me about a week before she moved into Rejuvenation." Frankie handed it to her. "She wanted you to have it, but she wasn't sure…"

Whitney nodded, the lump in her throat so big, it threatened to suffocate her. She fingered the row of beads, afraid to speak, to look at Frankie. Fear of the truth spilling out overwhelming her. This moment was bittersweet. Her mother should have been the one giving her this. Her cruel illness stealing this opportunity from them made Whitney angry…and now her own illness destroying what should have been a special moment with Frankie made everything seem wrong.

"I'm not sure if you've thought about your dress—and no pressure at all. I just want you to know that if you want to wear this, we can certainly find fabric at the shop in a shade that matches perfectly with the antique white. And I'm really good at embroidering beads."

The soft pleading in the woman's voice brought tears to her eyes. Frankie's kindness was pure torture. She was nervous that she wouldn't be a part of Whitney's plans, and she was so lovingly providing her support without overstepping that it just made all of this so much worse. Frankie was so patient and understanding. She wasn't pressuring her or asking for answers. She'd been so lucky to have her in her life this long.

After Trent, she'd miss Frankie the most if things ended.

"Frankie, I'd be honored to wear any dress that you make."

The "but" on the tip of her tongue refused to vocalize as she saw the look of joy on the woman's face.

Sadness and disappointment would come between them. But she didn't have the courage to cause it today.

• • •

"You missed the turnoff," Whitney said hours later, glancing up from her phone in the passenger seat.

"No, I didn't," Trent said, hoping this executive decision in the final seconds wouldn't blow up in his face. "I thought we'd take a quick detour."

Whitney sighed as she looked at him. "Where?"

"You'll see."

"Trent…"

"Whitney…" He echoed her tone. "Just trust me. I'll have you at the office in an hour."

She had agreed to come to dinner at his family's house today if he promised to be okay with her going into the office later to catch up on work, before the busy week started. He intended to keep the promise, but watching her at his mom's house, he'd seen her yawn at least a dozen times and saw her stretching her legs quite a bit. He'd noticed her massaging her temples when she didn't think he was watching, and despite participating in the family's conversation at dinner, she seemed distracted.

She needed a break. She needed to take a moment. And while he held her captive in the Jeep, he was going to make sure she took one.

"Fine," she said, but she shifted in the seat and checked her watch.

He was on the clock. He had exactly an hour before her butt needed to be in her office chair.

A few minutes later, he turned off the main road onto the familiar gravel road, and she lifted her head and scanned their surroundings. He studied her expression and waited.

Please be cool with this.

If there was one place he could take her where she might actually enjoy herself, it was here. If this didn't work, he was out of ideas.

A hint of a smile appeared on her tired-looking face, and her shoulders relaxed slightly. "The pumpkin patch?"

Whitney may not be a Halloween fan for its creepiness and frights, but she always loved visiting the pumpkin patch in the fall. They'd spend hours getting lost in the corn maze, enjoying the hayrides, and picking out the most perfect pumpkins in the field.

They hadn't gone the year before, and he'd missed their yearly tradition. He knew if he'd tried to schedule it in her calendar this year, the idea would be met with excuses, so kidnapping her for an hour was the only way.

And he was glad he took the risk, when her mood seemed to lighten as they drove under the archway into the parking lot.

She unbuckled her seat belt, and they climbed out. He took her hand in his as they made their way to the entrance and paid their admittance. He fastened the orange armband on her wrist before putting on his own, and then they headed through the decorated gates.

The familiar sight warmed him like a pumpkin spice latte. The old farm was decorated exactly the same way every year, with stacks of climbable hay bales for kids, a tractor hayride making its way through the fields. Tall cornstalks formed the annual maze that changed every year, which he and Whitney could never figure out without the help of clues. There were vegetable stands set up and a hot chocolate and cookie hut. Small gift shops sold fall and Halloween decorations and homemade fudge and a small, kid-friendly haunted house was in the old barn. Kids' crafts and activities were set up under dome tents along the edge of the property.

The crunchy fall leaves and the slightly muddy ground beneath their feet along with the slight chill in the air on the sunny, bright day was the perfect atmosphere for the outing.

He hoped someday they'd be taking their own children here. Continuing the tradition as a family. He kept that thought to himself, though, for fear of ruining the light mood that had wrapped around Whitney as they entered.

"What do you want to do first?" he asked.

"Um…I could use some hot chocolate for the hayride," she said with a small smile, as though reluctant to enjoy the moment but losing a battle with herself.

He struggled to hide his happiness and relief. In that moment, she seemed exactly like her old self. Her eyes, still tired, held a vibrancy he hadn't seen in a long time, and color had even seemed to return to her cheeks. Of course, it could be the cool breeze, but he'd take it. She was outside. She was relaxed. She was spending time with him without her cell phone in her hand, and she wanted to eat. Or at least drink hot chocolate.

He couldn't believe the transformation. If he'd known this place held this kind of power, he'd have brought her here sooner.

Damn, it was tempting to drag her butt there every day.

They approached the hot chocolate stand, and she pointed to the biggest cup they had. "I'll take one of those, please."

The young girl working behind the counter, dressed in a plaid jacket and matching hat, smiled. "Marshmallows, whipped cream, or chocolate sprinkles?"

"All of the above?" Whitney said.

The girl laughed. "Good choice."

"I'll have the same," Trent said. He sent a quick glance at Whitney as they waited. She was looking around at the festivities, and the expression on her face had his chest actually aching. He hadn't realized how much seeing her happy made him happy. He'd do anything to ensure that expression stayed as long as possible.

"Here you go. Enjoy!" The young girl placed their cups in front of them, and Trent handed over the three dollars, which did not seem even close to enough to cover the cost of watching his fiancée take a sip and close her eyes as she savored the rich flavors.

He'd empty his bank account to witness her lick the whipped cream and chocolate sprinkles off the top every day of the week.

"Hayride?" he said.

"Lead the way."

They carried their hot chocolate to the waiting farm tractor and climbed on board the hay bales in the back with several families. Trent wrapped an arm around her. She snuggled into him as they bumped along the uneven terrain, and he held her tight.

The kids across from them laughed as they were shaken around, and he was about to comment on how cute they were bundled in their little thermal vests and sweaters, hats, and mittens, but he bit his tongue.

No more mentioning children, which seemed to set Whitney off lately. Just like the wedding plans, he was leaving it to her. She'd bring up the subject when she was ready.

Unfortunately, she didn't even seem to notice the kids as she tilted her head back toward the sun, smiling as the fresh air blew through her blond hair. Disappointment threatened to ruin his mood, so he pushed thoughts of the future away as he held her tight and sipped his hot chocolate.

Enjoy the moment. This moment here with her right now.

The future could wait, and maybe he needed to stop living for what was next and focus on what they had.

The ride stopped a few minutes later, and he jumped down, extending a hand to her. She hopped off, and he checked his watch. Forty minutes and counting. "What's next?"

"The corn maze?"

He hesitated. "That may take a little longer than forty minutes. You know how we get lost."

Whitney stood on tiptoes and wrapped her arms around his neck. "I won't hold you to the time promise."

He had to fight to keep his jaw from dropping. If they could just stay here forever…

"Okay, well, remember you said that," he said, kissing her gently, his heart feeling as though for the first time in a long time, he had his fiancée back.

• • •

Whitney's sides ached from laughing as she and Trent hit another dead end in the maze. "Why are these damn things so hard?"

Trent turned in a circle and jumped several times, trying to use even more height to see over the cornstalks. "I could have sworn we were supposed to go left at the scarecrow holding a shovel."

Whitney moved closer and placed her hands on his chest. "I think you're getting us lost on purpose." And she didn't care one little bit.

She couldn't quite explain the magic of this place or its effect on her, but since she was a small child, her family had visited the farm every year, and the tradition and the wonderful memories always seemed to lift her spirits instantly, from the moment she smelled the hot chocolate, saw the pumpkins, and enjoyed the activities.

Trent bringing her here today had been just the break she hadn't wanted to admit she needed. Taking time off always seemed like a bad idea. As though the work would pile up and she'd fall further behind. Any other time, she'd be stressed and not enjoy the time off anyway. But today, she felt better than she had in a long time.

She'd forgotten how much she missed this time with Trent.

Wrapping her arms around his neck, she stood on tiptoes to place a kiss on his lips. The taste of chocolate lingered on him, and he smelled like the fresh fall air.

He wrapped his arms around her and lifted her off her feet as he kissed her back. She felt the passion and desire in his kiss but also a happiness and a sense of relief. As though he'd gotten her back.

But for how long...?

CHAPTER NINE

Now...

In her office the next morning, it was back to business as usual as Whitney opened the television network's website and followed the links to the location casting callout page. Scott had offered to do the application, but there was no way she was leaving this in his hands.

Though there really wasn't much to this preliminary stage.

Basic info about the town, its location and population, and a 140-character pitch about why they should be considered. Whitney filled in the required info and uploaded the best images she had on file of Blue Moon Bay, then hit Submit.

Now all they could do was wait.

Part of her hoped they weren't chosen to move on with a formal application and pitch. The holidays were coming up, and soon she'd need to focus on the town's festivities. Then there was the New Year calendar to plan, which she'd yet to come up with a theme for next year's layout.

Maybe they were overstretching with the *Race Across America* submission.

The day before had been nice. Not thinking about work, or at least not stressing so much about it. She'd gotten a rare glimpse into life outside her office, something she hadn't allowed herself in more than a year. Being with Trent, having fun, had reminded her of how much she was missing with her workaholic lifestyle.

And the world hadn't ended because she'd gotten off the hamster wheel for a few hours.

Her cell phone chimed with a new text message, and picking up her phone, she read the message from Sarah:

Are we still on for the haunted house promo photos today?

Damn, that was today. Sure enough, her calendar chimed with the reminder to be at the B&B in an hour.

She'd completely spaced on it. It was too late to arrange their usual photographer. He was almost always accommodating on short notice, but an hour was *too* short. It wouldn't have been had she been in the office the day before as planned. She could have called him.

She'd have to take the photos herself.

Shutting her laptop, she jumped up from the desk, texting Sarah as she went.

On my way.

She hurried out of the office and to her car. Climbing in, she put on her seat belt as her phone calendar chimed. She glanced down at it.

Meeting with the printers at two p.m.

Shit!

That didn't give her much time. It was already after noon. Twenty minutes in and out of the B&B, she'd have to hope not to hit midday traffic as she made her way across town. Her head ached, and she squinted in the sunlight's glare as she sped along the streets toward Dove's Nest.

Her phone rang, and seeing her boss's number lighting up the call display, she resisted the urge to scream as she hit the Bluetooth connection on the dash. "Hey, Mayor Rodale. I'm just on the way to the B&B to get the photos of the haunted house."

"The photographer meeting you there?"

"No…" *Think quick.*

"He wasn't available?"

She hadn't booked him. "These should be quick. I thought I'd just take them. No sense in paying the hourly rate."

"Okay, good thinking. When will you be back in the office? I have a new client coming by—they opened a new flower shop on Main Street and wanted to discuss some promotion opportunities."

"After the B&B, I have to stop by the printers to pick up the holiday promotional packs, but I should be back by three or three thirty?" As long as traffic was okay and there weren't any delays or issues with the promo packs.

"Oh dear…that's a little late," Mayor Rodale said. "You know what, don't worry. Scott's here. I'll ask him to meet with the client, and he can fill you in."

She swallowed hard, clenching the steering wheel tight. "Sure," she said through gritted teeth. Her head throbbed, a migraine coming on. "Sorry about that."

"Remember, Scott can help if you need him. Don't try to do everything yourself."

Great, her boss must have sensed her irritation. "Of course. Scott's a great assistant," she said before disconnecting the call. An assistant who could easily replace her if she took her foot off the gas for even a second.

Pressing the pedal a little harder, she got on with her never-ending to-do list.

• • •

His cousin was a true artist. Staring at the Halloween cake in the shape of Dracula, Trent couldn't believe it was made from cake, puffed rice, fondant, and sugar.

"It looks so realistic. Those eyes seem to be following me," he said, moving from side to side in her bakery later that day. The amazing spun-sugar eyes were seriously impressive. It was no wonder Jess's business was such a success. Her baked goods were the best he'd ever tasted, and her attention to detail in her decorating was second to none.

Jess laughed. "Here, try one of these," she said, holding out a tray of dark, round spiders with black licorice legs and white- and milk-chocolate-chip eyes.

Trent picked one up and bit into the thin, crisp dome shell. Chocolate mixed with a spicy hotness awakened his taste buds. "So good," he said, his mouth full. "Mexican hot chocolate?"

"Yep."

He took in the rest of the haunted house desserts she was boxing up—severed finger sugar cookies, Frankenstein's monster–shaped gingerbread, tombstone chocolate cookies…and hundreds of each.

"This is really impressive," he said. "I'm sure Sarah is relieved you didn't sell the bakery last year." Jess had turned down a million-dollar offer from a large chain store wanting to buy her out. She loved her small hometown and being close to family that much.

Jess checked her watch. "Speaking of...I have to get all of this over to the B&B."

"I'll help," he said, straightening.

Jess frowned. "I thought you and Whitney would be celebrating your birthday tonight. Happy birthday, by the way."

He shrugged casually. "I think she forgot what day it is." She'd left that morning for work without saying "happy birthday," and he'd yet to receive a text from her about whether she'd be home in time for dinner or any indication that she had anything special planned.

Jess's gaze was sympathetic. "Sorry, Trent."

He waved a hand. "You know I don't care about birthdays." He glanced around the bakery. "Where do you want me to start?"

But hours later, after helping Jess deliver the horror-themed baked goods to the B&B and enjoying birthday takeout with his cousin and Sarah and Wes, Trent still hadn't heard from Whitney. It was after ten p.m. when he left the B&B and still no reply from the text he'd sent five hours before. He'd only texted once, having learned over the years that when she was busy, more frequent texts just added to her stress. It did annoy him that when she went to work, it was as if she'd gone to another planet. Unreachable. But there wasn't much he could do about it.

He drove along Main Street and sighed. He didn't feel like going home and being there alone. A workout would be a good idea, but the gym was closed already.

Luckily, he owned a bar. If there was a place that could help drown out the silence of an un-ringing cell phone and quiet the nagging thoughts in his mind, it was Monday night at his bar.

Karaoke night.

As he pushed through the doors and entered the dimly lit space, the sound of unmerciful wailing over the speakers made him wince, and a memory of another birthday hit him hard.

• • •

THEN...

"What about karaoke?"

Trent shook his head so fast, he thought he might get whiplash. "Not a chance in hell," he told Whitney as they sat in the empty bar the week before the grand opening, planning the weekly entertainment schedule.

Shoes off, she was sitting cross-legged in the booth, looking comfortable and relaxed, while he was sweating bullets. In a few days, the bar would be open. He really hoped the town embraced the tavern as much as they'd once loved the old bar that used to be there, owned by Sarah Lewis's parents.

Whitney's pretty eyes widened. "What do you

have against karaoke?"

"Besides the butchering of perfectly good classics?"

"It's fun," she said with that seductive smile of hers that made it hard not to reach across the booth, grab her face, and kiss her until all planning was forgotten.

"It's never happening inside my bar," he said with a wink.

And yet somehow that beautiful woman who'd captured his attention in that past year got her way. And on opening night, too. Which also happened to be his birthday.

That year, there was only one thing he wanted. Standing near the bar, in the packed space, he couldn't tear his eyes off her as she and Jess did a duet of some classic rock song onstage. Dressed in black leather pants, a pale-pink oversize sweater hanging off one shoulder, and the sexiest heels he'd ever seen, she had him practically drooling. Her face was lit up as she laughed and sang terribly off-key and out of sync with the melody.

Jess was laughing too hard to cover for Whitney's fail, but the crowd thought they were adorable. Everyone seemed to be having an amazing time, and while he couldn't wait for karaoke hour to be over and the local band to take over, he had to admit, it had brought in an early crowd to launch the grand opening event with a packed house.

The brilliant, beautiful Whitney had been right.

Her gaze locked with his as the song ended, and the sight of her had his heart pounding in his chest.

He didn't even feel his legs move until he'd reached the stage himself and put in his own request to the karaoke DJ.

The next three and a half minutes were either going to change his life for the better or be his biggest embarrassment.

• • •

Whitney's mouth dropped as Trent climbed onto the stage and took the mic. The man who had been adamant about not having karaoke in his bar was actually going to participate? Her cheeks were still flushed from being up there herself with Jess, and she reached for her martini and took a sip before leaning toward her friend. "Can he sing?"

Jess looked just as shocked to see her cousin up there. "Guess we're going to find out."

Onstage, Trent looked nervous as the soft opening beats of a familiar country song started to play. He clutched the mic and cleared his throat. Loudly.

"Sorry," he said into the mic.

A silence fell over the bar as the opening lyrics appeared on the screen.

Whitney held her breath. Trent's gaze was straight on her as he sang Brett Young's "In Case You Didn't Know." And sounded amazing.

Not that it mattered. In that moment, he could have completely butchered one of her favorite songs and she wouldn't have cared. She couldn't take her eyes off him as he sang the lyrics straight to her heart.

This was it. The moment she'd been waiting for. She knew this was his way of finally telling her how he was feeling. And he was doing it with flair.

She'd known for months that she was in love with him, and to know he felt the same made her heart soar.

Next to her, Jessica swooned as she squeezed Whitney's hand. "I knew you two were perfect for each other," she whispered excitedly.

Her best friend was so right. They were perfect together. Over the past year, their connection had only grown more and more. The more she learned about him, the more she liked and admired him. He was self-made and motivated to succeed. Hard-working and driven, with a soft, compassionate side and a deep love for family and the people close to him.

Whitney couldn't erase the smile from her face while he sang, keeping the entire bar captive in the intimate moment.

That night, after the bar closed and they were all alone, he took her into his arms. Her heart was beating so loud, echoing against her chest. She was sure he had to hear it in the now quiet bar.

"You were really great up there tonight," she said, wrapping her arms around his neck. He'd been busy since he'd walked off the stage, so they really hadn't had time to talk. But all night, her mind had raced about what the gesture had meant. What she'd wanted it to mean. And whenever her gaze caught his across the room, it only became more evident how she felt about him.

His face flushed a little as he lowered his gaze.

"I, uh…j-just wanted to tell you…" he stammered, and she placed her hands on the sides of his face and smiled, staring into his eyes.

"I know. I love you, too."

CHAPTER TEN

Now...

She'd missed Trent's birthday.

Panic seized her chest when Whitney saw the date on her desk calendar the next day. She massaged her temples and took a deep breath. How could she have missed it? As forgetful as she was, she'd never missed a birthday before. She'd been so preoccupied with everything the day before that she hadn't even registered what day it was. She'd been at the office until almost midnight the night before, and Trent had been asleep when she'd gotten home. He hadn't even stirred when she'd slipped into bed next to him a little after one a.m.

How could she make this up to him?

Of course, he'd say it wasn't a big deal. But birthdays were special to the two of them. They always tried to outdo each other with a nice evening planned and the perfect gift. The last couple of years, they'd barely acknowledged the days, but they'd at least acknowledged it.

She couldn't text or call to apologize. She needed to do something meaningful. Make an effort to show him that he did matter to her, more than anything else in the world, despite her insensitivity the day before.

He truly did, and she was desperate to figure things out.

Not desperate enough, a nagging voice said in her mind as her gaze fell to the medical requisition form from Dr. Kyle still sitting in her open desk drawer. She'd yet to schedule the appointments at the local clinic. She had to soon. She couldn't keep putting it off, but a paralyzing fear of the results was making it impossible to make the call. What if things were even worse than she thought? There was at least some comfort in not knowing.

Logging onto her calendar, she scanned the to-do items on today's long list and struggled with the conflicting sense of obligation and commitment to her job and to her health and to her relationship. Something had to give. Right now, she was looking for a way to focus on Trent, allow him to be the priority. If she worked until six, they could still go to dinner somewhere. It wasn't enough, but hopefully he'd accept the peace offering.

Picking up her phone, she texted:

How about dinner tonight?

Unlike when he texted *her*, his reply was immediate:

Would love to but can't tonight. Football practice, then wings with the team.

It was Trent and Wes's tradition to take the boys out for wings after every practice. Team building and morale off the field made for a solid unity on the field. She admired his commitment to not only training the kids to be better football players but giving them a source of support they may not get elsewhere.

A few dots that meant he was texting…then:

You could join us.

When was the last time she'd gone to the field to watch him coach? Or hung out with him without a set reservation or having to schedule it in? Practice was at seven, so that actually gave her an extra hour than she'd been planning to have if he'd been available for dinner. She glanced at the calendar, mentally calculating how long each item would take. If she worked straight through lunch, she could do it. Get everything done and be out the door at 6:45.

I'll try to make it, she texted back.

And she really would.

As she set the phone on her desk, a new email appeared, and seeing the TV network's email address in her inbox, her heart raced. She wasn't sure what news she actually wanted.

Clicking on the email, she read:

Congratulations! Blue Moon Bay has been selected for the official pitch round...

"We got it!" she shouted before she'd even finished reading the message, practically bouncing in her chair. She couldn't believe it. This was the biggest promotional opportunity she'd ever had to manage—and they hadn't spent a dime.

Making it to the football field that evening was the last thing on her mind as she immediately got to work.

• • •

As Trent had predicted, Eddie was a natural.

Of course, getting the teen to play well out of skill instead of anger at being there, anger at the world, would be the biggest challenge. But he'd shown up to the practice, and that was a start. Wings with the team would help. Food bonded teenage boys.

"Thanks again for this, Trent. I think this is exactly what the boys need," Angel said as she stood next to him on the football field, watching the boys run drills with the team. Wes was warming them up, and the former high school football star wasn't going easy on the newcomers.

Liam was tall but thin. He would struggle with the bigger boys tackling...if they could catch him. He was damn fast. Eddie was shorter, stockier. More the traditional football player build. Trent was actually surprised that he had never played before. According to Angel, their father hadn't been a fan of contact sports, insisting the boys learn tennis and golf, things that emphasized individual talent and skills. The man either didn't understand or appreciate the value of being part of a team. The more Trent heard about Angel's ex, the less he liked the guy.

"They're good," he told Angel. "With some practice, I think they could both be great assets to the team." He laughed. "Hey, and if nothing else, maybe we can tire them out enough not to be so annoying."

She smiled the way only a relieved mom could smile as she tapped her folded forearms. "I owe you."

"Don't even think about it." He checked his watch. "You have a full hour to yourself. Why don't you do something crazy...like read that book you keep carrying around."

She laughed. "Maybe I will."

Instead, he saw her climb the stands and take a seat on the bleachers to watch the boys.

He scanned the gravel parking lot behind him. No sign of Whitney yet. He wasn't surprised, and he also wasn't upset. She'd offered dinner, and he was the one that evening with a conflicting schedule. He couldn't hold that against her, and he wouldn't. He suspected she realized she'd missed his birthday the day before and it had been an attempt to make it up to him.

At least she'd wanted to make the effort. That meant a lot to him.

Since the day at the pumpkin patch, he'd been hoping to keep that momentum going. She'd relaxed and enjoyed herself that day, and he thought that if she took more days like that, it might help her realize the importance of a healthier work/life balance.

He really hoped she made it this evening.

Wes jogged toward him, slightly out of breath. "Those new kids aren't bad." He opened a large duffel bag and started taking out the rest of the gear.

Trent nodded, returning his attention to the field. "Well, you know how it is. Anyone can do drills. Let's go see what they've got."

• • •

Whitney pulled into the gravel lot next to the football field and climbed out. There were only a few minutes left in the practice, but at least she'd made it. And she would join the team for wings. Leaving the office had been difficult with work unfinished, but it was one night, and everyone was right—she did put a lot…okay, too much time in. She deserved a break now and then.

She paused at the field entrance. Trent was demonstrating a defense technique, tackling poor Wes with ease. Wes might have been the local sports hero in town before an injury had derailed any chance at a professional career, but her fiancé had at least fifty pounds on him. He looked so amazing out there. His body was built for sports, so strong and capable and a force of nature.

He'd certainly stormed his way into her life.

The first time she'd seen Trent, she'd been a goner, and not only because he was naked. He was exactly what she'd looked for in a man—strong, confident, tall, and muscular. She'd often struggled with men feeling intimidated by her because of her ambition, but Trent had only ever been supportive and proud. He was the perfect partner for her.

But seeing him with the kids made her chest hurt. He was so wonderful with them, and it was obvious that the teens looked up to Trent and respected him. He was patient and fun, yet firm, and he let them know when they'd messed up. A lot of the kids on the team needed the discipline that came with being there. Organized sports were important, and she knew Trent was looking forward to coaching his own kids someday.

Whitney headed across the field, then paused, seeing Angel in the stands. She was watching the field, too. And it seemed the bar manager's gaze was locked on Trent, not her two teenage boys out on the field.

What did she expect? That just because Trent was her dream man, he wouldn't be anyone else's?

She shook off any feelings of jealousy. Trent was a hot guy who was constantly surrounded by beautiful women who would love to have his attention directed their way, but Whitney had never felt threatened or insecure. She knew he loved her. She could feel it with every ounce of her being. She had no reason not to trust him.

Angel was an employee. A coworker. And Whitney actually really liked her. She was an incredible manager and had helped take some of the pressure off Trent in recent months. She smiled at the woman as she climbed the stairs, then sat next to her on the bleachers. "Hi, Angel."

"Hey, Whitney, how are you?"

The look of concern on the faces of family and friends Whitney expected by now, but seeing it on an almost stranger's face made her stomach knot slightly. Had Trent told Angel about her accident? Had he mentioned Whitney's stressful, busy workload?

The woman was eyeing her with a look of someone who might have some insider, intimate knowledge of Whitney's relationship and personal life that *did* make her slightly uneasy. Was Trent confiding in Angel?

It was probably just natural, though. Trent and Angel spent a lot of time together. Probably more than she and Trent did recently. They would talk and open up, share stories about their personal lives. Trent had told Whitney all about Angel, too—her messy divorce with some Hollywood exec, the way she was struggling with the boys, who were having a harder time adjusting to their new life...

But sharing things with a significant other was to be expected.

"I'm great," she said, hiding her uneasiness. "Are those your boys out there?" She gestured toward the field, where two new teens played.

Angel nodded, shoving her hands into the pockets of her sweatshirt and shivering in the chilly, early evening breeze. "Those are my monsters," she said with a laugh. She looked so at ease, so natural sitting in the stands of a small-town football field, watching her kids play ball. Unlike Whitney, who was still dressed in her work clothes and definitely seemed out of place among the parents. She wasn't a parent and this wasn't her natural environment—a place she felt comfortable, where she belonged. Would she ever?

She shook the thoughts aside as she asked, "Did they play football in L.A.?"

"No. This was Trent's idea, actually," she said, and once again a look of gratitude crossed the woman's beautiful face. Whitney knew from Trent that Angel was in her late thirties or maybe forty, but she looked a lot younger. Soft, flawless porcelain skin and pretty green eyes, gorgeous hair.

"He's such a great guy," Angel said, then laughed awkwardly. "As you obviously know."

Whitney nodded and forced a smile. Her gaze landed on him now. She did know. She also knew that a great guy like Trent wouldn't wait around forever for her to commit. Time was running out, and she needed to tell him everything. That this lifestyle—sitting in the stands someday, watching him coach their own kids—might not be in her future. *Their* future. It hurt to acknowledge, but she couldn't keep pretending the life they'd once talked about was certainly in the cards.

He glanced their way, and a look of surprise registered on his face, seeing her there, before he offered a wave.

She waved back and tried to take comfort in the fact that it was *her* he was waving to, but for the rest of the evening, it was difficult to shake the odd feeling of unease in the pit of her stomach. Trent was the perfect person for her, but maybe she was no longer the perfect person for him.

• • •

THEN…

Lying on Trent's chest on her sofa, Whitney felt an undeniable sob escape him as the credits rolled on the heartwarming, inspiring sports drama they'd been watching. She lifted her head to glance up at him with a grin as he quickly wiped the tears away with his forearm.

"Are you crying?"

He shook his head and scoffed. "No. 'Course not."

She peered at him. "Yes, you are."

"Fine. I'm a big softie when it comes to these movies."

She snuggled closer. "I think it's sweet." She loved that there were layers to Trent. On the surface, he looked like a two-hundred-and-fifty-pound man who nothing could touch, but on the inside, he was thoughtful and considerate and in his own words, "A big softie." He was fantastic with kids, and while they hadn't talked about it since the pregnancy scare, she knew he'd been slightly disappointed. He was older than she was and had made life and career decisions recently that put him on the path he ultimately wanted. She was still young and figuring things out...

"It's just, that's the kind of life I want, you know? A simple, quiet, small-town life running the bar and raising a family," he said, confirming her thoughts. "It's a big part of why I wanted to finally settle down and have my own business. I don't want to be one of those parents who misses out on things. I want to be there for sports games or ballet or gymnastics... I don't ever want to miss a birthday, and I'm probably going to spoil them with love."

"I don't think you can spoil children with love," she said pensively. As an adoptee, she knew all too well how lonely it could be, feeling unloved. Luckily, she hadn't had many years to feel that way, and her parents had more than made up for anything her early years may have lacked in the way of affection. "How many children do you want? Eventually," she added quickly.

"At least five or six," he said.

Her eyes widened, and her head shot up. "Five or six?"

He laughed. "I want a big family like the one I was raised in. We drove one another nuts and fought all the time, but there was also lots of laughter and fun. I couldn't imagine what growing up would have been like without my sisters."

She nodded. She was an only child, so she'd never experienced that, but spending time with Trent's family definitely made her feel like that was a wonderful way to grow up.

"So, what do you say? Can you see five or six kids in your future...eventually?" Trent asked softly, twirling a piece of her hair around his finger.

Whitney smiled up at him and kissed him gently. "Let's start with three and see what happens?"

Trent grinned, holding her tighter. "Deal."

Whitney's heart swelled as she snuggled closer. Talking about starting a family with Trent felt right. She may not be ready for it just yet, but they had plenty of time, and she knew someday she'd be willing to give him a family like the one he'd had and the one she'd only dreamed of.

Someday.

CHAPTER ELEVEN

Now...

This humidity was torture. Despite the cloud cover and strong wind, the heavy thickness in the air was causing Whitney to melt. She unbuttoned the top two buttons on her tan blouse and, pulling her hair back away from her face, she tied it into a low ponytail at the base of her neck. It had to be eighty-five degrees outside, and her feet ached from walking in wedge heels on the sandy beach.

But the waves this morning were perfect, and the shots the photographer was able to capture in this early-morning lighting made all her discomfort worth it. These images would be perfect to use in her pitch presentation for *Race Across America* as well as next year's promotional calendar.

"Good morning. Sorry I'm late," Scott said from behind her.

He couldn't be late to something he wasn't invited to. Her jaw clenched as she turned around to face him. "What are you doing here?" She hadn't told him about the early-morning shoot. On purpose.

"Kim added it into my calendar," he said. "I brought you a pumpkin spice latte." He extended the cup to her.

"It's, like, a thousand degrees out here."

"You don't want it?"

The pumpkin spice aroma escaping the cup was too tempting, and after a night of unsettled tossing and turning, she was exhausted. She took it with a mumbled, begrudging "thanks."

Scott smiled brightly, unfazed by her attitude.

"I was capable of overseeing this shoot myself," she said. Maybe he'd take the hint and leave.

"It's no problem. I'm here now." He scanned the waves. "Wow, you couldn't have picked a better morning. Those breaks are fantastic."

She nodded, sipping the hot coffee. The caffeine was a needed jolt to her system, but the heat from the cup made her palms sweat even more. Why was she always so damn hot?

"I assume we're using these shots for our pitch?"

Our pitch. Truthfully, this was his pitch. He'd thought of the idea. She was just desperate to prove that she had the skills to pull it off. "Yep."

From the corner of her eye, she studied him. Unlike her, he was dressed for this. Khaki shorts, a white collared short-sleeve shirt, and sandals. Not exactly professional, but hell, they were practically the only ones on the beach.

Her pencil skirt and blouse must look ridiculous. She knew the mayor wouldn't care if she dressed more casually, but Whitney liked to look polished and put together.

She swayed slightly off-balance as a dizzy spell hit, and she sipped the coffee again. She hadn't eaten since the night before, that's all. She was fine.

"Is that Grant?" Scott asked, nodding to the photographer standing in the waves near the shore.

"He *is* the best." After years of working with different artists, Whitney knew their individual strengths and who to call for various projects. Grant was first on her contact speed-dial list.

"I agree. I just can't believe you were able to get him. He doesn't do much local work these days."

"That's why they pay me the big bucks," she said sarcastically. She wouldn't tell him that Grant's father was living just down the hall from her mother at Rejuvenation, so the two of them also shared a common bond as well as a working relationship. Let Scott believe she was a superstar.

"Will he have time to take a few shots of the diving cliffs around the south end? I thought they'd make a great challenge—"

She held up a hand, showing him her list of locations on her cell phone.

"Of course you've already thought of that," he said with a laugh. "I'm not even sure why you need an assistant."

She didn't.

Seeing Grant and the surfer walking toward them, she handed Scott her coffee. May as well put those assisting skills to use.

"Let's see what you got," she said to Grant, leaning over to view the slideshow of shots on the camera.

Scott's breath on the back of her neck as he peered over her shoulder was irritating, and she moved away slightly. She purposely hadn't invited him to this. She'd just barely been given the lead on this one, and she wanted to do it all herself.

She squinted to see the pictures and nodded.

"Great. They are exactly what I was hoping for. Just a few shots of the cliffs, and I think that's a day." She reached into her purse and retrieved an envelope with the surfer's payment and handed it to him. "Thank you."

"Those waves were sick, man. Can't believe I get paid for this shit," the young guy said, unzipping his wet suit a tad too far. Whitney averted her eyes from the six-pack and everything below it as he continued to climb out of the suit. No shame.

"Okay, so I'll… We'll meet you at the south end of the beach?" she asked Grant.

"Be there in five. Just need a new memory card," he said, jogging off toward his van.

"Wanna ride together?" Scott asked her as they walked across the sand to the parking lot.

Great. He was coming, too. She hesitated, but her vision was destroyed by the pounding in her head that had nothing to do with the time of day or lack of coffee. "Okay. You drive."

As they headed toward his Escalade, he said, "So I was thinking, for the pitch, you might want to use your office instead of the boardroom."

"All of the media equipment is in there," she said as he opened the passenger side door for her. She shot him an odd look at the gesture.

"What? My mom raised me right," he said.

He closed the door and crossed the front end, then got in behind the wheel. "I can set the equipment up in your office fairly easily. I just think your view of the bay is so much better than the view of Tommy's Board Shop's back alley from the boardroom window."

Good point. They *were* trying to convince these Hollywood executives that their town was spectacular. The graffiti in the back alley wasn't the image she wanted to present. "Okay," she said as he pulled out of the lot and they headed down the coast.

"Wait," Scott said, sounding shocked. "Did I just get something right? Did I actually think of something you hadn't?" He wasn't gloating, he was teasing, but her migraine didn't care—he was still irritating.

She ignored him, staring out the window at the movement of palm trees, other cars passing, and a cyclist on the side of the road—all a blur. At least the air-conditioning inside the Escalade gave a brief respite from the mugginess outside.

Scott pulled into the gravel lot of the viewing point at the cliff site, and they climbed out. Grant's van pulled up next to them, and he got out as well. "I'm thinking several shots from here, then we'll move closer."

Whitney nodded, swallowing saliva that had formed in her mouth. Her stomach felt nauseous, and she was close to throwing up. It had to be this humidity and lack of food. Once she hit the bakery on the way back to the office, raise her blood sugar with a muffin, she'd be fine.

"You okay?" Scott asked as they approached the cliffs.

"Yes." She forced a slow, steady breath as she focused on the photographer, pointing out various shots. She was a professional, and professionals didn't have bad days.

Besides, they were almost done.

They moved a little closer, and another wave of dizziness made her blink. She swayed, and her arms reached out to grab hold of something, anything to stop her from falling backward over the side of the cliff, but there was nothing but air around her.

Her heart raced before the feel of Scott's arm around her waist gave her a sense of relief. "Whoa...watch it," he said, dragging her away from the side.

"Damn, we almost got an action shot right there," Grant said with a laugh to ease the tense moment, but even he was eyeing her with concern.

Whitney stepped away from Scott, stumbling slightly on the gravel. "Yeah, I was trying to set one up for you, but Scott here ruined it," she said, making light of the situation as the nausea passed. She fought to calm her thundering heart as she avoided Scott's gaze. She could have fallen off the cliff to her death had he not just been there.

"Seriously, you okay? That was close," Scott said, obviously not in the mood to joke about the near-fall.

She waved it off. She did not need Grant mentioning this in front of her mother at the next Rejuvenation family picnic. "Now you know why I need an assistant," she said casually.

Scott annoyingly stayed close as Grant continued to snap the photos along the cliffs, and twenty minutes later, they were done. "Okay, I think we're good for today," Whitney said, handing Grant his payment envelope. "Thanks again."

"No problem. I'll have these over to you in the

next few days."

"Perfect." Whitney waved as she headed back to Scott's car and quickly climbed in, desperate for the air-conditioning.

Scott got in, but he didn't start the engine. Instead, he turned to face her. "What was that?"

"What was what?"

"That near-death experience."

Whitney scoffed. "I'm a klutz, and you grabbed me—thank you. Let's go." She put on her seat belt. Air-conditioning would be fantastic any second now.

"You didn't stumble. You almost passed out."

Prove it.

"No, I didn't. Can we go? I need to get to the office before a conference call with the East Coast." She was desperate to get out from under his scrutinizing gaze. His perceptiveness made her uneasy.

"Well, I guess for once, you'll be dropping the ball on something, because I'm not moving this car until you tell me what's wrong with you." He reclined his seat, folded his hands behind his head, and closed his eyes.

Was he actually serious? She clenched her jaw, unwilling to reveal anything. She didn't owe her assistant an explanation for anything. Especially not a guy who would use the truth against her to steal her job.

"Okay. Great," she said. "I'll just call Mayor Rodale and tell her why we won't be in today."

Scott opened one eye and raised an eyebrow. "You're going to tell my mom on me?"

She huffed. "Look, Scott, I'm just not feeling well today."

"Pregnant?"

"You wish." Within a three-month maternity leave, he'd have swooped in and repainted her office, filling it with sports memorabilia and a treadmill desk. Nope. Not happening.

"Stress?"

"Seriously? No! I could do my job blindfolded. It's probably the flu or something I ate."

"A flu that's lasted months that causes your joints to swell and your vision to strain?"

Her mouth gaped. How was he the only person to notice? To call her out on it? Probably because, ironically, she spent more time with him—even inadvertently just being at the office together—than she did with anyone else.

Her back sweat against the leather seat, and she craved a cool blast of air. Rolling down the window didn't help as the humidity just seeped in. "I have a water retention issue and…my vision is fine."

"Come on, Whitney. We both know you approved those brochures with the glaring typo and the date of the—"

She held up a hand. She didn't need to hear him replay her recent mistakes.

"I covered for you, but now you owe me the truth. Are you okay?"

His seemingly genuine concern could be fake, and he was the last person on earth she could trust with her secret. He'd use her illness against her the first moment he got. Yet, he hadn't used any of her mistakes against her…

She shook her head. "I'm really fine."

"What color are your shoes?"

She frowned, glancing down. She squinted. "Navy." She'd laid them out the night before; they went with this outfit.

"One is," he said.

Whitney leaned closer and squinted as hard as she could. Not only was her vision blurring, but colors had also started to become harder to detect.

Shit. The other shoe was black.

She had no idea what was happening, but it was terrifying. But she wouldn't admit how afraid she was to anyone. Especially not Scott.

"Whatever. I was in a rush this morning. The shades aren't all that different…"

"Whitney! Stop. Just admit you are sick."

Her lips clamped together, but she nodded slowly.

He brought his seat back to driving position and finally started the car. Then, turning to face her, he said, "I don't need to know what it is. I'm not going to ask if you need help, because you're you, and you never need anyone." He paused. "I'm also not going to say anything to anyone…"

"Thank—"

"Shhh."

She stopped talking.

"On one condition. You stop trying to block me. Let me do my job—assisting you. You are amazing at your job, now let me be good at mine."

She sighed. Guess allowing him to do his job wasn't too much to ask in exchange for his silence. "Okay."

"Great. Now let's get you to the office for your fake phone call," he said with a grin, putting the car in reverse.

• • •

As he pushed through the door of Sharrun's Construction on Main Street, Trent's head got caught in a wispy spiderweb, and he ducked back as a mechanical spider creeped toward him. "Whoa!"

Miley, Wes's new receptionist, greeted him with a warm smile. "Sorry about that. I guess we didn't anticipate seven-foot clients walking through the door," she teased.

"Ah, it's fine," he said. After the night before, he was practically floating. Whitney had actually come to the football practice. She'd been late and missed most of it, but she'd been there and had come along with them for wings. She'd actually followed through with leaving the office, despite how busy she was and she'd apologized for missing his birthday-in more ways than one. Maybe things were turning around, getting better.

And she and Angel had seemed to hit it off, chatting at the end of the table while the team devoured eight pounds of wings.

"Wes in yet?" he asked Miley.

"In his office. Head on in," she said, fixing the damaged spiderweb and resetting the attacker.

Trent took in the office as he entered farther. The space was the perfect size for his buddy's business, and he was so happy that the year before, Wes had been able to once again secure the office space needed to grow and expand his construction company. He'd had a rough few years after the death of his wife, raising his daughter on his own, but then reuniting with Sarah had changed all their lives for the better. He was thrilled for his buddy and maybe a little envious of the family Wes had.

He wished he and Whitney could reach that great balance of having careers and a family the way Wes and Sarah had figured it out.

He knocked once on Wes's open office door and entered. "Morning."

"Hey, man," Wes said, standing over several blueprints.

"Those the new cottage designs?" Trent asked, moving closer to peer at the sketches of the new Melendez Cottages rebuilds Wes and his team were working on. Thanks to a new website Wes's daughter had made for the company, showcasing Wes's impressive construction skills, Wes had landed the big contract to renovate and rejuvenate the old campgrounds into a more luxury glamping experience.

And by the looks of the designs, he was killing it.

Loft-style cabins with open-beam interiors and floor-to-ceiling windows, stone fireplaces, and Jacuzzi tubs... The old campsite was completely transformed.

"Yeah," Wes said. "We finished the main house rebuild last month, and the demolition crew is wiping out the old cabin structures this week. The storm along the coast had really done a lot of damage, so we weren't able to salvage a lot of the original materials, so it's a complete teardown. We hope to at least have three or four of these ready for the Christmas season."

"That fast? Really?" That was only two months away.

"Awilda Melendez has already booked them out, so yep," Wes said with a laugh.

If his friend was stressed about the tight construction timeline, it didn't show, but now Trent hesitated to ask what he'd come here for.

"What brings you by?" Wes asked.

"Well, I found a new location along the coast for the new bar. Right now it's a country saloon that's for sale because the owners have retired. Great bones, but it definitely could use a major remodel."

Wes nodded, immediately grabbing a Day-Timer and pen. Old-school almost to a fault. Trent would bet the guy didn't even know he had a calendar on his phone. "What's the address? I can drive out there in the next few days and take a look."

"There's no real rush…" Except he'd like to get the new location up and running as quickly as possible. With the two local locations, he was doing well. He'd paid off a lot of old debt and he had savings, but he hoped the third location would help springboard the income to a new level. But the first few months were always the slowest while the advertising and marketing took time to do its thing and people realized there was a new place.

"Don't worry, man. I got you," Wes said. His cell chimed, and he quickly glanced at it. "Unfortunately, I gotta jet. The baby's doctor appointment is in ten minutes."

The tug in Trent's chest was a familiar one at the mention of the baby. "Is Mitch his doctor?"

Wes nodded. "He's so great with babies. I swear him and Jess will have a dozen."

His cousin was so blissfully in love with the former Doctors Without Borders doc, who'd taken over his father's medical practice the year before, that Trent suspected Wes was right.

"Hey, can I tag along?" he asked. "Not to the appointment obviously, but I'd love to see the little rascal."

"Absolutely," Wes said, grabbing his keys. "Be back in an hour," he told Miley.

Trent followed Wes outside, and they headed toward the medical clinic down the street. "Heard you and Sarah set a wedding date."

"Yeah. January first seemed like a great date. Start the year off right, and it'll be an easy anniversary to remember," Wes said with a laugh.

Trent nodded.

Wes glanced at him. "Still no luck nailing down a date yourself?"

"No...but we're getting there. I'm not worried," he said, struggling to hide his disappointment. His future plans were at a standstill, while everyone else had exactly what he wanted.

CHAPTER TWELVE

Now...

The following week, the B&B haunted house officially opened, and as Whitney stood on the front steps, she was relieved to see the line of cars pulling into the parking lot and finding available spots along the street.

Families and groups of friends, some dressed in their own Halloween attire, started to form a line by the entrance where Wes stood dressed like a zombie to greet them.

"If I didn't know better, I'd say this house was actually haunted," Trent said, standing back to admire Wes's amazing handiwork on the faux exterior of the B&B. The wooden facade he'd created to look like a decrepit house with loose wood planks and broken windows, dark shadows behind torn curtains, and smoke that resembled a ghost rising from a crumbling brick chimney was truly amazing.

"You haven't even seen the inside yet," Sarah said, appearing next to them outside. She was dressed as a broken printer that was smashed in a fit of rage, and next to her, Marissa was dressed in a shirt and tie, holding the baseball bat.

Trent laughed when he saw them dressed in reference to *Office Space*. "You two look great."

Marissa giggled. "Dad is totally confused. He

thinks I'm a baseball player but can't figure out why I'm dressed in a shirt and tie," she said.

Poor Wes. Technology really wasn't his thing, and he was living with two techies. Sarah and Marissa had bonded the year before over their passion for coding, and the two were incredibly close now.

"And the best part..." Marissa said, turning Sarah around. Baby Henry was sleeping in a sling on her back, dressed as a black toner cartridge.

Trent immediately was enamored. "I'm totally going to wake him up."

Sarah laughed. "Doubt he'll stay asleep much longer anyway with these crowds coming through," she said, nodding her approval for Trent to take the baby.

Whitney swallowed hard as he carefully unwrapped Sarah's sling and took the still-sleeping baby into his arms. The tiny thing appeared even tinier in Trent's huge, muscular arms.

He looked so incredibly sexy holding the baby, Whitney had to look away.

Trent sniffed Henry's forehead and grinned. "Baby smell should be bottled so that when they are older and stinky, we can be reminded that at one time, they didn't smell so bad."

"Hey!" Marissa said, but then she sniffed her underarm. "Never mind. You have a point."

Trent winked at the little girl. "Want to give us a tour?"

She nodded excitedly. "Can I take them through, Mom?" she asked Sarah, and Whitney's stomach knotted even more. Marissa must have decided she was ready to start calling Sarah Mom. Wes and Sarah had told the little girl she could call Sarah anything she was comfortable with. Sarah looked just as pleased hearing it.

Would Whitney ever get that chance to hear someone call her Mom? Experience that sense of love and pride?

"I can stay out here and help Wes direct people," she said. "I already saw it when I took the photos."

Sarah shook her head. "No way. You have to see it now, all set up with the right lighting and the actors on-site."

Whitney hesitated.

"Go! Enjoy." Sarah was insistent. "It's the family-friendly hours, so you won't get too scared— there's no pop-out scares right now. The actors will behave until nine, then all bets are off," she said with a grin as she opened the front door and Marissa ushered them inside.

"I'm keeping the baby," Trent told Sarah as he followed Marissa inside.

"Figured you would," Sarah said.

Whitney reluctantly followed Trent, carrying Henry, and Marissa inside, and Sarah shut the door behind them. Already her palms were sweating just standing in the dimly lit foyer of the transformed B&B. If the outside was incredibly done, the inside was nothing short of a spectacular feat, and Sarah was right, it did look so different at night.

Dark bulbs had replaced the regular lighting, so the eerie glow of the house made her feel as though she'd stepped into a black-and-white dream out of the past. Directly in front of them was the B&B check-in desk that looked like an old-school hotel check-in. Skeleton keys hung on hooks behind the desk, and old, antique-looking photos hung on the wall—the creepy images a source of nightmares all on their own. Dark, shredded curtains hung in the entryways to the dining room on one side and the den on the other, preventing a view of what lay behind it, and ominous flickering candlelight lit the way upstairs. It looked professionally decorated, and she was impressed by all the work Sarah and Wes had pulled off in such a short time.

"This way first," Marissa said, leading them into the dining room through the flimsy, tattered curtain.

She motioned for Trent to go ahead, then stayed close to his back as they entered. Long tables with fake-bloodstained white tablecloths draped over them were set up inside, and on display were fantastically gory desserts, candies, and drinks, including the floating eyeball one Jess had shown her weeks before.

"Jess is so incredible," she said, feeling a slight tug of guilt. She'd barely talked to her friend in weeks.

"Help yourself to a spider. They're delicious," Marissa said, picking one up and shoving it into her mouth.

Whitney suspected the little girl would be buzzing on a sugar high by the end of that evening.

After tasting some of the delicious, if disgusting-looking, treats, they all followed Marissa into the den, which had been transformed into a witch's lair, where a frightening witch stirred some question-able-looking items in a large cauldron. The actress was quite convincing with the makeup and the haunting way she chanted her spell over the smoking liquid. She glanced up at them and crooked her finger at Whitney to come closer, but Whitney shook her head.

"I'm good here, thanks."

Trent laughed as he moved closer and peered inside the cauldron. "Looks delicious," he said, playing along.

"Just need a few more baby toes," the actress said, pretending to peer at baby Henry.

Trent cuddled him closer. "I'll protect this child with my life."

Whitney's gut tightened even more, and she moved out of the room.

Marissa continued the tour, leading them upstairs, in and out of the various guest rooms and hallways — all featuring a unique, frightening display — crazed scientists, zombies, vampires rising out of coffins, an insane asylum...

The amount of work Sarah and Wes had put into the event was truly something, and going by the squeals of delight and terror echoing throughout the B&B as guests started to flow through, the event was turning out to be a great success.

Whitney suspected they'd surpass their original money-raised-for-charity goal by the end of the week. They'd get a lot of returning visitors to the event, and once word of mouth spread, no doubt people would drive in from farther away to experience it.

"And lastly," Marissa said, leading them out the back door, through the overgrown garden, toward the gazebo, "is Madam Z, our on-site fortune-teller."

Sitting at a table inside the gazebo was an older woman dressed in a beautiful multicolored dress with mismatched patterns, a bandanna wrapped around her head, her long, dark hair loose around her shoulders. Gold necklaces, bangles, and rings reflected the light coming from a crystal ball on the table in front of her.

"Come and let Madam Z see what the future holds," the woman lured.

Whitney shook her head, but Trent nudged her forward. "Go on...it's all just for fun."

She sighed, then reluctantly stepped inside the gazebo and took a seat on the edge of the chair, ready to bolt at any second. What would this woman see? Did she want to know?

"Okay...what do you see?" she asked as calmly as possible despite her racing pulse. She clenched her hands on her lap and stared politely into the ball as the woman waved her hands over it in a dramatic display.

Whitney waited, but the ball went completely dark, and the woman's eyes held a real look of fear when she reopened them. Her gaze met Whitney's, and a shiver ran through her. She stood abruptly, knocking over the chair in the process, and stepped down from the gazebo.

"Hey, wait," Trent called after her as she headed toward the parking lot.

"I'm sure it was just a loose cable or something,"

Marissa said, crawling under the table to check the plugs.

"It's fine. We should get going. The real guests are all coming through now," Whitney said, trying to sound unfazed, but her heart was pounding and her palms were sweaty.

There'd been no future in that crystal ball…at least not one she wanted to know about.

• • •

The haunted house had definitely freaked her out.

Whitney was still quiet as Trent pulled the Jeep into their driveway half an hour later. She wasn't a fan of the scariness of the season, the gore and terror, he knew that, but the fortune-teller and the crystal ball malfunction had really frightened her.

He touched her hand gently as he turned off the vehicle. "Hey, it was just a bad wire connection." Marissa had managed to get it fixed again as they'd left the garden, but Whitney had had enough for one night.

She nodded. "I know. I'm fine."

She didn't seem fine, but he knew not to press the issue when she was already on edge. He opened the door, climbed out, then took her hand as they made their way up the walk and into the house.

He flicked on the interior lights and hung his keys on the hook near the door. "You hungry? Did you want me to make something? Coffee?" It was after eight, but he suspected she'd be staying up to work.

But he was surprised when she shook her head

and started to climb the stairs. "I'm tired. I think I'm going to call it a night."

"Oh...okay." He stood there awkwardly, finding himself in unfamiliar territory. She was obviously upset about something, and for the first time in almost a year, she wasn't heading straight to her laptop to work. She was going to bed. Did she want him to go to bed, too? Or did she want to be alone?

Damn, this shouldn't be such a riddle. They were engaged. They'd been together for seven years. He shouldn't have to question what his fiancée needed or wanted from him. He hated this feeling of walking on eggshells around her. He never knew what to say or do, fearful of saying or doing the wrong thing.

He swallowed hard and cleared his throat. "Would you like company or..."

She paused on the stairs, and her expression was more tired than she usually let him see. The dark circles under her eyes were evident, and she looked pale and even thinner. He wished he could protect her and keep her safe, fix whatever she was struggling with...if only she'd let him in.

"I know it's early, but do you mind?" she asked.

His heart soared a little despite the concern he had for her. "Don't mind at all," he said, joining her on the staircase.

When she reached for his hand, unexpected emotions strangled him as he held hers tight and they headed upstairs. This rare moment of her displaying any bit of vulnerability had him conflicted, but all he knew was that she was reaching out to him and he'd be there for her in whatever capacity she needed. If she wanted to talk, he was there to listen.

In the bedroom, she sat on the bed and bent to remove her boots, but he stopped her. He knelt on the floor in front of her and removed them.

She didn't protest the help, sending him a silent, grateful look as she allowed him to continue undressing her. He removed her sweater, lifting it over her head. Next, he unclasped her bra and slid it down her arms and away from her body. He took her hands and helped her to her feet, then removed her jeans and socks.

Opening his dresser drawer, he retrieved his oversize, faded football T-shirt that he knew was her favorite and slipped it on over her head.

He pulled back the blankets, and she climbed into bed, tucking her feet under the covers.

He undressed and slid in next to her and opened his arms. She moved in closer, and he wrapped his arms around her and held her close. He kissed the top of her forehead and lay awake until the sound of her breathing grew deeper, the muscles in her body softened and relaxed…and she was asleep.

CHAPTER THIRTEEN

Now...

The evening before had served as an epiphany.

Since Whitney's accident, Trent and everyone else had been encouraging Whitney to slow down, take a breather, work less, and try to reduce her stress.

But the constant nagging was only causing his fiancée even more stress. She already felt the pressures of her job, and instead of being there as a source of support the way she needed him to be, he'd tried to get her to change part of who she was. That hadn't been fair.

Her seeking silent comfort in him the night before had spoken volumes about what she actually needed. She didn't often ask for help, but she shouldn't need to. Maybe he needed to anticipate the help she might need but not be asking for, and then provide it.

Whitney may not even realize what she needed or how he could help, but the basics were obvious. She needed to eat, he knew that much, and instead of trying to "help" by suggesting dinner out or being home before nightfall to enjoy a hot meal with him, he'd bring food to her at the office so she could continue to work. He'd fork the food into her mouth while she typed if necessary.

Feeling more empowered and a lot more

hopeful than he had in months, Trent packed up her favorite rotini noodle pasta, grilled chicken breasts, and two pieces of her favorite pumpkin pie and left the house.

In the Jeep, he cranked the music up and rolled the window down. The October breeze felt great, and the sights of the changing leaves on the trees and the ones covering the ground made him smile. He loved this time of year. The changing of the seasons, the cooler temperatures.

A few minutes later, he pulled into the parking lot of the mayor's office, seeing Whitney's vehicle and Scott's Escalade in the lot. They were working on the pitch for the *Race Across America* show together, and he was happy that Whitney had finally started to accept assistance from the guy who was supposed to be her assistant. Maybe if they worked successfully on this project, she'd feel more confident letting Scott take lead on other projects. He knew she was worried that Scott might steal her job, being the mayor's son and having a degree from a reputable university, but Trent hoped the mayor saw Whitney's dedication and experience.

Getting out, he carried the food inside and entered the quiet office. The reception area was empty. Kim was gone for the day, and the office lights were all off, except for the one in Whitney's office down the hall.

He headed that way, following the sound of voices, and nearly stopped, hearing laughter. Whitney's laugh. Relief mixed with something else he couldn't quite pinpoint. When was the last time he'd heard her laugh like that? When was the last time she'd laughed with him?

Weeks ago, at the pumpkin patch...

Didn't matter who she was laughing with or why. The main thing was that she had found some joy in her working day, which he knew was often not the case. And it was a good thing that she and Scott were finally getting along. Maybe she wasn't feeling as threatened by the mayor's son anymore.

He felt better as he continued on and stopped outside the open office door. "Hey," he said, seeing her and Scott sitting at her desk. Papers and photos were spread across the desk, and on the computer screen, video footage of Blue Moon Bay, gathered by a drone, played.

And in their hands were takeout Chinese containers. A noodle dangled from his fiancée's mouth as she stared in surprise at him.

"Sorry to interrupt." In hindsight, he should have texted or called first to see if she'd eaten. Not that she would have responded to a text...

"Hey, Trent," Scott said with a nod. "Just took a break for a quick bite."

Yep, he could see that. It wasn't the sight of the food that surprised him, it was the fact that this guy had obviously talked his fiancée into stopping long enough to actually eat.

And laugh.

Whitney sucked the noodle into her mouth and set her food container aside as she stood. "What are you doing here?" she asked slowly as she walked toward him.

He held up the food. "I thought I'd bring you dinner, since you were working late, but it looks like I should have confirmed that you hadn't already eaten first."

"Sorry, I meant to text you, but I lost track of time," she said, glancing at her watch. "We still have so much to do before this pitch material is ready—"

"We can pick this up tomorrow morning," Scott said.

Whitney hesitated as she glanced at Trent. Obviously, she wanted to keep working.

"I brought the food to you. Eat it later if you get hungry. Stay and finish up," he said, handing her the food.

She hesitated as she took it. "You sure?"

"Absolutely. There's more than enough for two," he said to Scott.

"Thanks, man," Scott said.

"I'll see you at home," Trent said to Whitney.

He gave her a quick kiss on the forehead and left the office. He heard her tell Scott, "Give me a sec," before chasing after him down the hall. "Hey, wait up…"

He stopped and turned.

"I'm sorry…"

"It's okay," he said, and he meant it. He was just content that she was actually taking time to eat. Didn't matter that it wasn't the meal he'd brought or that she was enjoying it with her coworker. He wasn't at all jealous or intimidated by Scott. He had all the trust in Whitney and their relationship. He just felt slightly disappointed that what he'd hoped was a nice gesture had ultimately only made her feel bad.

That certainly hadn't been the intent.

"No, really, I am," she said. "I should have called or texted, but we were just wrapped up in this…"

"I get it. I was just worried about you, and you need to eat. I'm happy to see you were." He touched her shoulders and gave her a sincere smile that he hoped conveyed that he really wasn't at all upset.

"You can stay."

She didn't mean that. Whitney had always separated work from home life. The only time the two intersected was when she was working on promo for his bar.

Huh, maybe *that* was something he could use to bring them together again.

He'd been worried about adding more to her plate by telling her about the new location and asking for her help with a new marketing campaign, but now he couldn't sign on the dotted line and finalize things on the new location soon enough. "I'll just be in the way," he said. "Enjoy the food if you get hungry again later. Try not to work too late. I'll see you in the morning."

"In the morning?" She frowned.

"I'm going to head into the bar, finish up some paperwork." Sign the real estate agreement on the new building and hope to give the two of them something to work on together. "I'll probably stay to close up."

She nodded. "Okay…see you in the morning."

Trent kissed her quickly again and started to leave as she returned to her office.

"This chicken is delicious. If you don't marry him soon, I will," he heard Scott say, and Trent grinned as the door closed behind him and he headed back to his Jeep.

. . .

In his office at the bar, hours later, Trent reviewed the last page of the real estate contract, then signed the bottom of the page. He knew in his gut this was the right decision. But he'd never actually bought a new place before without mentioning the plan to Whitney. He hesitated before he stood and slipped the pages into the feeder of the printer.

He wouldn't second-guess this. Whitney would be happy when she found out. He'd have told her already if there had been an opportunity...a time when she wasn't already preoccupied with her own stress and work obligations. He hated to add more to her plate. He could handle this on his own.

Angel popped her head into the office. "You're still here? I thought you left hours ago."

He checked his watch. It was after two a.m. He'd meant to leave earlier, but he'd wanted to really comb through the details of the contract. Read all the fine print and make sure there were clauses in there that allowed him to back out, pending an inspection. Of course, he knew the place needed a lot of work, but in case there were bigger issues like electrical or plumbing that he hadn't been able to see by just touring the place.

He felt better knowing Wes hadn't noticed anything serious when the two of them had driven out to look at the place the week before. He'd asked Wes to keep the news that he was planning to expand to himself for now, until Trent had finalized everything and officially announced it.

"I'll be leaving soon," he said, running a hand over his tired face. "You can take off if you want. I'll lock up."

She hesitated. "You sure?"

"Absolutely. Get home to the boys. How's that going, by the way?"

She smiled. "Better. Really, the transformation in Eddie since he joined the football team is incredible. He even watched a movie with Liam and me the other night. I mean, he was texting his old friends on his cell phone, but he was at least sitting in the same room doing it."

"Good. I'm glad to hear it." The more he'd gotten to know Eddie and Liam at football practice the last few weeks, the more confirmation he got that they were actually really great kids, just struggling to adjust. Angel had raised them to be polite and respectful and hardworking. They were fitting in with the boys on the team, and Trent had seen Eddie hanging out at the arcade with several of his teammates when he worked the bar at the Game Room. No more fighting or causing trouble. "They are great kids."

"Too bad my ex is such an asshole," Angel said, a note of bitterness in her tone.

Trent frowned. "Still giving you trouble over the divorce settlement?"

She sighed, entering the office. "I wish it was just about the settlement. I actually don't give a shit about the money." She paused. "He's starting to contest the custody situation." She looked pained as she said it. "The boys don't know it yet, but he's filing an application to have them with him full-time in L.A."

"Thought the kids were cramping his newfound freedom?"

"Me too. Turns out his new girlfriend has three kids of her own and thinks him being a father is wonderful. She wants to meet the boys, have them integrate into their new blended family." She rubbed her forehead.

"That's not fair to the boys. They're just getting settled here, and they should be with you."

"Courts may feel differently. The boys might, too. They miss him. And they miss L.A." She sighed. "I'm not sure what I can offer—broke, single mom who's moved them to the middle of nowhere, away from their…father"—she stumbled on the word—"and friends."

Trent sat on the edge of the desk and touched her shoulder. "You're so much more than that. You're a fantastic mom who has their best interests at heart. Unlike their father, who sees them as a way to impress a new woman." What would happen to the boys when Angel's ex got tired of this new woman and no longer needed them around? Would he ship them back to Angel?

Angel looked unconvinced. "I don't know what I'll do if I lose them, Trent. Those boys are my world."

His heart ached for her. He couldn't imagine how hard this was. He loved kids, and he didn't even want to imagine how tough a divorce would be if he were only able to see his children part of the time. It would break him up inside.

"Hey, chin up. You'll get through this, and you'll come out on top." He paused. "And I'll try to make Blue Moon Bay a little more appealing for the boys."

She frowned. "How?"

"I could use some help with the construction on the new location. Sharrun's Construction is doing the reno, but the boys could learn hard work and earn some extra arcade cash by helping out at the jobsite." He'd need to run it past Wes, but he knew it wouldn't be a problem. Trent would pay the boys for the work himself.

"Really? That would be... Wait. New location?" Her eyes widened. "You found one?"

Trent took the papers from the scanner and handed them to Angel. "About an hour away. Prime location on the beach."

She scanned the pictures and the details. "Definitely needs some work, but I can see this looking great once you've turned it into a Trent's Tavern," she said excitedly. "This is really fantastic."

"Thanks." He appreciated her support. It felt good to tell someone... He just wished he were sharing the news with the most important person to him, the person this impacted the most, besides him.

His fiancée.

CHAPTER FOURTEEN

Now...

Whitney quietly slipped out of bed early the next morning, shutting off her alarm before it could sound and wake up Trent. She'd heard him slip in the night before, sometime after three. She stared at him now, sprawled across the bed on his stomach, his arms and legs sticking out of the blankets. Out cold. She'd never met anyone who could sleep as soundly as Trent.

Though it must be easy to sleep when there was nothing to keep him up worrying at night. Trent was such a great man, and karma treated him accordingly.

Bringing her dinner at the office the day before had been a sweet gesture, obviously spurred by her vulnerability she'd shown the night after the haunted house disaster. She would normally be disappointed in herself for having shown the moment of weakness, resulting in him wanting to take care of her, but instead she was actually feeling a lot better.

Maybe breaking down sometimes wasn't such a bad thing.

The day before, after a good night's sleep in Trent's arms, she'd felt refreshed and more motivated in the office as she and Scott had worked on the *Race Across America* pitch together. She was keeping her promise to let him be involved, and it actually wasn't so bad to have another opinion on the project. Scott was also funnier than she'd allowed herself to discover and an overall nice guy. He'd had her in stitches with stories of his own failed attempts at surfing. And it was true, laughing was therapeutic.

Getting out of bed, Whitney grabbed her work clothes she'd laid out the night before, and after kissing Trent gently, she left the room. She headed to the bathroom down the hall to get ready for work instead of using the en suite, not wanting to wake him.

She turned on the shower and undressed. Her vision blurred slightly as she went to step into the tub, and she closed her eyes tight, waiting for it to pass. She carefully opened them again and still, the little blue fish on the sea-themed shower curtain swam together.

She climbed in under the spray anyway and took several deep breaths as the water cascaded down her back. Her vision issues were always the worst first thing in the morning and late at night. Stressing about it only made it harder.

She reached for a shampoo bottle and poured the liquid into her hand, realizing too late that it was the conditioner. Damn bottles looked identical. Guess she was co-washing that day.

She lathered her hair, rinsed it, and by the time she shaved her legs, her vision was mostly back to normal.

As she reached for the tap to turn off the shower, she heard the bathroom door open. Trent peeked a sleepy-looking face around the curtain. "Want some company?"

"Why aren't you sleeping?"

"Because I heard there was a sexy, naked woman in here," he said with a grin.

Those damn dimples. She could never get enough of that grin. Whitney pulled the curtain back and nodded for him to get in.

He yanked off his underwear and stepped in with her, closing the curtain again behind him.

Her heart raced at the sight of his nakedness.

He took her into his arms and turned their bodies so that they were both under the hot spray.

Being in his arms had always made her feel the safest, and today was no exception. If anything, she craved the sensation even more.

He kissed her forehead, and she wrapped her arms around his neck and rested her forehead against his chest. "Sorry about yesterday. Dinner was a really nice gesture."

"I know. I'm a good fiancé," he said teasingly.

And right there was one of the reasons he was the most perfect man in the world.

She lifted her face up toward him, and he stared down at her lovingly. That look had never changed over the years, never dulled. Every time Trent looked at her, it was like he was seeing her for the first time. It gave her chills and butterflies in her stomach.

He leaned his head closer and placed a soft kiss to her lips.

And another one.

And another one.

She pressed her body closer, and when his lips met hers a fourth time, she tangled her hands into his hair and held him there. She ran her tongue along his bottom lip and separated them, deepening the kiss.

His hands trailed lower down her sides and around the back of her to cup her ass. He squeezed and pressed his lower half against her. She could feel him thicken against her lower stomach, and her pulse raced.

The craving she felt for him was unexpectedly intense as her body sprang to life. His desire-filled kisses revealed he felt the same way. There was always so much emotion in Trent's kisses—passion, lust, love, and a tantalizing teasing that always left her wanting more.

He broke contact with her mouth to lower his head to her neck, sucking and biting gently on her wet flesh. She clung to his back as he moved them toward the wall and continued his trek with his mouth down her chest, between her breasts, and lower along her stomach.

She closed her eyes, savoring the sensations flowing through her at his touch, his caress, his kisses. He was the best lover she'd ever had—caring, considerate, unselfish, undemanding, yet in gentle control and command. She'd do anything and everything he wanted. She had full trust in him…except for when it came to his reaction to her secret…

She pushed the thought away as she gently lifted his head back up to hers. "I love you," she said, because she desperately did, and yet there were so many other things she just couldn't say.

"I love you more," he said, gripping the back of her thighs and lifting her body over his erection. "You ready?" he asked.

She nodded eagerly. She was so ready to have him inside her. Needed it.

He lowered her slowly, forcing his cock in through her tight, wet opening. She moaned and clung to his shoulders as he went deeper, filling every inch of her with his long, thick shaft.

The water from the shower cascaded over them as he moved her body up and down over him. Slowly at first, then faster and harder as their passion rose.

"Whitney, you're amazing," he said, staring into her eyes.

"I believe you're the amazing one," she said, her breathing labored as he pleasured her in ways no one else possibly could.

"Whitney, if there's something else you need… anything you're not getting…" His voice was slightly strangled as he spoke.

He actually thought there was something more he could give her? Didn't he know he gave her absolutely everything she needed and so much more? It was her inability to give him what he deserved that caused her pain and hesitancy and doubt.

Not him. Never him.

"You are everything," she said, holding the sides of his face and staring directly into his questioning gaze.

He nudged them backward again until her back was against the wall. She used her legs around him to steady herself as he moved his hands to her breasts and massaged.

Damn, it felt so good. His cock inside her and his hands teasing her nipples.

She kissed him hard and bit his lower lip roughly, silently commanding him to move into a more intense direction.

Trent knew her so well and knew exactly what she wanted as his fingers pinched her nipples. Hard.

The combination of pleasure and pain searing through her had her gasping and clutching to him frantically, her nails digging into the flesh at his back as he thrust into her harder and faster against the shower wall.

Out of breath, she pulled back and leaned her head against the wall as he plunged in deeper, his orgasm reaching its peak the same time hers toppled over the edge. He pumped in and out of her body roughly a few more times before he stilled, pushing himself in as deep as possible.

This time, her vision blurred from the overwhelming sensation coursing through her body. She felt herself throbbing around him, and Trent released a deep moan as he came inside her.

Her body relaxed as she wrapped her arms tight around him. He rested his head against her shoulder as he slowly pulled out and gently put her back on her feet.

"Good morning," she whispered.

"Perfect morning," he said, holding her tight.

· · ·

An hour later, Whitney pulled into the lot at the mayor's office and headed inside. Entering her office, the heat from the sun coming in through the open blinds had her immediately reaching for the thermostat. Her body was still heated from the hot and steamy shower with Trent. She turned the air-conditioning to freezing before going to her desk. She opened her email and, seeing forty-six new ones in her inbox, she got to work.

She didn't look up again until Kim paged her office later that afternoon. "Whitney, you have a visitor."

"Who is…" The words hadn't left her mouth before her friend Lia appeared in the doorway.

"Surprise!" The booming, cheerful voice made her jump.

Her lawyer friend who now lived in New York was one of the biggest personalities Whitney had ever met. The year before, she'd come back to Blue Moon Bay for a family reunion they hosted at the B&B, and she and Sarah had finally put behind them a silly frenemy thing they'd had going on since high school.

Whitney had been relieved, as she'd always really secretly liked Lia, but her loyalty to Sarah had forced her to choose sides.

"Hey! What are you doing in town?" She hadn't expected to see Lia and her husband, Malcolm, until the holidays, so she was genuinely thrilled to see her.

"I have a legal convention in San Diego in a few days, so I thought I'd extend my trip. Was a little shocked to see the inn transformed into a nightmare house. Someone could have given me a heads-up about that…but I'm staying at the

Radisson, so it's all good." She entered the office and shivered. "Damn, it's freezing in here."

"Sorry…I'm always so warm," she said as Lia sat across from her, pulling her appropriately colored for the season orange cardigan around her thin, athletic frame. "How long are you staying?"

"Just two nights. Thought we could all get together for a girls' night?"

Whitney hesitated. She was far too busy for a girls' night, but Lia was rarely in town, and she really did want to hang out with her. Lia was their big-city friend, and Whitney always loved the chic vibe that exuded from the woman. It made her ache for that herself, having always hoped to live the fast-paced lifestyle in the concrete jungle before her mom got sick. If she couldn't get that fast-paced career Lia had, she was at least able to be in close proximity to someone who did.

"That sounds great," she said.

Lia's cell chimed with a message, and she smiled as she read it. "Perfect. Sarah and Jess are in, too. Halloween party at Trent's Tavern tonight it is."

Halloween party? She consulted her calendar. Right, today was Halloween. Where had the month gone? "Tonight…oh…um…"

Lia shot her a look. "Do not even think about trying to bail on me."

Whitney sighed. She didn't want to bail, and the last few days, she'd been learning to appreciate a bit more downtime. "Eight?"

"A little early, but we're all getting too old to be there when the twentysomethings crash in close to midnight," she said with a laugh. "And…I have the perfect group costume for the four of us," Lia said, her eyes twinkling with mischief.

Group costume. She knew there was no point in arguing. "Wonderful," she said with a forced smile.

• • •

That night, the place was going to be packed, so it was all hands on deck. Max was already positioned at the front door, and Angel was restocking the bar with extra bottles of everything. Trent filled the ice coolers as his additional help, Danielle, set up a shot table near the dance floor. The twenty-two-year-old had the friendliest, bubbliest personality Trent had ever come across, so he told Max to keep an eye on things. He preferred hiring older staff, but Danielle was saving for her film school tuition, and the tips she'd make working the shot bar that evening would definitely help.

"Man, I remember having optimism like that," Angel said with a tired laugh as she returned from the shot table, where she'd stocked Danielle with whiskey and tequila.

Trent laughed. "The joy of being young." He eyed Angel. "How are things?" They hadn't talked since a few nights ago, and he was curious about the situation with her ex.

"Well, Brad's working his angle with the boys. They're spending Halloween in the city with him tonight. The annual Halloween party tradition continues, apparently," she said, her tone slightly bitter.

"Don't worry. They'll see through their father's

bullshit," he said.

"At least I don't have to be worried about what they're getting up to tonight, left to their own devices."

That was one good thing. Halloween in Blue Moon Bay was usually fairly controlled and uneventful, with police surveillance circulating on the streets. In addition to Max, there would be an officer parked in front of the tavern as well, in case of any trouble.

Angel checked her watch. "I guess I should get my costume on. Do you need any more help before I change?"

Trent scanned the bar. Everything looked ready to go. "Nah, I'm good. I should get ready, too." He reached behind the door and grabbed a cowboy hat from the hook, then put it on. "There. Ready."

Angel laughed as she shot him a look. "That's your costume?"

"Every year."

His cell phone chimed with a text, and he smiled seeing it was from Whitney saying she'd be there that evening with Sarah, Jess, and Lia.

She hadn't been at last year's event, and he was thrilled she was going to make it.

See you soon, he texted, then put the phone away.

Picking up a box of Halloween-themed party favors—miniature trick-or-treat baskets shaped like pumpkins, skulls, and witches' cauldrons filled with candy and chocolate—he carried it around, positioning them on the tables already adorned with black-and-orange plastic tablecloths.

As he emptied the box and broke it down, he saw Angel coming out from the bathroom. Gone were the jeans and black T-shirt, replaced with a skin-tight, leather-looking black catsuit. On her head were cat ears, and the six-inch heeled leather boots she wore looked impossible to work in all evening. Someone else was looking to compete with Danielle for those tips.

"Jesus," he heard Max say, and when he turned toward the bouncer, the man's jaw was practically on the wooden bar-room floor.

Trent grinned as he walked toward him. "Close your mouth, buddy."

Max coughed and cleared his throat. "What kind of idiot let her go?"

"A big one," Trent said. He tapped his friend on the back. "Keep an eye on her, too, tonight, okay?" His locals he wasn't worried about. He knew they all knew he'd take no shit in his bar, so no one would act inappropriately toward his staff, but out-of-towners may not be as familiar with the rules.

"You've got no worries about that, man," Max said. "I'll be lucky if I can peel my eyes off her."

At that moment, Angel glanced their way and blushed as she caught Max's stare. Trent fought an irrational sense of longing at the way his employees were vibing each other. Could he and Whitney get back some of that spark *outside* the bedroom?

CHAPTER FIFTEEN

Now...

No one commented on the fact that Whitney's team costume for the *Charlie's Angels* theme Lia had decided on was basically the same outfit she'd worn to work that day minus the suit jacket. They were all just probably happy to see that she'd shown up at all and hadn't bailed at the last minute.

Luckily, her contribution was Bosley, while Jess, Sarah, and Lia had the harder costumes of the angels. The three of them had met that afternoon to scavenge through whatever was left at the local costume shop in town and had managed to find wigs, boot covers, and matching body-con dresses in different colors to pull off the looks. They looked amazing, and Whitney fought the small sense of longing that she'd missed out on the activity that day with the others. Lia was off work, and Sarah and Jess ran their own businesses, so they controlled their schedules. Whitney didn't have that luxury.

She was just glad she'd agreed to be here with them tonight.

The bar looked amazing as they entered just before eight. She hadn't been inside it in weeks. It looked like a professional had decorated the space for the event with the elaborate animatronic figures and the party favors on the tabletops. Trent had mentioned that Angel had taken lead on that part.

Whitney's gaze landed on the bar manager now, who was dressed as Catwoman in a tight black jumpsuit that looked like leather and sky-high-heeled boots that made her already fantastic curves even more pronounced. Nearly every man in the place was drooling.

"Holy smokes, Angel is wearing the hell out of that costume," Jess said next to her as they made their way to the "Reserved" booth Trent had kept for them.

"She sure is," Whitney said as Trent spotted them.

Dressed in his usual cowboy hat and plaid shirt—his annual Halloween costume—he waved and smiled at them.

"Ladies, the usual?" he called across the bar.

"Virgin martini for me," Sarah said. "Still breast-feeding," she told them quickly as explanation. "Not pregnant again."

Jess laughed as they all slid into the booth. "Only a matter of time. You and Wes plan to have another one within two years, right?"

Sarah nodded. "That's the plan. We like the idea of keeping them close in age…"

Whitney tried to silence her sigh. Another evening chatting about babies.

"And it makes sense to have the wedding early next year before you start showing again so you can buy that dress you saw at Dashing Bridal on Main Street," Jess said.

Sarah had found a dress already? Obviously, she and Jess had gone together. They hadn't invited her?

No, they had. She vaguely remembered the text from Sarah a month before, asking her if she was available. She couldn't remember replying to it. As much as it hurt not to be included, she couldn't expect her friends to put their lives on hold while they waited for her.

Besides, going wedding dress shopping may have given her an anxiety attack.

Sarah grinned at Jess. "I heard someone was perusing the jewelry counter at Bingly's last week…"

Jess's cheeks flushed. "Mitch was probably just looking for a gift for his mother's birthday next week," she said, but they all knew she was secretly hoping that Mitch would pop the question any day now.

Whitney rubbed her chest, and Lia caught her motion.

"You know," she said, "as much as I adore Henry and Marissa and all babies, in fact, and weddings are my favorite topic of conversation, tonight we're not moms, fiancées, girlfriends, or wives—we're four hot ladies out for a good time."

Sarah and Jess nodded their compliance, and Whitney sent Lia a grateful look.

And before long, that's exactly what they were. Within an hour, they were laughing and chatting like old times, and Whitney realized just how badly she'd needed this night out.

"Remember senior year when Kelli organized a protest against further frog dissecting in schools?" Lia said. "I think it was ten of us chained to that big tree in the schoolyard." She laughed and shook her head.

"And then we lost the key to the lock, and the school made us stay there for hours as punishment for the stunt," Sarah said, shaking her head.

If talking about Wes's first love bothered her friend, Sarah didn't show it as she reminisced about their high school friend they'd lost far too soon to cancer. Kelli had been Lia's best friend, and Lia was Marissa's godmother.

"Oh my God, this is my favorite song," Jess said as a fast-tempoed hip-hop song played. She jumped out of the booth and grabbed Sarah's hand. She waved to Whitney and Lia to join them.

Lia pushed her out of the booth, and Whitney gave in to the fun as she followed her friends out onto the dance floor. Moving her body, arms in the air, her hips swaying, she enjoyed the rare feeling of freedom.

Behind the bar, Trent looked their way, and his gaze was completely mesmerized as he watched her dance with her friends. Whitney smiled at him, and he leaned his forearms against the bar as he took her in, as though there was no one else in the room.

She hadn't felt as sexy as she did in that second in a long time. Not even during their more intimate moments. This connection in a public place, as though no one else was around, as though he was seeing only her, had eyes only for her, had her vibrating.

Unfortunately, as Lia took her hand and spun her, a wave of dizziness hit her, and she stumbled slightly off-balance. She blinked several times, trying to refocus and regain her stability, but the wooden floor beneath her feet seemed to be rippling like waves. The bright lights around her and the loud beat of the music now vibrating in her chest in time with her thumping heart had her feeling nauseous.

She released Lia's hand and hurried off the dance floor. "Pee time," she said weakly as an excuse and left them, not wanting anyone to follow her. She made it to the washroom just in time, and pushing through a bathroom stall, she retched, slumping to the floor.

This dizzy spell was the worst one she'd experienced. They typically threw her off, but this one had made her feel as if she was on an uncontrollable tea-cup ride. And it continued. She took several deep breaths, eyes closed as she fought against another wave of nausea. Sweat pooled on her forehead, yet a chill ran over her body.

A long few minutes later, Whitney peeled herself up off the floor and took a calming breath as she slowly opened the stall door and went out to the sink. Her reflection in the mirror was slightly pale, and her mascara had run.

The washroom door opened as she splashed water on her face. She quickly reached for a paper towel and dried her face as Angel entered and smiled at her warmly. "Hey, Whitney! Your friend Lia is a riot. She's like a little bit of city in this place."

Funny that Angel would feel the same way that Whitney did. Made sense, though, as Angel had always lived in L.A. before moving to Blue Moon Bay.

"Yeah, she's great," Whitney said, wiping away

the dark makeup from under her eyes.

Angel studied her. "You okay? You look a little pale."

"Totally fine." She forced a smile. "I think Trent might be pouring doubles."

"Hoping to get lucky, maybe?" Angel said with a wink as she reapplied her lipstick.

"Doesn't need to liquor me up for that," she said, suddenly feeling a desire to make sure this woman, and everyone else for that matter, knew that she and Trent were okay. They'd had a rough year since her accident…and a little before that. But lately, they were getting better. *She* was getting better. Unfortunately, her health was still an issue, but she vowed to make her test appointments that week and figure that part of things out. Once she had the test results and a game plan on how to fix herself, she'd tell Trent and her friends everything.

Things would be okay. She didn't need to lose Trent over this. She'd find a way. She had to.

"You must be excited about the new bar," Angel said as she slid her lipstick back between her breasts in the catsuit.

Whitney felt a new wave of dizziness. New bar? She frowned, but she refused to acknowledge she had no idea what Angel was talking about. "Oh yeah…"

"The location along the coast right on the beach is perfect, and sure, it needs work, but with Wes's crew, I know it will look great," she said, turning toward Whitney.

Angel knew about a new bar location and had seen pictures? Trent had talked to Whitney about another location on the coast, had talked about expanding...but Whitney hadn't thought he was actively considering it yet. It seemed to be a future plan, not an immediate one. And he'd found a place already? He hadn't told her anything. This was definitely one of those things a fiancée should know, have a say in.

And Wes knew?

She fought for a deep breath as she nodded. "I'm sure it will, too."

"See you out there," Angel said and then left the bathroom.

Leaving Whitney with another reason to feel ill.

• • •

"Want to tell me what's wrong now?" Trent said hours later as they pulled into the driveway.

"Nothing." After her conversation with Angel in the bathroom, Whitney's happy party mood had dampened. It was hard to have fun with the new information weighing on her mind. It wasn't the new bar that upset her or even the fact that Trent had ultimately made a decision that big without discussing it with her. He was entitled to make career decisions on his own. She did. What bothered her most was that he'd told other people before telling her.

But she'd yet to truly reconcile her feelings and thoughts about it and wasn't quite ready to have this conversation with him yet. Conversation in the heat of the moment, without adequate processing time, was sure to blow up into an argument.

Trent released a deep breath. "I can tell you're upset."

"I'm fine." He needed to drop it.

"Damn it, Whitney, that's three *nothing*s and four *I'm fine*s since we left the bar."

She turned in the seat to face him. Fine, if he wanted to do this now… "When were you going to tell me you bought a new bar?"

He looked at her as though she couldn't possibly be serious. "When were you going to have time to have that conversation?"

She scoffed. "Oh, no. Don't put this on me. I would have made time for an important discussion like that. A huge decision." She may put her career before everyday relationship things like dinner plans and…wedding discussions, but things like this took priority.

Trent's expression changed to one of annoyance. "Well, maybe you should make me a list of the topics that are important enough to make time for, because the wedding, and our relationship, certainly don't warrant the attention."

"That's not fair. Those are…"

"What? Whitney, what are they?"

She sighed. He was right, but she refused to let him turn this around on her. He was the one still in the hot seat right now. "I just think a huge financial decision should be something we talk about."

"I absolutely agree. But you're the one who refuses to combine our finances, remember? I would love to share these responsibilities with you, help you with the Rejuvenation fees and paying off any lingering debt—but you refuse to do it."

"My expenses are mine—"

"No, they damn well aren't!" His voice raised in frustration, and he took a calming breath. "I'm sorry." He paused and started again. "I love your mother as much as I love my own. Let me help take on the responsibility of caring for her, too."

Whitney swallowed the lump in her throat. "It's not that easy for me."

His expression softened. "To rely on someone. I know. I get it. But I'm not just someone. I love the shit out of you. You're my everything," he said softly but with determination to make sure she believed it.

"Why did you tell Angel before you told me?" That was the part that bothered her most, and as much as she tried to reason the slight pang of jealousy away, there was no denying that Angel was a beautiful, sexy single mom who obviously adored Trent, and Trent relied on her.

He ran a hand over his hair. "She was just there the other night when I was reviewing the real estate contract. I didn't even really think anything of it."

"You two seem close."

"I trust her to run the bar, and her boys needed some help." He turned in the seat and reached for her hand. "But she's no more to me than that."

Whitney looked down at their hands.

"Hey, look at me," he said.

She glanced up.

"Do you have a thing for Scott?" She could hear in his voice that he knew the answer to that. He wasn't jealous or asking out of any sense of insecurity. He was trying to prove a point.

"You know I don't."

"So we both have coworkers who sometimes are there at the right moment to catch some private info…or catch a laugh… It's natural. We're not the only people in each other's lives."

She swallowed and nodded. They were both their own people, and while they made a great team together, they were also strong individuals apart.

That was good, but it was also a little terrifying, the knowledge that they would both be okay without the other person.

He lifted her chin and moved closer. "I love you."

"I love you, too," she said.

"I'm sorry I didn't tell you about the bar sooner or discuss it with you. I should have."

She nodded, and he kissed her gently.

"So? We good?" he asked.

"We're good," she said.

How could she possibly stay mad at him when she was still keeping secrets of her own?

CHAPTER SIXTEEN

Now...

A week later, Whitney grabbed the biggest wineglass she could find, poured half the bottle of Merlot into it, and carried her laptop into the living room, where Trent was watching a soccer game. Her inbox boasted sixty-two unanswered emails, and if she waited until the next day to reply to them, there would only be more and she'd never get her workload under control.

The executives from *Race Across America* were super high-maintenance, and the contracts and documents they required signed and completed immediately to move forward were weighing on her. Their legal department had had several concerns, and she needed to finalize these negotiations soon. The mayor was on vacation for three weeks with her husband in Greece, and Scott had admitted that legal documents weren't his area of expertise.

Whitney sat on the opposite end of the couch and opened the laptop. Logging into her remote access, she clicked on the link to her email just as Trent lay down on the couch. He stretched out and placed his head against her leg.

She glanced at him and shifted more to the right, but he just repositioned himself. "Trent? I'm trying to work."

"Oh, sorry..." He sat up and shifted closer,

propping his feet up on the coffee table instead. A habit of his that drove her crazy.

On the television, the game was blaring, and blocking out the noise was challenging. She read and reread the first email three times before realizing it didn't even need a reply.

Shutting the laptop, she stood. "I'm going to go work in the bedroom."

"Is the TV too loud? I can turn it down," he said.

"It's fine. Enjoy the game."

Inside the bedroom, she sat cross-legged on the bed and opened the latest draft of the contract from *Race Across America*. Scanning it, the font swam together on the screen, and her temples throbbed.

Not now.

"Hey, I was going to run out to pick up sushi for dinner. You cool with that?" Trent asked, popping his head around the bedroom door.

"I'm not hungry."

"When was the last time you ate?"

Who knows? Breakfast? The evening before? She vaguely remembered a half-eaten protein bar melting on her desk from the sun shining through her office window, but was that today or a week ago? She had no idea. "I'm fine, Trent."

"I can get Chinese food instead from Wong's. Your favorite."

"Get whatever you like." She closed down the document and opened her email.

"Do you need more wine? I could swing by the—"

"Trent! I'm good." The look of surprise on his face made her soften her tone. "I'm sorry. I just have a lot of work to get done." Since the Halloween party, things had gotten even more hectic. The Christmas season was fast approaching now that it was November. It was as though on the stroke of midnight on the thirty-first of October, everything went from pumpkin spice everything to peppermint and pine trees.

With the *Race Across America* pitch demanding so much time, she was falling behind schedule on everything else on her to-do list.

Trent came into the room. "Anything I can help with?" He sat on the bed and shimmied closer, propping pillows behind his back, obviously intending to stay.

She couldn't work with him distracting her. He meant well, but just the sound of his breathing was irritating when she was trying and failing to focus on the complicated legal documents she could barely read without enlarging the font on her computer.

She forced a tight smile as she turned to face him. "You know, I am hungry. Chinese food would be great." Anything to get an hour to herself.

"Done." Trent jumped up off the bed. "I'll be back in a flash," he said as he kissed her forehead and then left the room.

"Take your time," she mumbled to herself.

• • •

"Hey, boss, you ready for the pitch meeting this afternoon?" Scott asked, popping his head around the corner of her office door the next day.

"Almost…" Whitney barely looked up as she answered. In two hours, they were meeting with the Hollywood executives in the hopes of selling them on the idea of Blue Moon Bay for a checkpoint stop as part of the race. The number of tourists an event like that would bring to the community during their non-peak season would give them another huge boost in becoming a better-known tourist destination. The television coverage of the beautiful small town would be worth a million dollars in advertising. It would help put Blue Moon Bay on the map, and while Whitney had been reluctant about the idea in the beginning, she was determined to succeed now.

"Need me to look over anything?"

She hesitated…

Team player, remember.

And as much as she hated to admit it, it might be a good idea to have a second set of eyes on the presentation, in case she couldn't trust her own. "Sure. Have a seat."

Scott sat across from her, and she printed the latest draft of the pitch, sliding it toward him while she cued up the slideshow presentation on her computer screen. He scanned the draft with all the key selling points and nodded. "This looks fantastic."

"Really? I mean, thank you." She cleared her throat. "It was a team effort." The tip that the show was airing for a third season and that producers were looking for new challenge sites for contestants *had* come from Scott. "This was a great idea."

He smiled. "Let's see the slideshow," he said,

sitting forward on the edge of the chair to watch.

Whitney pressed play, and the pictures and video clips of the town appeared. The surfing shots had turned out perfectly, and the drone footage over Main Street and along the jagged coast was breathtaking. The sandy shores and the clear blue water. Images of Dove's Nest B&B and the fantastic restaurants… It definitely featured all the best that Blue Moon Bay had to offer.

Ten minutes later, he was shaking his head. "I don't know how you do it. You make Blue Moon Bay sound like the best place on earth."

"Isn't it?"

Scott didn't look convinced. "I'm partial to more exotic locations."

Huh, maybe her job wasn't in as much jeopardy as she'd thought. Scott hadn't found a place in town, still doing the commute.

"And I get the feeling this small-town pace isn't quite your style, either," he said.

Damn, he was definitely perceptive. There was a time she couldn't wait to get out of Blue Moon Bay and see the world. But that was in the past and not something she wanted to share with Scott.

She cleared her throat. "Well, for today…this place *is* the best place on earth, and we need to convince those Hollywood execs."

He grinned. "Got it. You know, you and Trent should totally apply to be contestants on the show."

She eyed him. "Trying to get rid of me?"

"No way. I mean it—I think you two would win for sure, husband-and-wife team…"

"We're not married yet." Why had she said that?

"Okay, engaged-couple team. With your brain and Trent's muscle, you two would kill it at the checkpoint challenges," he said.

She could barely make it across the parking lot these days without her legs aching, "Racing across America" on a television show was not happening. "I'll pass."

"Just saying, you two are a power couple."

Were they? The last few months had been a little touch and go, but she wanted to continue to believe they would pull through.

Her cell phone rang on the desk beside her, and the Rejuvenation number lit up the screen. She hesitated, glancing at Scott. "My mom's senior facility."

"Go ahead," Scott said, picking up the pitch again and reading in an offer of privacy.

Whitney hesitated but answered on the third ring. "Hello?" *Please don't let there be anything wrong today.*

"Hi, Whitney, this is Marla from Rejuvenation."

"Yes, hi, Marla. Everything okay?"

"Everything's fine. We were just wondering if you were on your way."

Shit. What day was it? She opened her Outlook calendar, but there was nothing scheduled. "I'm sorry, Marla. What am I forgetting?"

"Dr. Tyler is here to see your mom."

She'd totally forgotten her mother's monthly doctor's visit was that afternoon. She looked at the clock. Could she get to Rejuvenation and back before the meeting? She had no other choice than to try. The doctor's appointments were really important. She needed the update on her mother's condition.

"Okay. I'm on the way. Please apologize to him for the wait. I'll be there as soon as I can."

"Thanks, Whitney. See you soon," Marla said before she disconnected the call.

Whitney slid her swollen feet back into the heels under the desk and grabbed her purse.

"Everything okay with your mom?" Scott asked, standing.

"Yes…I just need to head over there. I should be back in time for the meeting."

"Are you sure? I can take over as point person on this one if you can't make it back."

She hoped it wouldn't come to that. "I should be able to make it…but just in case…" She opened her email and sent him a copy of her slideshow. The one she'd spent weeks putting together. Four drafts and countless hours getting the visuals and wording just right. "I just forwarded you the presentation."

"Great. Don't worry. Go take care of your mom. I can handle it if you're not here," he said, following her out of her office.

She hesitated. That's what she was afraid of. "Okay. Thank you. But I'm sure I'll make it back in time."

* * *

Then…

The bar's grand opening event had been a huge success.

"You and Trent really pulled this off," Jess said to her as they collected empty beer mugs and wine-glasses from the tables throughout the tavern, well after midnight. "You two make a really great team."

Whitney smiled, exhausted but exhilarated by the amazing turnout that evening. "We really do." They'd worked together for weeks, planning and organizing the event, and with her marketing expertise and connections and his hard work and dedication, the event had been a bigger hit than they'd anticipated. The bar had been open a few months now and had been doing well, but that evening's official grand opening had really solidified the new establishment in the small town.

"I meant in more ways than one," Jess said, sending her a knowing grin.

Whitney blushed, catching Trent's loving gaze from across the bar. His tired, lopsided grin as he wiped the wooden surface made her heart race. She wholeheartedly agreed. They were perfect together.

Unfortunately, the next day, her commitment to the relationship was put to the test.

"Knock-knock," a male voice said, tapping on her open office door.

Whitney looked up in surprise to see the rep from Bacardi. She'd been working with the man from L.A. for weeks, as they were the official liquor sponsor for Trent's Tavern, offering prizes and free drinks, but had only met him face-to-face the night before at the event. "Hi, James…"

"The receptionist wasn't at her desk. Okay if I come in?" he asked.

"Sure, of course." She sat straighter as he

entered and took the seat across from her. He was dressed casually in jeans and a sweater, his peppered gray hair gelled back, but there was a definite air of business radiating from him. "Did you enjoy the event?" she asked.

Was he here to pull his sponsorship? Had they reconsidered? Her pulse raced, and she wiped sweaty palms against her dress pants, her mind already reeling with a list of other liquor suppliers she could reach out to.

"It was fantastic. Really great job," he said.

Her shoulders relaxed.

"But what really impressed me was you."

She blinked. Her?

James leaned forward and folded his hands on her desk. "The last few weeks have been one of the smoothest business transactions I've had in years. Your professionalism and knowledge of the marketing side of this business was ultimately what led to our decision to sponsor the location."

She wasn't sure what to say. The compliment was the highlight of her career, but she couldn't take all the credit. "Trent will make a wonderful business p-partner," she stammered.

"Oh, I know he will," James said. "But I'm here to offer you an opportunity."

Whitney swallowed hard. "What kind of opportunity?"

"We are looking for a new East Coast rep. You'd be essentially on the opposite end of these kinds of negotiations. You'd visit bars and restaurants all over the East Coast and discover the ones we should partner with."

She gaped. "Travel all over the East Coast?"

He nodded. "The job consists of about seventy percent travel. All expenses covered and a great starting salary. Perfect for a young, single, ambitious person starting out in their career. It's where I started with the company before I married and had kids," he said with a wistful longing that made her think he missed those good old days. "What do you think? Interested?"

"Oh…um…" Was she? A few months ago, she'd have jumped at the opportunity. No hesitation. Since completing her online degree, she'd applied to dozens of opportunities in the city with bigger companies, but she'd never gotten an opportunity to prove her skills and that she was just as capable as a candidate with a more impressive résumé.

Months ago, she'd already be packing her things. But now, things were different… "Can I think about it?"

He seemed slightly surprised, as though he'd actually expected her to sign an employment contract on the spot. And she wasn't completely sure why she wasn't. He was right. She was young, ambitious, starting out in her career…but she wasn't exactly single, and while the relationship with Trent was new and not something she should base huge life decisions on…it was important to her. She wasn't quite ready to make this leap without considering what it meant for them.

Which in itself told her almost everything she needed to know.

"Just a few days," she said at his silence.

He nodded and stood. "Of course. Think about it

and let me know." He headed toward the door. "But just a heads-up that we have a new trainee program starting in three days in L.A.…so don't take too long."

Three days to consider a whole new life path. "I won't," she said, trying to sound confident over the tightening of her chest. "And thank you."

He tapped the doorframe and left the office, and Whitney sat there conflicted.

The job opportunity of a lifetime had just presented itself. One she'd never dreamed possible, but one that was offering her the lifestyle she'd always said she wanted.

And all she could think about was if she could truly live without seeing Trent's loving gaze every day.

. . .

He'd be supportive of whatever Whitney decided.

The job opportunity was one she deserved, one she'd excel at…one that would take her away from him.

Trent's chest tightened at the thought.

Long-distance relationships were tough but not impossible. They'd make it work. He could take a few days off every month and visit her wherever she was on the East Coast. Though, he knew the first year in business at the bar was the most crucial, so in reality, that possibility was unlikely. But there was still calls, texts, FaceTime…

Not ideal, but it would be okay. He was determined to make it work.

But was Whitney? Was she contemplating the new position with the same thought in mind or would she end things to pursue the life she wanted without the complications and ties to Blue Moon Bay? To him?

His cell phone rang as he locked the bar that evening, and he frowned seeing his mom's number on the display. His stomach dropped. It was after midnight. She was never up this late.

"Mom? Everything okay?" he asked, answering the call as he headed toward his Jeep in the dark, empty parking lot.

"Your grandma had a heart attack," she said— and Trent's own heart shattered.

• • •

The day of the funeral was one of the saddest days of Whitney's life. Instead of sitting in a training room in L.A., beginning a new career, she stood next to Trent in the cemetery, while the spring rain poured heavy from a dark, thick sky. She held his hand firmly in hers as his grandmother was laid to rest, knowing this was where she needed to be, where she *wanted* to be.

By his side through thick and thin, better or worse. Always. There would be other business opportunities but only one Trent.

• • •

Now...

She didn't make it back on time. The appointment with her mother's doctor had been a lengthy one, the news not encouraging. Therefore, it only made her mood worse when she climbed into her vehicle and received the text from Scott:

We did it! Blue Moon Bay will be a checkpoint stop on the next season of Race Across America!

She should be happy and excited that they'd won over the client with her pitch and presentation, but all she felt was ill on the way back from Rejuvenation that evening.

Go have a celebratory drink! You've certainly earned one.

Whitney needed a drink all right, but she was hardly in the mood to celebrate.

Scott would get the credit for her hard work. Mayor Rodale would only remember that it had been him who'd delivered the pitch to the executives and won over the client. No one would remember that she'd been the one to put the entire thing together.

She massaged her temple with her left hand as she drove toward Trent's Tavern. Her migraines were getting worse, and stress made them that much more unbearable.

The news at Rejuvenation hadn't been good. Her mother's bloodwork from the week before indicated that the medications she was taking were having ill effects on her kidney and liver function. Dr. Tyler had recommended lowering the dose or switching to a new brand.

Both options had downsides, and it had taken hours of reviewing the possible alternatives to come to a decision to switch medication and see what happened after that. Her mother hadn't been lucid enough to weigh in on the decision, and Whitney hated making decisions without her input.

But it was only going to get worse, not better.

Pulling into a parking spot behind the bar, next to Trent's Jeep, she climbed out and went inside. It was only four in the afternoon, and she was grateful that the place was quiet and nearly empty and it was only Trent working.

"Hey, you," Trent said as she approached the bar. "So?" he asked expectantly. He'd known about that day's pitch, but she hadn't had time to tell him about the Rejuvenation doctor's appointment.

She nodded. "We got the contract. *Race Across America* will be coming to Blue Moon Bay."

"Congratulations!" His eyes widened with supportive excitement for her, even though she knew the reality show wasn't his thing. "That's amazing. Why don't you seem more excited?" He reached for a bottle of vodka and poured a double shot over ice, sliding it toward her. Then he leaned across the bar to kiss her.

Neither the drink nor the kiss made her feel better.

"I missed delivering the pitch. Scott did it," she said, draining the contents of the glass.

"What? Why?"

She explained the visit at Rejuvenation, feeling worse the more she talked about it.

"Shit, Whitney. You should have called. I could have met you out there." He reached over and took her hands in his. "You don't have to make these decisions alone. I'm here."

"You have the bar to run. You can't just close up

shop anytime."

"I can and I will," he said, studying her. "You get that, right? That I'd do anything for you. Anytime."

She did, but right now she didn't want support or reassurance, she just wanted to wallow. "I should probably head home before I drink an entire bottle of that stuff," she said, nodding toward her empty glass. She should be heading back into the office, congratulating Scott on delivering a great pitch, celebrate the success with her coworker, then launch into the never-ending to-do list she still had on her plate, but she lacked all motivation and energy and she didn't want to kill Scott's high regarding the win.

"Go home...take a bath, get some rest," Trent said gently, touching her hand on the bar. "And try to see the contract as a good thing. Mayor Rodale knows it was you who made this happen."

She nodded. She wasn't so sure about that. "I'll see you at home."

"I'm proud of you," he said, walking her to the door.

She wished the words made her feel better.

• • •

Enough was enough.

Trent couldn't stand to see Whitney this way. For weeks, things had been tense. He'd thought they were turning a corner around Halloween when she'd eased up a little and had seemed more like her old self, but then things had quickly returned to the fast pace business at the office as the pitch had drawn closer.

And today she'd hit an all-time low. Stress of the job, stress about her mom and the additional funding Rejuvenation was requiring for a private nurse to help with her mom, had reached its breaking point. He couldn't remember ever seeing her so down. Busy, preoccupied, yes, but never so depressed.

She was struggling, and Trent couldn't just sit by and watch the woman he loved deal with all of this on her own. That wasn't a partnership. All this time he'd been pushing and insisting on Whitney accepting help from him, and he'd allowed her to refuse. Allowed her to take on the heavy financial burden on her own because he hadn't wanted her to feel bad or as if she was indebted to him in any way.

Not anymore.

As her fiancé and someone she planned to spend her life with, he was allowed to make an executive decision in helping her. And he'd do it in a way where she couldn't prevent his help.

Picking up his cell phone, he dialed Meredith's number at the Blau real estate office, hoping it wasn't too late. He paced behind the bar as the call connected.

"Hey, my favorite client!" she answered on the second ring.

She probably wouldn't feel that way in a minute.

"Hey, Meredith. Unfortunately, I have some bad news." He paused, but there was no hesitation in this decision. He knew what he had to do. "I'm not going to be able to go through with the purchase on the new location."

She was silent for a moment, then, "Why the change of heart, darlin'? Was it the price? Because I'm sure with some haggling, I can get the sellers to come down another few thousand."

"No, that's not it. Well, I guess technically it is the money. Something else came up that I need to redirect those funds toward."

"Ah, okay…"

"Sorry about this. I know this isn't what you wanted to hear." He truly was apologetic. He wasn't someone to back out of a commitment or a contract, but sometimes unexpected things happened, and Trent knew he had to back out of this opportunity. It just wasn't the right timing. His motivation to expand had always been about having the ability to help Whitney more and provide the security he thought she needed in order to slow down her own pace, but he got it now. Whitney never would. This was who she was, and he loved her drive and ambition.

He just wanted to take away some external pressure.

"It happens," Meredith said with a sigh. "No worries."

He was grateful for her understanding. "Am I still your favorite client?"

"No," she said with a laugh. "Take care, Trent, and if you're in the market again, reach out anytime."

"Thanks, Meredith. I appreciate it." He disconnected the call and headed into the back stock room, where Angel and Max were busy doing inventory.

At least that's what they were supposed to be doing.

Trent cleared his throat loudly, and his two employees in the middle of a make-out session broke apart abruptly. Angel's expression held a flushed, guilty look, but Max was grinning from ear to ear.

"Oh, hey, Trent. We were just…"

He held up a hand. "I'm going to pretend I didn't see it." He was honestly thrilled for them, and he had no policies about staff not dating at the bar. But right now, his employees fooling around was the least of his concerns. "Can you two keep an eye on the bar for a while? I have to run out."

Angel nodded over her clipboard. "Sure. No problem. If it's not busy, I can teach Max some things," she said.

"Oh, you can, can you?" Max teased.

Angel shot him a look that said *cool it*, but then a small grin crept onto her face.

"Thanks," Trent said.

"Everything okay?" Angel asked. "I couldn't help but overhear Whitney out there just now."

Trent nodded. "She had a rough day." That's all he'd say. He'd realized that maybe he did share too much personal information with his bar manager, and maybe he shouldn't be as forthcoming about private matters at home. "She'll be okay."

"Good," Angel said, gesturing for Max to quit staring at her ass and get back to work.

Grabbing his jacket, Trent left the bar. A moment later, he jumped into his Jeep and cranked the music, feeling so much lighter at having made this decision as he headed toward Rejuvenation.

•••

THEN...

Trent walked up the front steps toward Whitney's family home, then turned and headed back toward his Jeep as sweat pooled on his lower back. He'd been in the house a dozen times; he'd met Whitney's mother—had dinner with her, played cards with her—but this visit was different. He paced in the driveway, the temptation to jump into his Jeep and drive away strong.

Nope. He couldn't chicken out. This was important, and he didn't want to put it off any longer.

But did he really need to do this? It was the twenty-first century. He didn't need permission to ask the woman he loved to marry him, but he did want it.

But was it too soon? Would Lydia approve?

He swallowed hard as a million thoughts and emotions spiraled like a whirlwind through him, and he took several deep breaths of contemplation. They'd only been dating a short while—but he knew how he felt. He was certain of how Whitney felt, too. They'd talked about the future. They'd talked about their goals and dreams. They were on the same page, and Trent couldn't imagine his life without Whitney in it.

And her mother was a huge part of her life— *their* lives. It was the respectful thing to do.

Squaring his shoulders, he took the steps two at a time and knocked on the front door before he could change his mind.

He ran a shaky hand through his hair as he waited.

Lydia answered the door a moment later, dressed in her usual baking apron and fuzzy slippers they'd given her for her birthday. Her hair in rollers meant she planned on going to bingo at the community center that evening. "Trent! What a nice surprise." She gave him a quick hug and looked past him. "Whitney's not with you?"

He cleared his throat as he shook his head. "I… uh…actually wanted to ask you something."

Realization dawned on the older woman's face, and Trent held his breath as he waited for any sign of encouragement. Would she be okay with this? Would she approve?

It felt as though there was so much on the line in that moment. His future happiness…

A slow smile formed on her expression, and his shoulders relaxed.

"Took you long enough," she said with a wink.

Lydia was right. It had taken Trent long enough to get the courage to propose, but now that he had her blessing, he didn't want to wait a second longer. And he knew exactly where and how he wanted to pop the question. It was going to take a little prep work and a little help from the local pumpkin patch.

• • •

Her annual pumpkin patch visit was the highlight of the season for Whitney. She wasn't a fan of Halloween with all its spookiness, but the cool evenings, the smell of pumpkin spice, and enjoying the harvest festivities at the local farm was her favorite fall activity.

Arriving at the farm that evening with Jess, she climbed out of her vehicle, feeling the usual excitement wrap around her.

Too bad Trent had to work late that evening. His last-minute text to let her know he wouldn't be able to tag along had disappointed her, but she'd still enjoy the evening with her best friend. Linking an arm through Jess's, they entered through the farm gates. The evening sun was low in the sky, casting a warm glow over the fields as families and friends participated in games of corn hole, made their own scarecrows from old farm clothes, empty vegetable sacks and hay, and launched pumpkins from a cannon. Watching the community come together to celebrate the season always made her feel proud to call Blue Moon Bay home. While she'd once dreamed of big city life, there was something about her small coastal town that would always truly feel like home, where she belonged.

"Hayride first?" she suggested as they approached the concession stand for the mandatory hot chocolate.

"Um…I was thinking we could start with the corn maze?" Jess said casually, but Whitney caught a hint of something she couldn't quite distinguish in her tone—mysterious excitement that had nothing to do with pumpkins and corn stalks. Something was up with her friend that evening.

"Okay, sure." She was up for anything and everything in any order.

They paid for their hot chocolate and Jess led the way toward the maze. Each year the farm created a new design, challenging locals with dead-ends and circular paths that could only be successfully navigated with the help of clues provided in the form of trivia questions. A correct answer would give the right direction through the maze to the next trivia stop.

"Hey, Whitney and Jess," Mr. Bennett, one of the farm owners said in greeting with a wide smile.

"Hey, Mr. Bennett, hope you have a challenge for us this year," Whitney teased.

The older man grinned and shot a wink at Jess. "Oh, I think you'll enjoy this one."

Whitney turned to Jess with a suspicious look. "What's going on?" She glanced around and noticed no one else approaching the maze. She peered inside, but didn't see anyone or hear the usual laughter as people got lost or debated the right direction.

"This year you're on your own," she said. She reached into her purse and retrieved an orange piece of construction paper and handed it to Whitney. "Your first clue."

Whitney's heart raced as she took it and read.

What was I wearing the first time we met?

A) A Clown Suit (Turn Right)

B) My Birthday Suit (Turn Left)

Whitney's eyes widened as she laughed at the question. "Clues from Trent? Why? What's happening?" she asked Jess, a whole new level of excitement enveloping her.

Jess shrugged, the mischievous gleam still in her

eyes. "Guess you'll have to complete the maze and find out."

"Enjoy," Mr. Bennett said.

Entering the maze, Whitney headed left. She hurried past the tall corn stalks, weaving along the path's twists and turns until she reached the next trivia question stop. The usual pumpkin patch trivia card was replaced with another piece of orange construction paper with another one of Trent's handwritten questions on it. She picked it up and read.

What song helped me confess my feelings for you?

A) In Case You Didn't Know (Turn Left)

B) Love Stinks (Turn Right)

Whitney laughed as she headed left again through the maze. She brushed corn stalks out of her way as she moved quickly, eager to reach the next trivia stop.

Trent had created her own maze challenge that year. She couldn't believe he'd done something so incredibly special for her. Making these direction clue trivia cards and convincing Mr. Bennett to give her exclusive access to the maze must have taken so much time and thought. Her heart swelled as she reached the next trivia stop.

She picked up the next card and read.

Where did we have our first kiss?

A) The parking lot of a local Denny's (Turn Left)

B) Dancing alone in the bar (Turn Right)

Whitney headed right and continued to follow the correct path through the maze, guided by the answers to Trent's trivia questions about their relationship. With each one she was reminded of all the special moments they'd shared since the day they met, and her pulse raced as she drew near the last stop.

Cards in hand, she drew a deep breath as she rounded the last corner of the maze and found Trent standing there at the trivia stop. Dressed in jeans and collared shirt, he looked amazing and more than a little nervous as he smiled at her. Her mouth went dry and her heart pounded loudly in her chest. He was there. She'd suspected he would be, but it still felt slightly surreal as she approached him.

"Hi," she said.

"You figured out my maze," he said, his voice full of emotion as he moved toward her.

"It was the best one yet," she said softly, gazing up at him.

He reached for her hands and drew her closer. "Sorry I said I couldn't make it here tonight. I wanted to surprise you."

"You're forgiven. This was definitely a nice surprise." She wrapped her arms around his neck and kissed him gently. Her body was shaking slightly as a feeling of anticipation overwhelmed her. He'd gone through a lot of trouble to do this for her… Was there more to come?

He stared into her eyes and took a deep breath. "Whitney, the last year with you has been the best year of my life."

She nodded. For her too.

"My life has changed so much since moving

back home and starting the business, but the biggest change is the one I feel inside. I love you and being with you has made everything else that much better. You're everything to me," he said, releasing her slowly and dropping to one knee.

Whitney's hand covered her mouth and tears welled in her eyes.

Trent took her hand in his and retrieved a small ring box from his pocket. He opened it and held it out to her, revealing a beautiful solitaire engagement ring.

Whitney's mouth gaped as the diamond sparkled in the evening setting sun.

"Marry me?" Trent asked.

Whitney nodded quickly, and the word "*yes*" escaped her lips on a strangled whisper.

Trent smiled and kissed her hand before sliding the ring onto her finger. He stood and took her into his arms, and Whitney's heart felt like it might explode with happiness. "I love you," she said, hugging him tight.

Trent pulled back and kissed her softly. "I love you more."

There was no way that was possible, but Whitney wasn't about to argue with her new fiancé.

CHAPTER SEVENTEEN

Now…

How long would the clinic keep her on hold?

Whitney tapped her fingernails against her desk, the urge to hang up overwhelming. She couldn't put off scheduling the tests any longer, but she was hoping the clinic in town was booking several weeks out. Now that she was actually a step closer to the appointment, she needed a little more time to summon the courage to go through with the tests.

Not knowing the severity of her condition had given her at least a false sense of security. But there was no denying that her sight was getting worse a lot faster in the last few weeks, and no amount of painkillers was helping with the migraines.

"Hello, Ms. Carlisle, you still there?" a clinic attendant asked.

Barely. "Yes, I'm here."

"Great. Sorry to keep you waiting. The soonest opening we had for an MRI appointment was in February…but I noticed a cancellation for tomorrow, so would that work for you?"

February or tomorrow. Wow, nothing in between, and neither appealed to her. February was too far away, but tomorrow was…tomorrow.

She hesitated. Putting this off would only make things worse in the long run. "Okay, yes. What time tomorrow?"

"Eleven a.m. We ask that you arrive fifteen minutes before your scheduled time."

"Okay." Whitney listened to the rest of the preexam instructions, then disconnected the call. Sliding her feet back into her ballet flats under her desk, she headed toward her boss's office. She rarely asked for time off, so she shouldn't be as nervous about it as she was.

What excuse could she give for needing the day off when they were right in the middle of contract negotiations with the producers and designing the calendar for the upcoming year? Admitting to a doctor's appointment would cause concern, and a personal day always raised suspicion.

She paused outside the mayor's office door that was slightly ajar. Hearing voices inside, she turned to leave, but she stopped at hearing Scott speak.

"I'm just not sure I'm ready to take over this responsibility yet."

Whitney's pulse raced, and she leaned closer.

"Of course you are," Mayor Rodale said. "With your degree and experience, you are the most qualified candidate—it's a no-brainer decision."

"I've only been back here for six months...how will it look to the residents here?"

She held her breath.

"Everyone in town loves you. They love our family. They also see the need for some changes around here, and so do I."

Shit. What was going on? Had Scott used her mistakes to steal her job? Or had the pitch presentation solidified him as a more capable head of marketing and tourism? Either way, it certainly sounded as though she was soon to be replaced.

"Whitney...um, I think they are in a private meeting," Kim said behind her.

She turned quickly and hurried away from the door as Kim stepped forward to close it.

Obviously, the mayor's niece knew what this private meeting was about. And she didn't want Whitney hearing it. "Oh, yeah...I can talk to her later. It's not important," she said, rushing past the receptionist and back into her office.

At her desk, she forced several deep breaths.

Just relax. They can't fire you for no reason or over a few mistakes.

Had Scott told his mother that she was sick? She never should have let her guard down and trusted him. How many times in her life did she need proof that she could depend on no one before she stopped taking chances on people?

She sat straighter and reached for her cell phone.

Forget taking the day off, she was now more determined than ever to prove she was still the best at her job. She'd get those contracts back to *Race Across America* by lunch and then design the entire calendar herself before she left for the day.

Dialing the medical clinic, she waited for the options.

"...to cancel an existing appointment, press two..."

Whitney pressed two.

• • •

Arriving back in town just in time for football practice, Trent grabbed his gear from the back of his Jeep and climbed out.

Wes's truck pulled into the lot next to him, and he waited for his co-coach. "You made it," Wes said as he got out and locked the doors.

"Yeah, the errand didn't take as long as I thought it would." Marla and Dr. Taylor at Rejuvenation had been relieved at the decision to hire a personal nurse for Lydia, and paying the full year's cost had been more than appreciated by the senior facility. He felt really good about the decision. He just needed to find the best way to tell Whitney so that she didn't freak out and get upset with him.

It had been a risk doing it without consulting her, but he hoped it was one of those times when the crime could be forgiven based on the sincerity of the intent.

"Hey, man, unfortunately I'm not going to need your help with the new location renovation after all," Trent said as he and Wes crossed the football field.

Wes frowned as he readjusted the duffel bag on his shoulder. "Decided not to buy?"

"For now." Eventually he'd still like to expand, but there was no rush now that he'd relieved some of Whitney's financial burden a different way. "Just think it's probably best to focus on the locations I have," he said. He didn't want to tell anyone where the savings had been relocated to. It wasn't anyone else's business.

"No problem. I totally get it. I'll admit, I wasn't

sure when I was going to find the time. Melendez Cottages are taking more time and resources than I'd originally thought."

"About the cottages, I have a favor to ask," Trent said as they dropped the gear onto the field and opened the duffel bags.

"Name it," Wes said, reaching inside for a stack of traffic cones.

"Angel's boys are still struggling a little. Their father is making a ploy to get them to live with him in L.A., and I'd offered to help her with maybe setting them up with some part-time work here in town. Give them more motivation to choose to stay and also help her show the courts that they are doing well here."

Wes glanced at him as he positioned the cones. "And you're wondering if I could use a couple of apprentices?"

Trent nodded. "I'll cover their wages. I'm not asking you to pay them."

"Sure," Wes said. "The Melendez Cottages are a no-go. I can't have unskilled minors on-site at a job like that one. But I can give them some cleanup work around some local jobsites after construction is completed."

"Thanks, man, I appreciate that."

Wes looked like he wanted to say something but then got to work setting up the tackle dummy.

"What is it?" Trent asked as he helped.

Wes hesitated. "Look, it's none of my business, man, but you seem to be awfully concerned with helping Angel out."

Naturally, that might come across as suspect.

Trent took zero offense at Wes's non-direct questioning. "There's absolutely nothing going on there." He paused. "It's a big brother relationship thing. I feel compelled to help her, that's all."

"And Whitney's okay with all this help?"

He remembered the conversation in the Jeep the night of the Halloween party and nodded. "We've actually had the discussion. Everything's cool. Whitney knows I'm completely devoted to her." And he hoped his actions that day proved it to her even more. "But you're right. I'll back off a little. Angel's not my responsibility." The only person he felt a responsibility to was Whitney. Normally, he wouldn't care what his helping Angel looked like to the outside world, but he never wanted to disrespect Whitney in any way, and if their friends were starting to look at Trent's friendship with Angel sideways, maybe it was best to put some distance there.

Wes seemed appeased. "It's your relationship, man. I just care about the both of you."

He was lucky to have a friend like Wes. They all looked out for one another in their circle of friends. Trent fist-bumped his buddy. "I appreciate it."

"I'll ask the boys to stop by the office," Wes said as the team started to arrive.

"Great. I'll give Angel a heads-up."

Trent greeted the boys as they geared up and scanned the field for Eddie and Liam, but he didn't see them.

He checked his watch and gave them a few extra minutes, but the boys were a no-show.

Odd of them to miss a practice.

He reached for his cell phone and started to text Angel but then stopped. If any of the other kids missed practice, would he call their parents to check in on them? Maybe he *was* too involved with Angel and her family. He knew there was no attraction between them, but he also knew how things could and would be perceived.

He had to be careful there.

He put his cell phone away and blew the whistle hanging around his neck, catching the team's attention. "Okay, guys! Bring it in!"

CHAPTER EIGHTEEN

Now…

Trent did what?

Sitting on her living room sofa late that evening, her swollen feet propped up on several pillows, Whitney stared at the email from Rejuvenation with the paid invoice attached. Her mother's housing and new nursing requirement costs had been paid in full for the year. She blinked, not trusting her eyes.

That's one keeper of a fiancé you have there, was Marla's message.

Whitney's conflicted heart made her chest tighten until it was hard to breathe. Such an amazingly thoughtful gesture…but something she couldn't allow him to do. And he knew that—that's why he'd done it without talking to her first.

The funds must have come from the money he'd been saving to buy the new location along the coast. He'd backed out of the real estate contract.

It was time. This made it painfully obvious that Whitney had to tell him the truth right away.

Hiding her deteriorating health was getting harder, and she didn't want to keep lying by omission. As soon as he got home from football practice, it had to happen. She couldn't be with him knowing there was such a big possibility that she'd never be able to give him the family he wanted, the one he deserved. She'd been keeping things from him for too long, and even though it was going to break her heart, she had to let him go.

And find a way to repay him for the Rejuvenation costs.

Focusing on the other emails in her inbox was impossible, so she lay back against the sofa cushions and closed her eyes until she heard the sound of his Jeep pulling into the driveway. The headlight beams illuminated the living room through the window, and she sat up as she heard him unlock the front door.

"Whitney?"

Controlling her trembling body took all her strength, so she didn't answer. Instead, she sat waiting on the edge of the sofa until he entered the living room. Her engagement ring caught her attention, and with trembling hands and unshed tears burning the back of her eyes, she reluctantly took it off. This would be the only way to show him she was serious. The only way he'd believe it was truly over.

"Hey…you feeling okay? I wasn't expecting you home from the office yet or I would have come home earlier." He set his football gear down, the duffel bag against the wall in the hallway, where it would stay until next week's practice.

Another habit of his that drove her crazy. Something else she'd miss.

"I came home early." In her hands she clutched her engagement ring, the edge of the diamond cutting into the flesh at her palm. Removing it had been one of the hardest things she'd ever had to do, fueled only by the fact that giving it back to him was the right thing.

"Are you sick?" he asked, running a hand through his hair, still wet from his shower at the sports facility.

Yes.

The word was on the tip of her tongue, but she shook her head. He wasn't getting that version of the truth. One he could argue with, make her change her mind...or try anyway. "Trent, I need to tell you something." Her voice wavered and she swallowed hard. She refused to cry, to give in to the tearing sensation in her chest. She had to be the strong one while she still had enough strength left.

Sitting next to her on the couch, the look of concern on his face was almost enough to break her, but she forced a neutral, unfeeling expression of her own. This was for the best. For both of them.

"Whit, you're scaring me. What's going on?" He reached for her hand, but she kept hers in tight fists on her lap.

"I haven't been honest with you." She cleared her throat when the words came out a whisper.

"About what?"

Everything.

She opened her hand to reveal the engagement ring.

Trent's expression clouded with a mix of confusion and hurt. "What are you saying, Whitney? You're breaking off the engagement?"

More than that. The relationship. "I'm not able to be the person you need, Trent."

"What I need is you." He knelt on the floor near

her knees and took her sweaty hands in his. "Look at me, Whitney, please."

She couldn't for fear of caving, so she shook her head. "This is for the best, Trent. I want my career, and I'm not sure I'll ever be ready for mother-hood." It wasn't even an option for her unless there was some miraculous cure for her sickle cell ane-mia, and her bitterness at the injustice of it helped give her voice the hint of coldness she needed.

"Okay, so we wait awhile. See how you feel in a few years. Just because you're not ready right now doesn't mean you'll never be. And calling off the engagement makes no sense. This is something we can work through together."

She couldn't. Not anymore. "This will never work, Trent."

"You mean us—*we* will never work?" he said, reluctantly taking the ring.

She nodded, her eyes on her now empty hands. Looking at him was too hard. Breaking both of their hearts was torture, and the stress had her vision turning blocky again.

"No," he said. "That's not good enough."

She forced a breath. "You don't get a say in this."

"The hell I don't," he said, standing and pacing the living room. "I'm not going to let you throw us away. I love you, and we will find a way to work through this."

"I'm not the right woman for you."

He took her hands and pulled her into his chest. "Don't say that. You're perfect for me. We are perfect together. Whitney, we will get through this.

We can get through anything. Together." He titled her chin upward, forcing her eyes to his.

Every part of her soul wanted to sink into his arms, into his words, into the faith that he had in them, but she couldn't. "You deserve a life I can't give you, and in time, you'll only resent me for it."

"That will never happen. I love you, Whitney." He rested his forehead against hers, and she shut her eyes tight, unable to see the pain on his face when she delivered this final blow.

Her tongue was heavy in her mouth, and air refused to get to her lungs. She was drowning…and she wouldn't bring him under with her. "I don't want to marry you, Trent."

His heart breaking reflected in his eyes, killing her. "That's a lie."

"It isn't. I thought it was what I wanted, but it isn't. I thought kids were what I wanted, but they aren't, and you have been very clear that you want a family. One I can't give you." She removed her hands from his and turned away.

"Whitney, let's just talk this through." Tears glistening in his eyes destroyed the last of her willpower.

"There's nothing to talk about. I'm not changing my mind on this. And while I'm grateful for your offer to pay for the nursing costs as Rejuvenation, I can't accept that gift. I'll find a way to repay you."

"You're upset because I forced you to accept my help."

She took a breath and nodded. "It just further confirmed that I'm not ready for this relationship. Leaning on you, depending on you…is not who I am. I thought you knew that." It was so messed up that ultimately it seemed as though she were punishing him for the most incredible, altruistic act, but she was simply trying to be fair. Even if she couldn't explain it all right now.

His chest heaved as he stood there, staring at her. Confused, hurt, questioning... He shook his head and ran a hand through his hair, then he looked at the engagement ring in his hand. "And there's nothing I can say? Nothing I can do to change your mind?" He sounded like he'd move heaven and earth to have her reconsider, and it took all her remaining pride not to.

"I'm sorry, Trent," she said.

And she really was. About so much.

He nodded slowly, then turned and left the living room. A second later, the front door slammed, and all she could see was him jumping in the Jeep and driving away, his taillights blinking out in the distance.

• • •

THEN...

This day was even harder than she'd anticipated.

With shaky hands, Whitney folded her mother's favorite cardigan and went to put it in the open suitcase on the bed.

Lydia stopped her. "Leave that one here for when I visit," she said.

The lump in her throat threatened to choke her as she nodded, avoiding her mother's eyes. She couldn't meet them for fear the truth would be reflecting in hers. Her mother had to be frightened about this move to the senior facility and what that meant, but Lydia wasn't allowing Whitney to see it.

There was no question who Whitney had inherited her strength from.

"Okay, good idea," she said, hanging it back in the closet of the room her mother had been staying in that year since her first few episodes had made it dangerous for her to live on her own. A year after Whitney's dad passed and her mother's health was deteriorating quickly.

She hated that they were even contemplating moving her into a home for assisted living, but after her mother's fear the week before when she hadn't recognized Whitney or Trent or her surroundings in the new home, they'd been forced to make the difficult decision. It was the best thing for her.

They finished packing the clothes, and Lydia reached for her photos on top of the dresser. She placed them carefully inside and then zipped the suitcase. She took a second but then squared her shoulders and said, "I'm ready."

Whitney wasn't. She didn't think she could possibly ever be ready.

But she, too, concealed the intense emotions raging through her as she picked up the suitcase. They met Trent in the driveway, where he was loading a box of Lydia's personal items into the Jeep.

"There're the beautiful ladies," he said, but his voice broke slightly, and he quickly stopped talking.

Unlike Whitney and her mom, Trent's emotions

about this whole thing had been on full display since the week before, when they'd made the decision and toured the facility. He'd clutched both her hand and her mother's as they'd sat in the exterior courtyard at Rejuvenation and discussed what came next. It made Whitney love him even more, knowing how much he cared about her mother.

They climbed into the Jeep and drove in silence along the coast.

Settling her mom into her new room was made much easier by the amazing staff, who were obviously very used to these situations and worked to give the family space but also offered the needed support for the transition.

Whitney and Trent stayed with her mother for hours until she insisted they leave. "Gotta go see if there are any hot old guys living here," she said with a wink. "There's nothing better than a first date, and given the circumstances, I suspect I'll have a lot of them."

Her mother's humor was helping her get through this difficult time, and the three of them hugged for a long time before she pushed them out the room door. "Go live your life," she whispered to Whitney. "I'm going to be just fine here."

Trent was a sobbing mess as they signed the papers at the front desk.

But when he pulled out his credit card to leave on file for the monthly payments, Whitney frowned, stopping him. "No. This is my expense."

"*Our* expense," he said.

She shook her head. "No, Trent."

"Whitney, we're in this together."

"I can't accept help with this."

"It's not accepting help. I love you. We're in a relationship. We're engaged now and planning a future together. For good. For bad. I'm all in."

But she stood firm. "Not in this."

He looked annoyed but allowed her to set up the payments on her own credit card.

In the Jeep moments later, the air was thick and heavy, adding to the tense pressure of the sad day. "Look, I appreciate your wanting to help…"

"It's stuff like this that makes me question your commitment to our relationship," Trent said, staring straight ahead through the windshield as he started the vehicle.

The words felt like a slap. "You know I'm independent."

"You're also stubborn and proud. Those aren't always virtues."

Her mouth dropped. "Well, you're sometimes overbearing and insistent on 'your way or no way.' Those aren't always virtues, either."

Hurtful words spouted, fueled by the emotionally exhausting day, and they drove in silence back home, both battling their own pain.

But entering the house, Trent turned to her, an apology in his expression. He didn't need to say anything and she didn't, either. He opened his arms, and she walked into them. He held her tight while she finally let the tears fall.

• • •

Now…

This time, he wasn't there to hold her as she cried.

• • •

The springs of the tiny cot Trent had rolled into his office at the bar dug into his back as he lay staring up at the ceiling for long hours into the night. He was no stranger to nights like this. Countless nights couch surfing, sleeping on friends' floors over the years in the city when he was competing, hadn't made him dependent on comfort for a sense of security or happiness. So it wasn't the fact that he was lying there on a too-small, uncomfortable cot that made it impossible to sleep. It wasn't the eerie silence, either. And it wasn't the thought of being alone.

Before Whitney, he'd never met anyone he'd fallen so hard for. He'd been okay with the prospect of being a bachelor. Then everything had changed for him. She was everything he'd never known he was searching for. She was the one person he'd needed more than air. The only person he didn't know how to live without.

How could he move forward without her, knowing life would always suck just that much more? That real happiness had existed with her, in her. That he'd never again be filled with the love he'd had with her.

But she didn't want to be with him anymore. He'd thought her pushing him away for the past year had been because of the stressful job and the pressure she was under. He'd believed she was putting off wedding plans and talks of forever because she'd been too busy to make space and time for it.

But that hadn't been the case at all.

Whitney had simply stopped loving him. Stopped wanting all the things she'd once told him she wanted. She'd been looking for a way out and a way to tell him she'd had a change of heart. He couldn't wrap his mind around it. He didn't want to believe it.

He knew they were struggling lately, but there were still moments throughout the past year when their connection was just as strong—maybe even stronger—than it always was. Remembering those brief glimpses into the love they had for each other made it that much harder to accept this.

Accept the fact that as hard as he clung on as he'd felt her drifting away, he'd still somehow lost her.

Trent rolled to his side and stared through the open office door toward the bar. He'd had everything he'd ever wanted. His successful business, a wonderful family, and the love of his life who'd made everything else matter that much more.

What would he do now, without her?

CHAPTER NINETEEN

Now…

Trent pulled on the handle of the door to Delicious Delicacies early the next morning. The door wouldn't budge. He pulled harder. Nothing. He placed his hands on the glass and peered in. He could see Jess behind the counter. He knocked and held up his hands as if to say, *What gives?*

She sent him an odd look and yelled, "Push!"

Ah, right.

He pushed and stumbled slightly as he entered, tripping over the small step that he couldn't remember ever being there before. "What's up with your door?"

"It's always been that way," Jess said, eyeing him.

"You should get that fixed," he mumbled, his words slightly slurred.

"Are you drunk?" His cousin sounded shocked. Obviously, his beautiful ex-fiancée had yet to inform her best friends that she'd crushed his heart into a million little pieces.

"You betcha."

Jess glanced pointedly at the clock. He knew what time it was. It didn't matter. "What's going on?" she asked, concern in her voice.

The bakery floor felt wobbly beneath his feet, so Trent pulled out a stool at the counter and sat.

"Did you know?" he asked.

"Know what?" Jess asked, but he heard the faintest hint of guilt in her tone.

"About Whitney not wanting babies anymore. Not wanting us anymore."

"No. That, I did not know, and I'm sure it's not true," she said, looking concerned. She held up a finger and went to pour a mug of her darkest, strongest roast. She placed the mug in front of him. "Drink this—it'll help sober you up."

"I'd rather be drunk, thanks. It hurts less," he said, pushing the mug away. "Did you know she was starting to feel this way, Jess?"

She sighed. "I knew something was going on with her, but she hasn't exactly been forthcoming with a lot of things lately." Jess paused as though weighing something. "I know she's not feeling well. She blames it on stress and pressure from work, but I really think it's more than that. The weight loss and dark circles under her eyes…"

He shot his cousin a look, but the gesture hurt his throbbing head. "You said you'd tell me if you knew something was going on with her."

"I know, and I would have told you if I had actual proof, but it's just a gut instinct."

"We're family. Cousins. We're like this," he said, intertwining his two fingers. "We stick together."

She nodded slowly. "Yes. But I'm also like this with Whitney," she said, wrapping her hand around his intertwined fingers.

He stood up and wavered slightly off-balance as he paced the bakery. "The hardest part is I feel like I didn't know her. If it's true that she doesn't want children or to get married or be with me, then I was totally blindsided." He reached out to pick up a muffin from a basket on the delivery shelf and knocked several items onto the floor.

"Of course you were," Jess said, taking the coffee cup and forcing it into his hand. "You need to sober up before I'm here all day redoing the deliveries for tomorrow morning."

He barely heard her. "She said she doesn't want kids." No matter how many times he repeated it to himself, out loud, he didn't fully believe it. She'd been all in before…before her major car accident the year before. That's when so much had changed. He thought she'd still been recovering. He was giving her time and space. Then work took over her life… He shook his head. "You think she'd have mentioned it before, right?" He gave a humorless laugh, finally sipping the coffee.

"This is going to ruin the pleasant numbness I'm feeling," he said, handing it back to her.

Jess took it, but she looked even more worried now. "You aren't driving, are you?" She looked outside for the Jeep.

"Nah. 'Course not. I walked from the tavern." Stumbled his way over in a haze of heartache, more accurately.

"Who's watching the bar?"

"Closed today."

"It's Friday, Trent. Everyone expects the bar to be open…"

"I expected to get married and have a shitload of kids with the woman I love more than life itself. No one gets everything they want," he said, sitting back on the stool.

"Fair enough," his cousin said, reaching across and touching his hand. "Fair enough."

• • •

Throwing herself back into the pile of emails in her inbox was the only way Whitney was going to survive the day. She'd emailed Mayor Rodale and said she'd be working from home that day to avoid distractions as she finalized the New Year's calendar. Truth was, there was no way she could hide the deep sorrow she was feeling, and she knew if anyone asked if she was okay, she'd probably collapse into a sobbing mess.

Avoiding people right now was her only option. She could break down in the privacy of her own home when the tidal waves of despair hit—like when she saw his clothes hanging in the closet and realized he'd have to come get them, that soon the closet would be half empty. Or when she saw his favorite coffee mug in the sink, one she couldn't yet bring herself to wash. Or when she smelled the scent of him lingering on his pillow. She'd be sleeping on the couch until she was sure that smell had faded.

For months, she'd been struggling with the knowledge that she either needed to find a way to fix herself or she had to end the relationship with Trent. She couldn't follow through with a future with him when the plans they'd had for the future had changed for her and he was unaware. The day before, the decision had been forced to be made, and it was done. She'd broken it off. It was the only thing she could do. She should have had the strength to do it months ago when she discovered her illness would likely prevent her from having children and could affect her ability to raise them if she was sick or her vision couldn't be trusted... She knew her illness was getting worse all the time, and she was terrified of what that meant for her future. Her self-preservation had her moving away from wanting kids because she felt that wasn't an option. It wasn't fair to Trent to keep him waiting on forever any longer.

Her mother always said decisions were the hardest in the moments leading up to them, but once made, it felt like a weight was lifted. That wasn't the case this time.

She'd had to fight every urge to go after Trent as he'd driven away. Reaching out to him would only make everything worse. She needed to give them both space and time to let this seep in. The fact that seven years together had ended.

Even if the love she had for him hadn't.

He'd paid her mother's medical bill for the year. The incredibly generous gesture was something she was still trying to reconcile. She knew he loved her and supported her, had always wanted to do more than she'd allow him to, but it wasn't until he'd actually gone and made such a huge commitment to her—to them—that she realized she couldn't be with him if she couldn't hold up her end of the bargain, doing the same for him, giving him the family he wanted.

Though she desperately wanted to.

That fact hadn't been so apparent until it was truly gone.

Work. Focus on work.

It was all she had left…

She forced a deep breath and opened her email from the *Race Across America* show executives requesting several release forms to be completed and signed. She clicked on the DocuSign link, but the forms said "completed." Scrolling through more recent emails, she saw the finalized copies. With Scott's signature on them. She sighed, annoyance flowing through her.

Good. She'd cling to the feeling. Any other emotion would do.

Since overhearing Scott and his mother talking in her office a few days before, she hadn't been approached by anyone to fill her in on any new chain of command at the office. She hadn't been demoted yet… It was almost worse that they weren't telling her the plan to advance Scott. As though she didn't have a right to know or be given an opportunity to prove she was still the right person for that position.

All of a sudden, it seemed she was losing everything that was important to her. Air trapped in her chest, and she rubbed the spot, feeling her collarbone protruding even more.

Trent was gone. Her career was at stake. And her health was deteriorating faster every day that she put off the tests and treatment. And she had no one to blame but herself. Her stubborn independence, something she'd once thought of as a strength, had been her downfall, her greatest weakness.

Her phone chimed with a message, and seeing Jess's name on the display, her stomach twisted. Had Trent told his cousin about them? She didn't know for sure where he'd gone the night before. When he hadn't returned all night, she suspected he'd slept at the bar on the old cot he'd set up in there for late nights if he was too tired to drive home.

Where would he go now? Where would he live?

The house was in her name. She'd been adamant about not purchasing a new place together until they were married. She'd been so damn adamant about everything, and now none of it seemed to matter. Why had she been so stupid? Why hadn't she been able to let go and trust and accept the help and support from someone who loved her more than anyone else ever had?

Picking up the phone, she read the message from Jess:

I love you and I'm here when you want to talk.

Whitney sat back and rubbed her aching forehead.

What did this mean for all of them now? She and Trent had the same friends, same community. They'd been a unit for so long. Could people see them as individuals now? Apart? Could their friends reconcile this? Or would things be awkward and tense?

In most breakups, there was a divide.

Sarah was her friend. Wes was his.

And Jess. Who got Jess?

Tears burned the back of Whitney's eyes as she thought of everything she was losing. Her best friend may not choose sides, but Trent was family, and Whitney was a recently terrible friend who had pushed her away.

Frankie. Dear, wonderful Frankie. She'd never be welcomed into Frankie's open arms and heart anymore. Her surrogate mother who'd been there for her when her own mom couldn't be, who loved her... She no longer had her, either.

The effects of a breakup trickled to so many innocent bystanders, and it broke her heart that she was now the cause of so much hurt and sadness. She was responsible for so many people having to adjust to a new reality, a new situation. They'd all be fine without her, sooner or later. But could she *ever* be fine without all of them?

Whitney slammed her laptop shut. Pushing it aside, she reached for a blanket on the edge of the sofa, curled into a ball, and let fresh tears fall.

CHAPTER TWENTY

Now...

All evening, he heard the sounds of patrons outside the bar, tugging on the locked door, knocking, the bar phone ringing with people obviously wondering why the tavern wasn't open, but he didn't care.

They were closed, and they were staying closed.

There was no way he could see familiar faces laughing and having a good time that evening. No way he could hear the music blasting or fill drink orders when all he wanted to do was punch someone.

He'd moved on to a new stage of grief—anger. And it was almost a welcome relief. He knew it wouldn't last, but for now, he was clinging to the strong emotion that at least made it possible not to feel as though an elephant were sitting on his chest.

Behind the bar, he emptied the dishwasher, stacking clean beer glasses along the ledge. Twenty-four hours and not a word from Whitney. He wasn't sure what he expected, but complete silence wasn't it. He'd held out hope that she'd come to him or call or even a damn text to say...

What?

What did he expect her to say?

He picked up a beer mug and threw it across the bar, the glass shattering into a million pieces as it hit the pool table. Resting his hands against the edge of the bar, Trent let his head fall forward. His body trembled, and the myriad of emotions running through him had him all kinds of messed up.

He sighed and straightened, the tense twisting in his gut never easing. He wasn't sure it ever would. How could it?

Breakups in a small town were torture. A seven-year relationship that everyone had seen as the perfect pairing was going to be the death of him. Shared friends would be caught in the middle. Family was going to be disappointed. He hadn't gotten the balls to talk to his mom yet, because she was going to be destroyed by the news.

And they would still see each other all the time. How was he supposed to survive running into her on the street? At the grocery store? At Sarah and Wes's wedding and Jess and Mitch's wedding…

Too many damn weddings that weren't his.

He roughly grabbed the broom and headed toward the shattered glass. The bristles collected the shards into a large pile, and he sighed seeing his fractured reflection in them.

"Hey, do you know the door is still locked and there's a mob of angry, sober people outside?" Angel's voice said behind him.

He sighed as he turned. "Bar's closed tonight. You can head on home." He'd sent Max away an hour ago and told him to relay the message.

"Max told me what happened," she said sympathetically as she walked toward him, her heeled boots echoing on the empty air. "I wanted to stop by to make sure you were okay."

He resumed his cleanup. "Fine."

"I'm sorry, Trent."

He was, too, but for what, he didn't know. He didn't owe anyone any *sorry*s. He'd been loyal, faithful, honest, supportive, respectful, and loving for seven long years.

Seven years that she'd simply thrown away as though they meant nothing.

Angel reached for the broom, but he held it away. "I got it."

She shoved her hands into her jeans back pockets and rocked back and forth on her heels. "Okay…well, why don't I make us some food? I know you probably haven't eaten."

He had zero appetite. Just the thought of food made him nauseous. "You don't have to be here. I'm fine."

"The closed bar and the broken glass on the floor suggest otherwise."

"Really, Angel—"

"Trent. Stop," she said, touching his arm. "I know what you're going through, and I may not know how to help, but I can make food and just… be here."

He hesitated. Finding comfort in Angel wasn't a great idea, but he was a mess, and she did know what he was going through, having suffered a similar fate. If anyone could help him try to make sense of this shit, it was her.

"You've been there for me and the boys; I just want to return the favor," she said.

He swallowed hard and simply nodded.

Twenty minutes later, the smell of hamburgers and fries had his stomach growling. When she placed a plate in front of him on the bar, he begrudgingly reached for a French fry and popped it into his mouth, burning his tongue. "Hot."

"That's typically what happens when things come out of a deep fryer," she said, sliding the ketchup bottle toward him.

He squeezed some onto his plate as she climbed up onto the stool next to him. "So, want to talk about it?"

"Not really." He didn't even know where to begin, and rehashing things would only make him feel worse.

Angel leaned over the bar and reached for a bottle of bourbon. She held it up, but he shook his head. Leaning back on the alcohol was a bad idea. He'd finally gotten over the buzz he'd had that morning.

"None for me," he said, shoving more fries into his mouth.

"Well, I'm going for it," she said, pouring a shot.

"You okay?" he asked.

"Better than you, but only slightly," she said before tipping the alcohol back. "My kids have informed me that they want to go back to L.A. and live with Brad. They left last week, and until we can get a court date where I can fight for custody or Brad gets tired of having them underfoot, that's where they will be staying."

That was why the boys hadn't been to football practice. "Damn, Angel, I'm sorry…"

"Apparently, they told Brad that I'm dating Max, so I was the lucky recipient of nasty text messages."

Trent's jaw clenched. That prick. His anger and sympathy for Angel's situation gave him a momentary respite from his own troubles. "Why didn't you tell me all this?"

She sighed. "I kinda got a vibe that you wanted to keep the working relationship professional. We'd already blurred lines, becoming friends, and technically you're my boss..."

So she'd caught that. Trent felt like an idiot. Of course he could be friends with Angel. There'd be no harm in it, and he'd let some insecurity make him unavailable when she could have used someone to talk to. Luckily, she'd had Max, but he wasn't sure his buddy was a great listener when he struggled to keep his lips and hands off the woman. Max meant well, but it was his ear that Angel might have needed.

"Sorry about that. It was..."

She waved a hand. "I get it. It's hard for some people to believe that a man and a woman can just be friends," she said, and there was an odd note in her voice that he couldn't quite figure out.

He nodded, and they continued to eat. As he cleared away their dishes a little while later, she turned on the music and poured two shots of bourbon. This time, he accepted it. "Just one," he said.

She held her glass up. "To shitty situations."

He'd toast to that all day long. He clinked his glass to hers, and they tossed them back. Angel set her glass down on the bar and climbed off the stool. "Let's dance."

He shook his head. "No."

"Oh, come on. Dancing is one of the known cures for heartache."

He doubted that, but she yanked his hands, pulling him from around the bar, then dragged him toward the dance floor as the fast-tempo song ended and a sad country western ballad started to play.

He raised an eyebrow. "This is supposed to cure my heartache? A song about a dude losing everything?"

"It's not an exact science," she said with a laugh, taking his hand and slipping into his arms.

His chest tightened as she forced his arm to wrap around her.

Whitney loved to dance. She'd pull his awkward ass out onto the dance floor all the time. He'd fallen in love with her in his arms in this very spot years before.

Angel started to sway, and he struggled to breathe as he forced his own feet to shuffle across the wooden floor. The sultry twang of a guitar and the soulful sound of the singer's pain echoed, resonating in Trent's head.

Time wasted on a love that was never his...

He swallowed hard as Angel rested her head against his chest. "The only way to heal is to give in to the pain," she said.

He was afraid if he did that, he'd never survive.

He breathed in the scent of her hair, and it only reminded him of how much he missed the smell of Whitney's hair when she was lying on his chest in bed. His grip tightened on Angel, but all he was envisioning was holding Whitney in his arms as they swayed to the music, late after the bar was closed and they were all alone…

He cleared his throat and started to move away. He couldn't do this. This drowning in sorrow in an effort to kill the pain and resurface a new man, without the lingering, torturous heartache wasn't a method to healing he wanted to go through. He wanted to keep pushing down the pain until it was buried so deep, it could come back in moments of weakness.

And he certainly didn't want to lean on a friend like Angel.

"Trent, there's something I've been needing to tell you," she said, and he immediately tensed at the serious, apprehensive tone.

"What is it?" As he pulled away, a loud, smashing noise interrupted whatever she'd been about to say, and the bar door burst open a second later. An angry-looking man in a suit entered and stalked straight toward them.

"The bar is closed," Trent said, meeting the guy halfway and preventing further access to the place. Were people really so pissed he was closed that night that they were breaking his damn door down? This guy was definitely an out-of-towner.

"Brad? What the hell are you doing here?" Angel asked, rushing up behind Trent.

Brad? Her ex? Trent took in the tall, thick man in front of him. Made sense, actually. He'd never seen Angel's ex, but this guy was exactly what he would have pictured, if the guy had warranted any of Trent's headspace at all. Expensive suit and shoes. Rolex on his wrist. An arrogant ego that filled the room.

"This the asshole the boys were telling me about?" he asked Angel, glaring at Trent.

"No, and it's none of your business anyway," Angel said, attempting to step between them.

Trent held her back carefully. The guy reeked of alcohol, his pupils were dilated, and he looked more than ready for a fight. Angel hadn't told him everything, but he suspected the guy was abusive.

Brad turned to her. "Not my business? Damn right it's my business. We're still technically married. And you're shacking up with someone else, in front of the boys?"

"You have a girlfriend living with you," Angel countered.

Trent gave her credit for not wavering. This man was trying to intimidate her, but she was standing strong.

"She's not living with me, and it's different," Brad said. "Do you really want the boys to see their mother like that? Hooking up with strange, random men?"

Wow. Double standards. Even if that wasn't at all what Angel was doing, she was entitled to live her life any way she wanted. She owed this clown absolutely nothing.

"Get out of here, Brad," Angel said.

"We need to talk," the man said, moving closer to her.

"We'll talk through our lawyers. Please leave." She folded her arms across her chest, and Brad reached for her, obviously changing tactics as his expression softened.

"Come on, Angel, let's just talk."

Angel moved away from him. "No. I'm not letting you do this to me anymore. This manipulation and gaslighting. I'm done, Brad."

"I'm the manipulator? You're trying to destroy the relationship I have with my sons. All the lies you're telling them about me. And actually, I don't even care about Eddie—he's not even mine…"

What? Angel had never mentioned that. He glanced at her, and she looked more than a little panicked.

Angry once again, Brad advanced on her, and Trent had had enough. The guy had definitely picked the wrong day to break the door of his bar and start this shit. Angel was handling it quite well, but the man didn't seem to be taking the hint. He'd try making the message clearer.

"Hey, Angel said she's not interested in talking. This is my bar, and I'm asking you to leave," Trent said, standing between Angel and her ex.

The guy scoffed, looking amused. "Do you know who I am?"

"I know you are trespassing, and I could call the police about you damaging my door."

Brad glared at him as he moved closer until their faces were inches apart. "I'm not leaving without Angel."

"Oh, I think you are," Max's voice behind Brad caught all their attention.

And a strong right hook caught Brad's chin as he turned to face Max. The guy reeled backward, holding his jaw. "Motherfu—"

"Max!" Angel said. "What the hell?"

Brad staggered slightly, but he made a beeline straight for Max. Trent intercepted and caught the hit that was intended for his friend. The blow to the eye was a lot harder than he'd anticipated. This shit ended now.

A quick struggle later, he and Max had restrained Brad and tossed him out of the bar. "Don't ever come back here," Trent told the guy.

"And do not go near Angel again," Max added.

"This isn't over, Angel!" Brad called to her where she stood, slightly shaken inside the bar entrance.

Max and Trent blocked any access, and Brad climbed into his Beemer and peeled out of the parking lot.

Going back inside, Trent shot a look at Max through his quickly swelling eye. "Dude, what the hell? I had it under control."

Max shrugged. "I just really wanted to punch the guy," he said. "Angel has opened up to me about…a lot."

So Trent's suspicion of abuse was right. He couldn't exactly stay pissed with Max now.

Apparently, Angel could, as she delivered a lecture once they were back inside. Though Trent could tell she wasn't entirely upset that her ex had gotten what he deserved.

"I'll go find something to use as a temporary fix for the door," Max said.

"Thanks, man," Trent said, going back behind the bar. He opened the ice cooler, but Angel pushed him out of the way.

"Go. Sit," she said.

Trent sat on a stool while she made an ice pack for his eye and poured another shot of bourbon.

"Thanks for your help," she said. "Sorry about the door."

"It's nothing. A quick fix. And you were holding your own."

She nodded, but her hand trembled as she sat next to him and placed the ice pack against his face.

"About what he said about Eddie...is that true?"

She avoided his gaze as she nodded. "That's... um, what I was trying to say. Before."

"What do you mean?"

She sighed as her gaze met his. "You didn't recognize me when I came in here months ago, looking for a job, and I was going to tell you then... but it was awkward."

Trent's heart raced, and his palms sweat. What the hell was she saying? He peered at her face, but just as before, he didn't remember ever having known her before recently when she moved to town.

"We met before. One night fifteen years ago... Settling here in Blue Moon Bay wasn't a coincidence. It wasn't just a random spot on the map."

He swallowed hard as realization sank in. She'd purposely moved there to be closer to him. For what exactly? "Why... What... You never reached out." He felt woozy, and it had nothing to do with the shot or the punch. At least not the physical one from Brad.

"I met Brad right after, and he's been in my life—in Eddie's life ever since." She shook her head. "It may have been wrong, but it was just one night…" Her voice trailed.

She was saying he had a son? That Eddie was his? The room swayed all around him as he tried to understand. She'd been there for months. Allowed him to get to know Eddie… He swallowed hard, and his heart echoed in his chest. "Does Eddie know?"

"No!" She shook her head. "And I want to keep it that way. For now." She ran a hand through her hair, looking almost as conflicted as he felt. Conflicted, guilty, remorseful… A long, awkward tension filled the silence between them.

"Please say something," she whispered.

What the hell did she expect him to say? He was still in complete shock. His entire life had been upended in a matter of days. Over and over again. He had a kid. A fifteen-year-old son. One he'd known nothing about. One he may never have known about…

"I…uh…"

The sound of heels on the bar floor made them both turn.

Who the hell was there now?

His eyes widened as he saw Whitney enter. Then things moved as if in slow motion as she took in the scene in front of her. One she was completely misreading if the hurt and confusion in her expression were any indication.

Shit.

But no. He wasn't doing anything wrong. He'd been in the bar thinking about her, missing her, mending a crack in his heart that kept reopening with every memory that surfaced. And just moments ago, his world had once again been knocked off its axis.

But he could see how she might misread things right now. Him and Angel in the bar alone together and the other woman tending to his busted eye.

He stood up so quickly, he knocked the stool over. "Whitney?"

"Sorry…" she mumbled.

"What are you doing here?" Had she come to talk? To tell him she'd reconsidered? His heart raced as he walked toward her, a brief moment of optimism, before she shut it down.

"I just came to make sure you were okay…" Her gaze drifted toward Angel, then returned to his. "But it looks like you've got things covered," she said before turning and walking out of the bar.

"Whitney!" he called after her, but she was gone.

• • •

The weather had quickly taken a turn for the worse as Whitney jumped back into her vehicle and drove away from the tavern. A sob nearly strangled her, and she swallowed it down.

What had she expected? Certainly not the sight of Angel and Trent together, alone in the bar, that she knew would burn in her mind for a long time. All this time she'd told herself that there was nothing between Trent and his coworker. She'd ignored any gut instincts she felt about that situation and continued to believe in the love and commitment they'd had.

But she hadn't been completely truthful, either, so maybe neither was Trent.

She wasn't even sure why she'd gone to the bar anyway. She'd left the office in a haze, and the vehicle had seemed to have a mind of its own, heading toward the bar...toward Trent. She missed him, and she'd just wanted to see him...

Then, noticing the broken door, she'd been worried.

She flicked on the wipers faster as the rain got worse. A rumble of thunder echoed in the distance before a flash of lightning lit up the dark, stormy sky. Her hands shook on the wheel as the eeriness of the memory of the night of her accident caused goosebumps to surface on her skin.

Sarah and Jess had been reaching out to her that day, offering support and letting her know they were there for her if and when she needed them. She knew she would. Eventually. And while she'd been a terrible, distant friend lately, she knew they would be there for her without question. But right now, she just wanted her mom.

It might be a horrible idea. But she was desperate for comfort, for her mother to hug her and lie to her and tell her things would be okay, like when she'd suffered her first broken heart years before.

Funny, at age fifteen, she hadn't thought pain could cut any deeper, that her shattered teenage heart would never recover.

She'd had no idea the pain life could bring.

Pulling into the parking lot of Rejuvenation just as the darkest night closed in around her, she got out of the car and jogged through the puddles of rain and mud toward the door. Her swollen ankles were throbbing, and her struggle to focus and to act like nothing was wrong was giving her a migraine.

Pretending everything was fine was exhausting. Soon, she'd be forced to give up the charade, but at least now, there would be fewer people around to see her fall apart, to fuss over her and treat her differently.

"Whitney, what a surprise. We weren't expecting you today," Molly, an evening-shift nurse, said as she approached the desk. "They say the roads are terrible for driving." She wrapped her cardigan tighter around her body over her uniform as she nodded toward the storm.

"It's treacherous out there, for sure. I know Mom doesn't like nights like this… Is she awake?" It was only a little after nine, but her mother spent a lot of time sleeping these days.

"I think so. Go on in and check. Mary's making the rounds soon for lights out, but feel free to stay as long as you want," she said. Her forehead wrinkled. "Whitney, is everything okay? You look really pale, dear."

She nodded, demanding her voice not to break, hoping the rain could be blamed for her running mascara. "I'm fine. Just tired from long hours at work." It wasn't a lie, but it was just the tip of the iceberg. But how could she admit that her deteriorating health was slowly killing her?

"Okay…well, if you need anything, let me know. We can roll in a cot for you if you want to stay the night."

It was a rare exception she was offering, and Whitney was grateful. "I'll let you know. Thank you."

Walking down the hall, her chest tightened. It was quiet, and the activity rooms were empty. From several open room doors, she saw residents sitting in their chairs or getting ready to call it a night. They all had their own pain, their own heartache, their own illnesses... How had she thought she could find a sense of peace here? Maybe she should just leave. Could she handle her mom not knowing her right now?

Pausing at the door, she quietly opened it. Her mom was in her usual chair near the window, and she turned, hearing her enter.

The smile that spread across her face gave Whitney a sense of relief, and her knees sagged a little beneath her.

"Whitney!"

"Hi, Mom," she said, rushing over to hug her.

She wrapped her arms around Whitney and squeezed tight. Her mother's hug was the only thing keeping the pieces of her heart together. "I didn't expect you tonight. I'm so glad you're here. Though this weather isn't great for driving..."

Her mother's eyes shone with clarity when she pulled away, her face beamed, and Whitney hated that she wasn't able to fully appreciate this rare moment with her. She longed for times like this when they could talk, reminisce about the past, plan for an uncertain future without allowing reality to give them doubt.

But she was overcome with gratitude for this

opportunity that came when she needed it most. Selfishly, she needed this.

"You're upset," her mother said.

Whitney shook her head, but it was no use. She'd never been able to keep things from her mom. Growing up, the woman had known everything she'd tried to hide.

"Where's Trent?" she asked, looking at the open door behind her.

"He's not coming," she said, a sob escaping her. He might never be coming again. Wasn't that how it worked after a breakup? You also broke up with the family. Her mom, both in her lucid and non-lucid state, would miss him, but it was too much to expect that he'd continue to visit now.

"Darling, what's wrong?" Lydia studied her face, brushing her damp curls behind her ears, the way she had when Whitney was a child.

Unable to speak over the lump in her throat, she knelt on the floor and rested her head in her mom's lap.

"Oh, sweetheart," her mother said, stroking her hair.

Whitney closed her blurry eyes and allowed her body to sag. Her mother's soothing touch and words helping to ease the ache in her chest. "It's okay… Whatever it is won't seem so bad in the morning."

She always said that. That troubles always looked darker and more insurmountable at night. Daybreak brought with it a new perspective, a new hope…

Unfortunately, these troubles weren't something that the light of day could chase away.

CHAPTER TWENTY-ONE

Now…

He had a kid.

No matter how many times he repeated that in his mind, Trent couldn't quite believe it. The night before, there had been no resolution to the discussion with Angel. After Whitney's unexpected entrance, he'd needed to just shut it all down.

He'd needed to shut *himself* down.

But now, he knew he had to address the matter head-on. Right away. He had no idea what to do with the knowledge or what Angel expected…if anything. They hadn't made it that far.

Damn, he wished he could talk to Whitney about this, but he suspected this new information would only solidify her feelings about ending their relationship. She'd see it as just another reason their lives didn't line up for a future together. He had no idea how she would react to this. He'd have to tell her eventually, but right now, he had to come to terms with it himself and sort out what it meant.

For his life. For Angel's. And for Eddie's.

He cradled a coffee cup in his shaky hands as he waited for Angel the next day at the bar. He hadn't slept a wink after locking up and crashing on the cot in the back. He'd laid there, staring at the ceiling, a new, different numbness enveloping him as self-preservation.

There was so much he wanted to say, to ask, to clarify... But he wasn't even sure where to begin. All these years, she'd never reached out.

How was she even sure Eddie was his? It had been a one-night stand so long ago. One he didn't even remember. That made him feel guilty as shit. He hadn't recognized her at all when she'd walked into the bar months ago. He hadn't been a saint in his younger, body-building days, but he was disappointed in himself for never knowing this had been the outcome of one of his more impulsive decisions. Poor Eddie deserved more than that.

And despite only learning about it less than twenty-four hours ago, he felt sad that he'd missed an opportunity. It may have been complicated and messy, but he still wished he'd known. How would his life have been different?

The bar door opened, and he swallowed hard, seeing her enter. Then relief flowed through him when he saw that Max was with her.

"Hope it's okay that I brought Max," she said carefully as they approached.

He nodded, sending a grateful look at Max. "Of course." It was actually better to have the other guy there. A buffer of sorts. "You know?" he asked his friend as they sat across from him.

"She told me last night," Max said.

Trent nodded slowly.

"I was trying to get the courage to tell you for a while..." Angel said nervously. "I was going to the first day I walked in here, then I chickened out and asked for a job instead. I hadn't even really had a plan to stay here in town. It just went that way.

Then the timing was never right, and then when you started helping out the boys—helping out Eddie—I thought maybe I shouldn't tell you. Leave things as they were. Let you two be friends." She took a breath. "But then after everything you were going through…" She shrugged. "I couldn't not tell you the truth you deserved to know."

Trent nodded again. He wasn't quite sure what to say. Where to start…

"Should I not have told you?" she asked, and he saw her squeeze Max's hand tight.

"No. I'm glad you told me." The timing was terrible and maybe fifteen years too late, but he was happy he knew. He cleared his throat. "What do we do now?" He had no idea where they went from here.

"I don't know," she said. "I'm not sure we have to do anything drastic or quickly. Just maybe figure it out as we go along?"

He sighed. What else could they do? He knew he wanted to be in Eddie's life—that had been crystal clear since the moment she'd dropped the bomb on him. And he was already there in some capacity, as a friend and someone Eddie could count on and trust. Maybe that was enough for now. Maybe it was all he'd ever really be.

"With the boys in L.A. there's no rush, but eventually…"

"We'll tell him?" The boy deserved to know. His reaction may not be the most positive at first, but he deserved to know the truth, and it would be up to him if he wanted to have a relationship with Trent.

Whatever that looked like.

Angel nodded, a look of remorse in her expression as she said, "I really am sorry, Trent. I thought I was doing the right thing."

And who was he to say she hadn't? He offered the best version of a reassuring smile he could muster given the circumstances of the last few hellish days. "You did the best you could. We'll figure this out."

Ten minutes later, after a slightly awkward parting, Trent locked the door to the bar and headed down the street. There was only one person he could talk to about this right now. Only one person he could go to for advice.

The bell chimed as he entered Frankie's Fabrics, and one look at his mom's smiling, welcoming face had his guard crumbling and the emotions falling down his face.

CHAPTER TWENTY-TWO

Now...

"Wow. He looks like shit," Mitch whispered as he picked up a bowl of seasoned ground beef from Jess's kitchen counter the following evening.

With a tray of cheese, salsa, and fixings, Jess followed him. "Two bottles of whiskey will do that to a person."

"I can hear you two," Trent said from where he slumped on the sofa in Jess's living room. His head ached from too much alcohol, lack of sleep, and an unrelenting sense of doom. He hadn't told anyone other than his mother about Eddie, and she was in enough pain over the breakup with Whitney and shock over his fatherhood for the entire family. He wasn't ready to tell anyone else yet. In time, he would. Baby steps.

"I'm glad you came over tonight, buddy," Mitch said, a concerned look on his face, which made his cousin swoon at her boyfriend's thoughtfulness. Jess wore that expression a lot around Mitch.

And while he was happy that she'd finally found "the one," maybe hanging out with them that evening wasn't such a great idea. Seeing Jess and Mitch together was torture. For so long, his cousin had been the one watching Trent and Whitney's relationship with a slight envy for what they had.

Now *he* was a third wheel with a close-up view

of real love.

Trent reached for an empty taco shell and took a bite. The carbs would soak up the alcohol.

Jess sat next to him on one side, and Mitch took the armchair next to her. They had little choice in the seating arrangement as he'd sat on the middle cushion on her sofa, and his overly muscular frame and long legs took up most of the space. He was really good at unintentional cock-blocking. But he just couldn't deal with seeing the two of them cuddled together right now.

"You two sure you wouldn't rather watch a comedy or something?" Mitch asked after they'd made their tacos.

"Nah, I'd like to see the photos," Trent said, more out of politeness than real interest.

They were watching slides of Mitch's latest trip overseas. He was only going on one short trip a year now that he'd met Jess and had taken over his father's medical clinic.

But an hour later, Trent was fascinated. And much soberer. "Where were these taken?" he asked, sitting on the edge of the couch, his elbows resting on his knees.

"Cambodia," Mitch said as photos of an orphanage appeared on the screen.

"None of those kids have homes?" His heart ached as he stared at the happy faces of children who had nothing, not even a real family, and his paternal instinct, which was always really strong, was on full speed ahead these days.

"Unfortunately not. The parents either die or can't care for them properly, so they end up here.

There's so much overcrowding, though, and there isn't a ton of resources to help," Mitch said.

Jess wore a sad expression as she shook her head. "These photos are always the most heartbreaking," she said, gesturing for Mitch to maybe keep moving forward, knowing that with Trent's deep love of children, these might be too much to see right now given the circumstances.

She had no idea…

Mitch hit the button to move the slide forward, but Trent said, "Can you go back for a second?"

"Sure."

Trent stared at the picture for a long moment before asking, "And all these kids—they are looking for homes?" He jotted down the name of the orphanage on his cell phone.

Jess's eyes narrowed. "Are you thinking about this? You'd consider adopting?"

He shrugged. "I don't know, but looking at these little kids kinda makes me want to do something, you know?" He couldn't quite explain it, but somehow, now knowing that he'd missed out on being a father these last fifteen years had him yearning to be one even more.

"I think it's a fantastic idea," Mitch said. "Just do your research and really be prepared for the challenge. It's so rewarding, but it's not easy. These kids leave their homes, everything they know… Some of them have been abandoned by people they love, so it's scary for them at first, and it takes a while for them to trust."

Trent nodded and sat back as Mitch continued to flick through the slides, but he couldn't erase the images of the children from his mind or let go of the thought that maybe the family he'd always wanted may not come in the traditional sense. Maybe it would come a different way.

A messy, complicated, but full of love and good intentions way.

• • •

As Whitney turned onto Main Street late that evening, she could barely keep her exhausted eyes open. Long hours, getting lost in work, was the only way she was able to dull the ache in her chest and resist the urge to respond to Trent's attempts to contact her. He said they needed to talk, but she couldn't do it. Not yet.

She surveyed the local businesses. All the places she'd helped support over the years. All the familiar faces and families. Everyone seemed to have something good—a thriving business, a family, a significant other… Everything good *she'd* ever had was slipping away through her fingertips, and as she'd desperately grasped to hold on to what she could, she'd let the most important ones fall.

She needed to start rebuilding her life. A new life. The first step was getting healthy, and she'd made her doctor's appointments for her tests for the available February date. It was a small step but one in the right direction. She'd focus on one thing at a time.

Mayor Rodale still hadn't said anything about her position, but if she lost it to Scott, she'd figure something out. She had to stop stressing about things that were out of her control.

Her stomach growled, and she pulled into a parking spot near the diner. She hadn't had much appetite in days, but that evening she was actually hungry. She climbed out and headed toward the front door but paused as her gaze landed on a couple sitting in a booth near the window. Tall, thick guy with his back to her and Angel. Hand in hand, they looked lost in each other as they laughed and talked. She couldn't be certain because of her sight, but her gut told her the man was Trent.

Her heart raced, and the lump in her throat refused to go down. She'd seen them together in the bar, so this sighting shouldn't be inducing this thick anxiety in her chest. It wasn't a surprise that the two of them might find each other. Angel was everything she wasn't. She could give Trent everything he wanted. He'd immediately move into a stepdad role for Angel's kids. Hell, he'd already gotten close to the boys.

This would happen all the time. They lived in a small town. There'd be no way of avoiding running into them together.

"Going in?" a man asked behind her as she stood frozen in place, blocking the entrance.

"Oh…no," she said, moving quickly out of the way to let the man enter.

Through the window, her gaze met Angel's, and her pulse pounded even harder as recognition dawned on Angel's face. Whitney saw the other woman stand, and she quickly headed back toward her car.

"Whitney! Hey, Whitney, please wait," Angel's

voice called behind her.

She desperately wanted to run away. Get as far from the woman and this awkward situation as possible, but she couldn't run forever, and this conversation needed to happen sometime if they were all ever going to be able to move forward.

She turned slowly and clenched her trembling hands.

"Hi. Thanks for stopping," Angel said, coming up to her. "I just wanted to say I'm sorry about the other night."

Whitney shook her head. "It's none of my business." She'd broken things off with Trent. She was the villain in this story. What right did she have to be upset that he may have already started to move on? Or that Angel had seen an opportunity to move in? They were both single people, and they were entitled to be together if that's what they wanted.

"It wasn't what it looked like," Angel said with a remorseful look. "My ex showed up, and Trent was defending me…"

"That's Trent," she said awkwardly, glancing at him still sitting in the booth in the diner. Hearing about how he was Angel's knight in shining armor hardly made her feel any better. And if he'd wanted to talk to Whitney, he certainly didn't seem like he wanted to in this moment. "I should go."

"Whitney, I really am sorry," she said and paused. "Trent's really broken up about this. He misses you, and he loves you."

Whitney stared at the ground. This wasn't a discussion she wanted to have with anyone right now. Especially not Angel. The other woman could say what she wanted, but Whitney knew before long, Trent and Angel would be together. If they really weren't already. They'd looked awfully cozy in the diner together. "I'm sure he'll get over it and move on with his new life," she said, turning to leave.

"We haven't even figured out what to do about him being Eddie's father yet," Angel said.

Whitney froze.

Eddie's father.

The words echoed in her brain, but they seemed far away, as though in a dream. Trent was Eddie's father? What the hell was going on? Had he known? Had he been keeping this from her? She'd been feeling so guilty for not telling him about her illness...and he was keeping something so important, so life-changing from her?

Trent was a father?

Her mind raced, and her pulse pounded. It made sense now that he and Angel shared a connection, but the thought had never crossed her mind it would be something like this.

Angel gasped slightly. "Oh my God, you didn't know. He didn't tell you."

She had to get away. She had to put some distance between herself and this truth she wasn't ready to face. She turned quickly and headed toward the car.

"Whitney, wait! Please!"

She kept going.

She heard the woman sigh behind her, but she kept walking, her appetite suddenly gone again.

Reaching the car, she climbed in, and her gaze involuntarily drifted toward the diner as she backed out of the parking spot.

And her heart stopped.

It was Max with Angel. Not Trent. The other man was now standing on the sidewalk, his arm draped across Angel's shoulders as he ushered her back inside.

Max. Not Trent.

But either way, Trent was the father of Angel's son.

CHAPTER TWENTY-THREE

Now...

The atmosphere at the B&B was awkward when Whitney arrived for Marissa's birthday party that Saturday afternoon. She'd been expecting this first get-together with her friends to be slightly intense, but she hadn't anticipated the feeling that being the dumper, not the dumpee, she was seen as the villain. Rationally, she knew her friends didn't think of her that way, but she still hadn't really reached out to any of them to talk about everything that was going on, and today wasn't the right time, either.

Trent was a father. To a fifteen-year-old. To Angel's fifteen-year-old. He hadn't told her, so she suspected none of their friends knew, either, and the knowledge was eating her up inside. But she'd ended things with Trent, so what right did she have to be upset by this?

Loud, kid-friendly versions of pop songs played, and she followed the sounds of laughter and voices toward the ballroom.

She'd contemplated not going at all, but she was really trying to make an effort to change her ways moving forward. Work was only one aspect of her life, and while it may feel like the only thing she truly had anymore, she needed to reconnect with her friends.

She was grateful that Trent hadn't arrived yet. She wasn't quite ready to be in the same space with him, even if separately. The revelation that Angel and Max were dating still left her with an unsettling feeling. She'd read the situation wrong, but that didn't change anything. Especially not now. Trent was the father of Angel's fifteen-year-old. The thought kept going around and around in circles in her brain. She had no idea what to do about it.

"I'm glad you're here," Sarah whispered to her, wrapping an arm around her waist as Whitney entered the B&B's ballroom where Marissa's party was in full swing.

Whitney squeezed her friend's hand. "I can't stay long, but I wanted to drop off her gift and say happy birthday. You two really went all out." Whitney took in the beautifully decorated room with at least two hundred pink, purple, and white helium-filled balloons and matching streamers hung across the ceiling. A large HAPPY BIRTHDAY banner was hung on the wall, and the tables were covered with party hats, favors, and candies. A unicorn-shaped piñata hung from the ceiling, and the kids hovered around it, eager to break it open.

Across the room, she met Jess's gaze, where she sat next to Mitch, and her friend offered a conflicted-looking smile. Whitney gave a quick wave in return. That relationship was probably going to be the hardest to figure out. She hated that Jess would feel as though she had to take sides. She didn't, and Whitney wanted to reassure her friend that she'd never expect that. She also wanted to ask Jess if she could apologize to Frankie for her... In time, she'd like to talk to Trent's mom herself, but she wasn't sure if the woman would want to have anything to do with her after breaking her son's heart.

She noticed Lia across the room as well, laughing and dancing with a group of Marissa's friends. As Marissa's godmother, Lia wouldn't dream of missing the party. No doubt, she'd flown in just for the event and would be leaving the next day. The other woman didn't notice her yet, but Whitney found a comfort knowing Lia was in town, and she'd definitely plan some time with her before she went back to New York.

"How you holding up?" Sarah asked.

"I'm okay," she said with a forced smile. Except that her heart was a mess and she'd recently learned that the man she'd been building a life with had a son.

This wasn't the right time to talk, and she wouldn't be a buzzkill at a child's birthday party. "Really, I am. We'll get together and talk soon," she promised.

"Okay," Sarah said as Wes arrived from the kitchen, carrying the birthday cake full of sparklers.

"Happy birthday to you…" the happy dad started to sing, and everyone joined in.

Whitney even managed to croak out a few whispered lyrics, but all she could think about was how many of Eddie's birthdays Trent had missed. He loved children. He must be devastated to know that he hadn't been there for Eddie all these years. Hadn't known. She knew he must not have known, because Trent was a good man, and he would have stepped up. He would have wanted to be a father…

So when did he find out?

She brushed the thoughts away, focusing on the birthday girl.

Marissa beamed, and her eyes widened, seeing the beautiful cake shaped like a flying unicorn that seemed to defy gravity. Jess must have made it for the event. It was absolutely incredible, with majestic wings and a sugar-worked gold horn. The little girl sent Jess a look of appreciation before she closed her eyes and took a deep breath, then blew out the candles. Everyone cheered and clapped.

The baby monitor in Sarah's hand crackled with static before the sound of Henry's cry came through the speaker.

"Ah, he must have smelled icing," Sarah said with a laugh. "I'll be right back."

"Can I get him?" Whitney asked.

Sarah couldn't hide her surprise. "Sure... I mean, are you sure?"

Whitney nodded. It was time to start stepping up as Auntie Whitney. It may be the only role she ever played in regards to children, and she needed to get used to that idea. Embrace it. Be the best darn aunt to all the kids her friends had. "I'm sure," she said.

"Okay. He'll need to be changed," Sarah teased, calling out after her.

"I think I can handle it," she said with much more confidence than she actually felt. She didn't have much experience with dirty diapers. But she'd figure it out.

She climbed the winding staircase to the living quarters section of the inn, but when she reached the top landing, an unexpected dizzy spell hit, and she struggled with the wave of nausea as the entire house seemed to spin all around her. She swallowed the saliva in her mouth and shut her eyes, but it didn't help. The music from downstairs sounded like it was getting farther away, and the floor rippled under her feet, knocking her off-balance. Her body swayed, and she reached out all around her for something to grab hold of, but she couldn't reach the railing in time—

Because she was falling, tumbling down the staircase, her body violently crashing against the wooden steps all the way down.

• • •

Trent couldn't even remember the drive from the bar to the hospital. He'd been moving on autopilot, in a foggy haze of worry and pain, his thoughts racing a million miles an hour and his heart beating out of his chest.

Entering now, he hurried toward Jess, sitting in the waiting room with Sarah and Wes. "How is she?" he asked, still trembling. His entire body was breaking out in a sweat despite the cool temperatures today, and he felt as though someone had a vise tightening around his lungs.

Jess gave him a quick hug. "She's going to be okay," she said, trying to sound reassuring, but Trent heard the deep concern in his cousin's voice. "Mitch is in with her now and so is her regular doctor. A few broken bones and a nasty blow to the head."

The fall down the B&B stairs could have killed her. His hands fisted at his sides, and his jaw clenched. "That stupid job." If Whitney had been a workaholic before, he suspected she was working even longer hours since the breakup. He saw her vehicle in the mayor's office parking lot all the time.

"I'm not entirely sure the job is to blame," Jess said softly.

Trent frowned. "What do you mean?"

"Mitch suspects there might be more that Whitney hasn't been telling us."

Trent's heart sank. "Like what?"

Jess shrugged. "A medical condition she may have been hiding. He's not sure yet, but they're running tests and he's reviewing her file."

A medical condition? One she hadn't told anyone about.

Trent ran a hand over his face as he slumped into a chair next to Sarah. She reached for his hand and squeezed it. "At least she's finally in the right place to get whatever help she needs," the other woman said.

Trent nodded. It was little consolation when the love of his life was lying in a hospital bed with severe injuries for the second time in a year. "What do we do now?" he asked, looking at Jess.

His cousin sat in the empty chair beside him and gave him a helpless look. "All we can do is wait."

CHAPTER TWENTY-FOUR

Now...

They were all back here again.

The sight of everyone she loved and their worry-filled expressions when she opened her eyes made Whitney wish she could go back to sleep. She owed all of them an explanation and an apology, but her mind was foggy, and her head ached.

"Hi..." It was Jess who spoke. Her concern was mixed with the sound of guilt, and that made Whitney feel so much worse. Her friend had nothing to feel badly about.

She was the one at fault. The only one. The distance between them lately had been Whitney's doing. She'd pushed them all away and had neglected her friendships.

"Hi, Jess..." Her voice sounded foreign to her own ears. The notes of fear and uncertainty were ringing loud. She looked around the room, her gaze settling on Trent.

His expression was so pained, so hurt, she could barely breathe as their eyes met and locked. He was pale, and the dark circles under his eyes said he hadn't gotten any sleep. He looked even more devastated now than he had when she'd ended things a week ago.

Because now he understood.

Understood that she was sick, what her

condition meant, and knew that there was nothing either of them could do about it.

He stood and touched Jess on the shoulder as he looked at Sarah and Lia. "Hey...um...could we get a minute?"

"Of course," Jess said, gathering her sweater and purse from the chair. "We won't be far," she said, kissing Whitney's cheek. Sarah approached and gave her a gentle hug.

Gentle. As though she might break.

Lia squeezed her hand. "You'll be back to the office in no time, so just chill," her friend said, and the fact that the other woman knew her so well caused another lump to form in the back of her throat.

Wes and Mitch sent her sympathetic, supportive looks as they ushered their partners out of the hospital room.

They all knew. Tears welled in her eyes. Why not cry? They all knew how weak she was now anyway. No more pretending.

When the door closed behind her friends, she stared at it, terrified to look at Trent. His sadness was breaking her the most.

He cleared his throat and shoved his hands deep into his pockets as he moved closer to the bed. "You broke an ankle and an arm in the fall, lots of bruising, and you have a concussion," he said.

She couldn't feel her injuries. A small silver lining. "I guess I was lucky." She couldn't remember anything after her vision had blurred at the top of the stairs and the dizzy spell had taken complete hold.

The stairs! She'd been on her way to get the baby. Her gut twisted. Thank God it had happened before she'd reached the baby's room. What if she'd been holding Henry when it had happened? More tears burned her eyes at the thought that she could have hurt the beautiful child. Not to mention the fact that she'd probably ruined Marissa's birthday party. So much for getting off to a good start as Auntie Whitney.

"I was listed as next of kin," Trent said.

"Yeah, right. Um, I guess I'll have to change that right away." Unfortunately, it meant that the doctors would have filled him in on everything. By now, she knew Mitch had also told her friends about her secret illness. She wasn't upset. They all needed to know. They all should have known a long time ago. Keeping it to herself had been wrong.

"It's fine," he said, but despite his presence in the room, she already felt him pulling back. The thick tension in the air around them was suffocating. She'd ended things. They were no longer together. He didn't need to be there, and she wasn't sure if she wanted him to be, because what was the point? They were no longer planning a future together, which was harder to fully accept than anything she was going to be facing now.

Who would be there for her now?

She swallowed the lump in her throat and straightened her spine against the too-soft bed. She'd get through this on her own. Her inherent stubborn streak was the only thing she could rely on in that moment to prevent her from crumbling, so she clung to it.

"Why didn't you tell me?" Trent asked quietly.

"Because there was nothing you could do. Why didn't you tell me you had a son?"

The words hit their mark, and his expression changed to one of conflicted remorse.

"I only just found out. But you've known about this illness for…how long, Whitney?" The deep hurt in his voice made tears gather in her eyes. He sat in the chair next to the bed and lowered his head in his hands. His shoulders shook, and she looked away toward the window. Watching him break down was too much. Her already shattered heart couldn't take it.

"I'd like to be alone," she said, forcing as much strength into her voice as she could muster. It wasn't much, but obviously it was enough as he stood up and wiped his eyes with the back of his hand.

Instead of leaving, he came closer, looking unsure, hesitant, uncomfortable…

So different than the man who'd claimed to love her, who swore he'd always be there for her, who'd told her there was nothing they couldn't overcome together.

He must have realized now that he'd been wrong.

"Whit…I…I want to be strong about this. I want to be here. There's so much going on right now. Both our lives are so damn complicated."

She heard the uncertainty in his voice. He knew the truth now. He knew she was broken, that she couldn't give him what he wanted most. A family. But she knew the truth now, too—that he already had one. He truly didn't need her anymore.

"It's okay, Trent." Forcing her voice steady, she summoned every last inch of the strong person she once was. "You can go." No matter how much she longed to beg him to stay, she wouldn't. "And please don't come back."

He hesitated but slowly nodded as he turned and left the hospital room.

CHAPTER TWENTY-FIVE

Now...

The next day, Whitney felt a little better. Induced sleep and an IV to keep her fluids up were the reasons for it. As well as her best friends, who had been by her side for hours. Telling them to go home was futile, so Whitney had stopped resisting their support. Lia had gone out for a food run, but she, too, had prolonged her stay in Blue Moon Bay to be there for Whitney.

Her doctor entered the room, and Jess looked up from the magazine where she was forcing Whitney to take a quiz called "Which pop star would my BFF be?" It was her friend's attempt to keep the mood light and Whitney's mind off the test results she would be getting that day, but now her friend put the magazine down, and a serious expression crossed her face.

"Do you want us to wait out in the hall?" Sarah asked him.

Dr. Forester shook his head. "No. I think it's best if you two were with her right now."

She swallowed the nerves in her throat. Obviously, the doctor didn't have good news.

Sarah and Jess sat on the edge of the bed, and Whitney shuffled over slightly to make room. "It's going to be okay," Sarah whispered.

"Is it?"

"I don't know," she said, "but you won't be alone."

Whitney nodded, eternally grateful for their support.

They all listened, not fully understanding as the doctor explained the results. "Without treatment, the symptoms of the sickle cell anemia will get worse over time. This collapse was your body's way of telling you that you can't keep ignoring your health, Whitney."

This lecture was long overdue, and all she could do was listen. Listen and really hear it this time. No more putting things off.

"So what kind of treatment do I need?" Whitney asked.

Dr. Forester sighed. "I'm afraid the test results weren't as positive as we hoped." He paused. "You are going to need a bone marrow transplant. Currently, your bone marrow is producing blood cells with defective hemoglobin, but if we replace your cells with healthy ones from a donor, you'll hopefully be able to produce healthy hemoglobin again."

Jess reached out to touch her hand at the same time Sarah did, and Whitney's gaze fell on the three hands connected.

Best friends. They'd always been there for one another, and despite Whitney's exterior toughness and insisting that she didn't need them—she desperately did now. She was terrified, and she didn't even try to hide it.

"The process requires us to kill your existing bone marrow and replace it with a donor's," the doctor continued. "Then we monitor your recovery for a month or so to make sure your body doesn't reject it or there isn't an infection."

"What does that mean? What do we do first?" Whitney's voice held only confidence when she spoke, but her grip on her friends' hands tightened.

"We'll need to find a donor. I know in your case, because you were adopted, it rules out family members, who would normally be our first line of candidates for a match. Friends are next," he said, looking at Sarah and Jess.

They both nodded.

"Absolutely," Jess said. "How do we find out?" She was ready to go.

Support by being by her side was one thing, but this was too much. "Jess… Sarah, no. I can't ask you—"

"Shhhh…you're not asking. We're doing it because we want to," Sarah said. "I'm in as well," she told the doctor.

"The likelihood that either of you will be a match is slim, I won't lie, but at least we have a start. I also have an intern searching through an online donor bank registry to see if there's anyone local or nearby."

"Count me in, too," Lia said as she entered with the bags of food. She turned to Dr. Forester. "I'm Lia Jameson. I'm already registered on the match database. I was a donor before; maybe we'll get lucky with me this time."

Lia had donated bone marrow before? Then realization dawned. For Kelli, when she was going through her cancer treatment.

But Whitney still shook her head. "Lia, I appreciate the offer…"

"Whitney, will you just stop?"

Mouths dropped in the room at Jess's out-of-character outburst.

"Seriously. Quit acting like you're Superwoman. We don't need a superhero in Blue Moon Bay. We need *you*. Our best friend." Her voice broke, and tears threatened in Whitney's eyes. "I need you. So stop being so freaking stubborn and accept our help. *Lia's* help if that works out," Jess said, her voice softening.

Whitney nodded quickly. "Okay. Yes, I'm sorry. Lia, I really do appreciate this. From all of you." She relaxed back against the bed and closed her eyes. "Thank you all for being here."

Sarah and Jess hugged her, and Lia's smile was wide as she wrapped her arms around the outside of the group hug, squeezing tight.

"We are going to get through this," Jess said. "Together—the four of us."

Whitney didn't know how she'd ever gotten so lucky to have three of the most amazing friends, but she knew she'd never make it through this without them.

CHAPTER TWENTY-SIX

Now...

Concentrating on anything else while Whitney was lying in a hospital bed across town was impossible. He couldn't sleep. He couldn't eat. Working used to provide a distraction, but being at the bar only made him feel guilty and stressed that he wasn't by her side at the hospital.

But she didn't want him there. She'd pushed him away. He had no idea where things stood between them, and now their relationship was the least of his worries. She was sick and needed a bone marrow transplant. He'd gotten tested along with all the others, but unfortunately, he hadn't matched.

Feeling helpless was the hardest damn thing.

"Hey, man. Why don't you go home and get some sleep?" Max said, coming up behind him.

Home.

The only home he had was the one he'd shared with Whitney. One he was pretty sure wasn't his home anymore. He'd been staying at the bar, showering at the sports facility after workouts, and hadn't even started to look for a new place yet. A part of him had been holding out hope of the two of them getting through this, reconciling, and getting back together. He hadn't truly believed that it was over.

But her not wanting him to be there for her

during the hardest part of her life made things that much more real. She really didn't want a future with him, and he knew she was pushing him away, had ended things because of her illness, but he wasn't sure what he could do to try to change her mind.

He should have tried harder at the hospital to force her to let him be there, but seeing her so tired and sick, asking him to leave, he hadn't been able to add to her pain.

He shook his head. "That won't help." Staying busy at least allowed him to stop focusing solely on the what-ifs plaguing him.

What if they didn't find a match? What if she didn't get better? He'd lost her a week ago. But what if he *really* lost her?

He couldn't even think about that.

"You know, I think I will head out," he said, grabbing his jacket from the hook and tossing the bar keys to Max. "Lock up?"

"You got it," Max said. "Take care, man."

Outside, he climbed into his Jeep and drove across town to his family home. It was the only place he'd find any comfort right now. His mom knew everything, and therefore she was the only person he could truly talk to. Or sit in conflicted silence with.

Going inside, he found his mom in the kitchen. Plastic Tupperware containers filled the counter space, and several pots were simmering on the stove. The smell of roast and pasta and stew all mixing together. This was what she did when she was worried: She cooked. And by the looks of the recipes, she was as worried as he was.

"Hey, Mom," he said, slumping onto a stool at the counter. His shoulders sagged, and every muscle in his body ached with tension.

"How is she?" Frankie asked, turning to face him as she stirred a pot.

"Same. They're still waiting to find a match."

"I got tested the other day," she said. "I wanted to go see her while I was there, but I wasn't sure…" Her voice trailed, sounding sad.

He nodded his understanding. This couldn't be easy on his mom, who loved Whitney like a daughter. They were all navigating this with confusion and sadness and no freaking idea how to proceed. What was the right protocol to follow in an emergency situation after a breakup?

"Jess is keeping me posted," he said. "Whitney doesn't want me there." He ran a hand through his hair, then rested his elbows on the counter, clenching his shaky hands together.

His mother sent him a sympathetic look. "This has to be torture on you. I don't know what to do with myself when I'm not at the shop." She gestured to the cooking.

"It's the hardest thing I've ever had to survive. I don't know what to do. I want to barge into that hospital room and insist to be there next to her through this whole thing, but I know that will only make things worse. I want to respect her wishes, but it's so damn hard." Whitney was strong and independent, and he knew she'd never lean on him right now.

"You look exhausted," his mother said. "Why

don't you go lie down in the living room, and I'll bring you something to eat."

Trent wasn't sure he'd be able to sleep, and he certainly didn't have an appetite, but he nodded and headed into the living room.

When he did finally doze off, his dreams were all about Whitney.

· · ·

As promised, Lia, Sarah, and Jess hadn't left her side in two days. Normally, having them there, feeling vulnerable and needy, would have irritated her, but this time, Whitney was truly terrified, and she appreciated the love and support surrounding her.

Everyone she knew in town had gotten tested over the last few days. Even Trent, which made her even more conflicted. She missed him so much, craved the sight of him, the sound of his voice, his reassuring embrace... It physically hurt to think about him, so she tried to push him to the back of her mind as much as possible. Right now, she needed to focus on her health and use her strength to try to get through the next few weeks.

All she could do was hope. Which made her feel bad. If one of her friends was a match, they'd be going in for the procedure of the bone marrow transfer. She'd heard the process was much harder on the donor than it was for the recipient. The idea of putting any of them through that upset her, but she didn't have a choice. Her own research into the state of her condition had revealed that without the transfer, she would only continue to get sicker, and eventually she would die.

She scanned the hospital room now. Jess slept in a chair, Sarah was curled in a ball at the foot of her bed, and Lia was sitting on the window ledge, her gaze somewhere out the window. She glanced her way, and seeing her awake, Lia got up and approached. "Hey, need anything?"

Whitney shook her head. "You three being here is more than enough."

Lia gave a small smile. "There's nowhere else I'd rather be...except maybe on a girls' trip to Maui."

Whitney laughed, grateful that Lia was there. The other two were great sources of support, but Lia helped to keep the atmosphere light, despite the fact that she knew Lia was just as worried as everyone else.

"I promise, if I make it out of this bed, a girls' trip to Maui is on the immediate agenda." She meant it. No more prioritizing work above all else. No more skipped holidays and vacations for the sake of her career. Yes, she needed to be financially stable, but there was more to life. She deeply regretted that it had taken this to make her realize it. If she thought of all the things she'd missed out on and could potentially miss in the future, it was hard to breathe. She'd just focus on how she would approach things moving forward.

"*When* you get out of this bed. Not if," Lia said. "We're going to figure this out." She sounded determined despite a hint of lack of confidence.

This had to be tough on Lia for other reasons, too. Whitney knew Lia had been a huge source of support for Wes's first wife, Kelli, when she was sick with cancer. Lia had spent a lot of time in Blue Moon Bay back then at Kelli's bedside. She hadn't been a bone marrow match for Kelli, and Whitney knew Lia was really hoping she could be a match this time.

The doctor entered the room a few minutes later, and Lia woke the others. "Do you want us to leave?" she asked Whitney.

Whitney shook her head. "Please stay." She never knew what kind of news to expect from Dr. Forester, and either way, she could use the support. The four of them stared at the doctor expectantly.

Dr. Forester smiled. "So…I have some good news."
Oh, thank God!

Whitney's heart soared, and she swallowed hard. "We have a match?" she said, barely more than a whisper.

Dr. Forester nodded and then turned to Lia. "Ready to do this?"

Tears rimmed Lia's eyes. Her knees seemed to give way slightly in relief and she sat on the edge of the bed. She smiled and squeezed Whitney's hand. "Let's do it."

In matching hospital gowns hours later, Lia and Whitney held hands as they were prepped for the procedure. IVs were injected, and they were briefed on the process.

"You sure?" Whitney asked Lia. This was such a big sacrifice her friend was making, and as much as she knew she needed this, it felt like such a big ask.

"There was never any question. I got you," Lia said.

And for the first time in a long time, Whitney let go of the need to be in control, and she let her friend try to save her life.

• • •

The love of his life was getting a bone marrow transplant.

In the hospital cafeteria, Trent wrapped shaky hands around a coffee cup, the contents long ago having gone cold. He didn't want to add any unnecessary stress to Whitney by going to see her, but he needed to be there in the hospital. Close by. He couldn't do anything. But just being there felt like the smallest thing he could do. He couldn't think about or focus on anything else. All he could do was sit and wait and pray.

He ran a hand through his hair and checked his watch. Jess had texted to say Lia and Whitney had been prepped right away and were going in for the transfer an hour ago. He wasn't sure how long it would take, but he'd stay there all day. And all night.

"Hi." Jess's voice next to him made him glance up. "Thought you'd be here."

"I didn't want to come up…"

She nodded her understanding as she sat. "She's going to be okay, and then the two of you can work this out."

He swallowed hard. He desperately wanted to try to work things out, but did Whitney? Would this result in her wanting to try again or would it only solidify her claims that they weren't right together?

He knew she worried about not being able to give him the family he wanted. Would he be able to convince her that it didn't matter? Would she give him that chance?

He should be the one next to her during all of this, but he also knew he needed to give her the space she'd asked for even when it left him with a huge hole in his chest.

"I'm glad she's allowed you and Sarah and Lia to be here for her," he said, squeezing his cousin's hand. That was a huge step toward progress for Whitney. It also told him just how terrified she must be, and that made his chest ache even more.

"We're all here for you. We're rooting for you both," Jess said gently.

He nodded, not trusting his voice to speak.

They sat in silence for a while, both lost in their own thoughts, drawing comfort from each other as they waited.

He had almost summoned the nerve to tell his cousin about Eddie when Jess's cell chimed with a new text message. She reached for it quickly and read. Her face held a look of relief as she glanced up at him. "It's Sarah. They're out. The transfer went great."

He released a sigh of relief. "What now?"

"More waiting and hoping for the best."

Seemed these days, that's all he could do.

CHAPTER TWENTY-SEVEN

Two Weeks Later...

Waiting for Dr. Forester was excruciating. Whitney checked the clock on the wall again as she paced the hospital room.

"Your pacing is driving me crazy," Lia said through the laptop Zoom connection. She'd gone back to New York a few days before, unable to take any more leave from work, but she'd insisted they connect her in for this appointment.

"I know. I'm sorry," Whitney said. "I just can't sit still. What's taking him so long?" Her body had accepted the bone marrow transplant, and the day before, Dr. Forester had sent her for more tests to see if the new hemoglobin was producing healthy blood cells. Keeping her emotions intact was a challenge, and she refused to get her hopes too high yet, but she was feeling better.

Better than she had in more than a year. Her eyesight wasn't perfect, and the damage done was irreversible, meaning she'd be wearing glasses from now on to correct her vision, but her body aches had disappeared, the headaches were a rare occurrence, and the swelling in her joints had gone down. She'd gained weight, and the dark circles under her eyes had disappeared. She looked and felt like a new person. She'd been sick and struggling for so long, she'd forgotten what healthy felt like.

Granted, she was under less stress not being at work and having everyone dote on her hand and foot the last two weeks. That had to be having an impact as well. She'd almost gotten used to being taken care of.

Almost.

"I'm sure he will be here soon. But seriously, Lia's right—the pacing is annoying," Sarah said, flipping through a magazine so fast, there was no way she was seeing anything on the pages.

Whitney reluctantly sat. The pacing was making her dizzy.

"Here he comes," Jess said from her perch in the doorway where she'd been waiting. She hurried into the room and sat on the edge of the bed. "Everyone, look casual."

Whitney laughed. God, it was good to have them there with her. If the news was good, they'd celebrate it together. And if it was bad…they'd get through that, too.

"Hello, hello," Dr. Forester said, closing the door behind him.

Good mood…good sign? Closed door…bad news?

"Hi, Dr. Forester," Whitney said. "I brought in moral support."

"Perfect. I'm glad everyone's here. Good to see you, Lia. How are you feeling?" he asked, peering through the computer screen.

"Feeling great." Lia waved a hand as though to say, *Get on with it.* "Give it to us straight—did the transplant work?"

Whitney could hear the nervousness in the

other woman's voice. They all wanted positive news that day, but she sensed Lia needed it almost as much as she did. The last few weeks as she'd gotten stronger and healthier, her mindset had also continued to change, and her hopes had risen for a chance to live her life better.

She hadn't heard from or seen Trent. He was respecting her wishes. But she did miss him more and more each day. He'd never been far from her thoughts, and she regretted pushing him away, but she hadn't known what else to do. Her heart and mind had been conflicted and she'd needed to finally prioritize her health above all else, focus on getting better.

Dr. Forester nodded. "Yes, it did."

Relief caused Whitney's shoulders to sag as she fell back against the pillows on the bed.

"Thank God," Jess said.

Sarah reached into her oversize purse and produced a bottle of champagne. "Too soon?" she asked as the doctor shot her a look. "We'll wait until you leave," she said, tucking it away again.

Whitney laughed. Her friends were the perfect brand of ridiculousness when she needed it most. She took a deep breath. It wasn't over yet. Nothing was ever that simple. "Okay, so what does it mean? Will I still need medication? A future transplant?" Her body was producing healthy blood cells now, but for how long? She was afraid to get too optimistic.

"You'll need your anti-rejection drugs a little longer, and I want you in my office every three months for routine bloodwork." He pointed to Jess,

Sarah, and Lia. "You three will remind her?"

"Yes, sir," Jess said.

Sarah saluted her agreement.

"Scheduling it into my Outlook right now," Lia said.

In the past, having babysitters would have irritated Whitney, but she was so fortunate to have this new chance at life that she didn't mind.

"But as long as you reduce your stress level and don't ignore any symptoms, there's no reason to think you'll require another transplant."

"So I'm cured?" Was that possible? She'd read about children being able to have the disease cured from a transplant, but the research on adults was still inconclusive. They were still researching alternative methods. Though she knew how rare bone marrow transplants in adults were, so maybe she'd really just been extremely fortunate.

She wouldn't forget that or take it for granted.

"Not exactly cured, but better," her doctor said. "And if your body continues to produce healthy cells...who knows?" He smiled.

"But I'll have to reduce my stress at my job."

"As I said, you'll need to take some time off...or consider a new position."

Darn, she'd been hoping he'd changed his mind. But that was okay. She'd figure it out. Time off wasn't the worst thing in the world.

"The pace you were keeping before was no doubt what triggered the symptoms to start appearing in the first place."

She swallowed hard. It would be tough walking away from a career she loved. But she'd made a promise to herself to do whatever was necessary to live a long and full life.

"Consider yourself hired as my marketing manager of events at the B&B until you decide what to do career-wise," Sarah said, producing the champagne bottle again.

Whitney smiled her appreciation.

The doctor shook his head. "Fine. Go ahead. But don't tell anyone I said it was okay," he said. Then, touching Whitney's shoulder, he smiled. "You're going to be okay."

"Thank you, Dr. Forester." She paused. "Um… what about children? If my cells continue to be healthy…" She had to know. It was the part of having this disease that crushed her the most. If her health continued to be okay, if her body continued producing healthy cells, could she potentially have kids someday?

"Anything's possible. Let's take it day by day, okay?"

It wasn't a yes, but it wasn't a no, either, and her heart filled with the tiniest bit of hope. She smiled through tears as she nodded. "Okay."

"Bye, ladies," the doctor said, leaving the room.

The second the door closed behind him, Sarah popped the cork on the champagne bottle.

"I've got mine, too," Lia said, holding up a tiny bottle to the computer camera.

"To friendship," Jess said as Sarah handed them plastic hospital glasses filled with the bubbly liquid.

To second chances. To hope.

"To friendship," Whitney whispered.

• • •

"Next round's on the house!" Trent yelled across the crowded bar that evening as he received the text from Jess that said Whitney's appointment had gone well.

Angel sent him a surprised look. "Trying to go out of business? The place is packed."

"Whitney's transfer went well. Doctor says she's going to be okay," he said, his hand trembling on a whiskey bottle as he poured three shots and waved his bar manager and bouncer toward the bar. Despite everything they had going on between them, they'd put it all aside and had been a source of comfort for him the last two weeks. He hadn't seen or talked to Whitney while she was recovering, as per her wishes. But he'd thought of her every second of every day for the last two weeks, and he hoped there would be an opportunity to talk to her…reconnect…tell her everything… He was afraid of getting his hopes up for a chance at a future together, but he couldn't help it.

Now that she was better, maybe she'd have a change of heart? If she could deal with the new situation he found himself in.

"To Whitney," he said, raising his shot glass high into the air.

Max and Angel looked as happy and relieved as he was as they all clinked glasses and tossed the alcohol back.

He reread the text from Jess several times. Whitney was going to be okay. It meant some life changes, but at least she was going to get better.

Now, he just had to hope he could be a part of the new life changes. And that the love of his life could accept his.

• • •

"Knock, knock, can I come in?"

Whitney zipped her bag as Scott entered the hospital room. "Hi," she said, surprised to see him there. She hadn't spoken to him since her accident, but Mayor Rodale had sent flowers from the office, wishing her a speedy recovery.

She had no idea where her career stood in light of everything, but her main focus right now was getting better. She was leaving the hospital that day with renewed hope and a different outlook on life.

Scott extended a small potted cactus toward her. "For you."

"This is…different." Cards, flowers, chocolates were customary — what was the significance of a thorny plant?

"You're a workaholic, I assumed anything other than a cactus would require too much attention and would probably die."

She laughed harder than she had in weeks, not even caring about the mild pain it caused to her still-healing ribs. She was feeling better, and each day she found new strength and a reason to find happiness. Today it was the cactus. "I think you're holding out too much hope for the cactus," she said, but unfortunately, she knew her eighteen-hour workdays had come to an end. She couldn't keep up the pace anymore. Not at the risk of her health.

And if that meant Mayor Rodale let her go when she put in the request for an additional month's leave, then she'd have to learn to be okay with that. She'd land on her feet. She always did.

Scott shoved his hands into his pockets and rocked back and forth on his heels. He looked nervous when he spoke. "So, I'm not going to be your assistant anymore," he said.

Her heart rose into her throat. She'd expected this. She'd overheard the conversation between them at the office, and she'd been away from work for a month; it was to be expected that Scott would move into her job. But she'd assumed they'd wait until she was at least out of the hospital before firing her. She cleared her throat. "Because you're taking my job. Mayor Rodale sent you here to let me go."

He frowned. "What? No. Shit, Whitney—you think I'd fire you while you're barely out of a hospital bed?"

Her cheeks flamed. "But you are planning to?" Weren't they? "I mean, that's what you meant about not being my assistant anymore. Right?"

He shook his head. "I'm planning to run for mayor."

Her jaw dropped. Ahhh, that's what they had been talking about. Changes…replacement. Not for Whitney. For Mayor Rodale.

"Oh my God. That's such a relief," she said, sagging back toward the pile of pillows. Embarrassed by her wrong assumptions but definitely relieved.

"You really thought I was after your job?"

"Yes!"

He laughed. "That's why you were being 'mean boss' all the time? I thought you just didn't like me."

More embarrassment crept up her neck. "Sorry about that. You just impressed me…and intimidated me," she said, the truth hard to admit.

"Well, ditto."

His smile was kind and sincere, and she felt like a fool for thinking the worst. She touched the tiny spikes on the cactus and slowly glanced up at him. "So…you'll be my boss now."

He nodded. "Yep. If I win, which should be fairly easy since no one else is running so far."

She slapped his arm. "You don't have to gloat."

"Sure I do. Payback will be fun," he said with a wink.

"Just so you know, I'm going to need more time off to recover. And when I do come back, I won't be able to keep up the frantic pace and schedule."

Scott waved a hand. "I'd take you at fifty percent over someone else at a hundred and ten any day."

A warmness filled her with a sense of gratitude. "Thanks, Scott."

"Get better, okay? And take care of that cactus," he said with a wave as he left the room.

Whitney released a deep breath when she was once again alone. Her job was secure if and when she could return to it. All her worry and apprehension over it had been for nothing.

Grabbing her coat and personal belongings, she left the hospital room, ready to take on this new chapter of her life. Forever grateful that there was one.

CHAPTER TWENTY-EIGHT

Now...

Trent paced the living room of his family home, where his entire family was gathered for dinner. The kids played ball in the yard, but he felt too nauseous to join in the fun. Conversations and laughter drifted from the kitchen, but he couldn't bring himself to participate when his mind was preoccupied.

Angel had told Eddie the truth the day before when he'd come back from L.A., and she was supposed to text to let him know whether they were coming to dinner with his family that evening or not. They thought it might be the next logical step. Let Eddie meet everyone. Let everyone meet Eddie...his son. Trent still couldn't quite get the news to settle. He was happy about it but sad about the lost time. Lost opportunity.

Apparently, the teen had taken the news okay. He'd always known that Brad wasn't his biological father, so it hadn't been a huge shock. But Angel had said that he'd voiced his disappointment at her not telling him sooner. Especially since they moved here and he'd gotten to know Trent under somewhat false pretenses.

Trent shared that sentiment with the kid, so maybe that was one thing they could connect on. That and their passion and skill for football. It wasn't a lot, but at least it was a starting point. He wasn't sure what he expected from the relationship, but he was keeping the bar low and being open to Eddie's pace, Eddie's boundaries. He'd follow the kid's lead. With Angel's help, maybe they could form a deeper connection in time.

He wanted that.

His sister Kara approached and wrapped an arm around his waist as he stared outside the window, hoping to see her car approaching. "Either way, things will be okay," she said.

He squeezed her tight, appreciating the strength from his tiny baby sister. "Thank you for being here." She was taking the weekend away from school to be here, and that meant a lot. This was important to all of them.

"Look, the kid is family now. So is Angel. We'll figure it out. Families come in all shapes and sizes, right?" she said.

The words registered with him more than she could possibly know.

"Speaking of family, have you spoken to Whitney?" Kara asked, sounding pained. He knew his sister was missing Whitney almost as much as he was. She'd texted him nonstop while Whitney was recovering, and he knew she'd been hoping to see her here today.

That would have been far too much to expect. He needed to sort these things out separately first, then maybe someday find a way to merge the important aspects of his life together. He was holding on to faith that he could.

"Not yet. I'm respecting her wishes for space."

"I respect that. But remember that sometimes there's such a thing as too much space."

He nodded, considering her words. He knew she was right. He needed to make his next move soon or risk letting too much time come between them. One more play to get her back into his life...then, if she still rejected him, he'd find a way to move on.

His phone chimed, and he jumped. His mother entered the room, a hopeful expression on her face. "Read it," she said when he stood there slightly frozen.

He took a deep breath and, with a shaky hand, opened the text from Angel:

Sorry, Trent, he says it's too soon.

His heart fell as he shook his head and showed Kara the text.

"Well, maybe it is. Finding out about you was one thing. Meeting the entire family is another. Give him time," Kara said supportively.

Then dots that Angel was typing....

But he said he will be at football practice tonight.

He released a sigh of relief. That was something, at least. "He's still coming to football," he told them.

Baby steps, he texted back.

Baby steps, she agreed.

Trent tucked the phone into his pocket and, feeling slightly more hopeful than he had in weeks, he joined his family in the kitchen for dinner.

• • •

In her office the next day, before anyone else had arrived, Whitney packed up her personal items.

During her leave, Scott was going to hire a temporary assistant to take over and keep things running until she was ready to come back. She picked up the picture of her and Trent at the pumpkin patch the night they'd met and hesitated. What did she do with it? The memory of that day still hurt, and despite the weeks that had passed since she last saw him, her heart still hadn't started to heal.

Would it ever?

She still loved him as much as she ever did, but he had some life-changing things going on, and as much as she wanted to be there for him, his silence the last few weeks made her think that maybe he didn't want or need her support. She'd asked for space and he'd given it...but now she realized maybe that had been a mistake.

In the time and distance, had he started to move on?

She sighed, placing the photo inside the banker's box. Then picking it up, she glanced around the office a final time. "Bye for now," she whispered as she headed out.

Outside in the crisp late-November air, she put the box in the trunk of her car and climbed in. She pulled out of the lot and headed toward Rejuvenation. She was looking forward to seeing her mother, and the nurses had said the new medication and the full-time nurse had really made a big difference. The knowledge warmed Whitney's heart, but she was still conflicted, knowing she had to find a way to repay Trent.

Damn, she missed him so much.

Driving past the tavern on Main Street, it took all her strength not to stop and see him. Jess had told her that Trent had been at the hospital the day of the transplant procedure and that he had requested daily updates about her healing progress. The idea that he was still concerned, still there, gave her a hope she wasn't sure she was allowed to have. A hope she wasn't quite sure what to do with. They'd eventually talk…but what would be the ultimate outcome?

She still loved him, and she would always love him. For her, there was no one else but him…but was that enough?

She pulled into the parking lot at Rejuvenation twenty minutes later and wiped tears from her eyes that she hadn't even realized she was crying.

She was okay. She *would* be okay.

But as she climbed out of the car and saw Trent walking toward her, her legs felt a little unsteady beneath her. "Hey…" he said.

Dressed in a pair of tan pants and a white collared shirt unbuttoned at the top, he was too gorgeous for her broken heart.

Why was he there now? Had he continued to visit her mom?

The thought killed her.

"I know you're upset with me," he said.

She shook her head. "I'm the one in the wrong. All of this was my fault…"

He took a step forward. "I heard everything you said about us, and I understand why you broke things off. I even understand why you pushed me away these last few weeks." He paused and stared straight into her eyes. "But if you even feel the littlest bit of love for me still, somewhere deep down, please just trust me one more time."

What was he talking about?

Littlest bit of love? She had so much love for him—that's why she'd let him go.

"Please, Whitney. I just want to ask you something."

Her cell phone rang, and she sighed. Of all the bad timing. She ignored it. "Go ahead. Ask your question." Her heart raced, and it was so damn hard not to wrap her arms around him and sink into him. Not seeing him had made things easier, but now, face-to-face...moving on without him would be impossible.

"I think you should get that," Trent said as the phone continued to ring.

"Why?"

"It might be important."

There was something suspicious in his tone, as though he knew who was calling. "What's going on?" She glanced at the caller ID and, seeing her mother's number from inside the senior facility, she answered. "Mom? Everything okay? I'm just in the parking lot. I'll be right in." Her mother's new medication was working so much better, and the time they had together was more frequent than it had been before. Dr. Tyler said it might not last as her body got used to the new drug, but for now, they'd take it. Anything to prolong their time together.

"I know. I can see you from my window," Lydia said.

Whitney glanced toward the building and saw her mom wave. She waved back, then returned her attention to Trent.

What were the two of them up to?

"Sweet girl, I'm not sure how much time I have, so I'm pulling the mom rank while I can. Whatever Trent asks you to do—do it," she said.

Whitney's mouth gaped. "How do you...?" She stared at Trent, her heart racing.

Dial tone. Her mom had hung up on her.

"What's going on?"

Reaching into his pocket, Trent took out two plane tickets and a folded set of papers. He handed her the tickets first. "I've booked us a trip."

"A trip?" She glanced at the destination. "Cambodia?" She couldn't go away with him. They'd broken up. They hadn't spoken or spent time together in weeks. Not that she hadn't been desperate to...

She glanced toward her mom's window and saw her holding a sign. SAY YES, it read. "What's in Cambodia?" she asked carefully.

"This," he said, handing her the papers next.

Whitney read the pamphlet for an orphanage in Cambodia, her eyes widening. "This is an adoption application form."

Trent nodded, a look of hopeful apprehension on his gorgeous face. "I've already started the process. With or without you, I'm adopting a child...but I hope like crazy, it will be *with* you."

Her mouth gaped and her eyes teared. Trent was adopting a child? From Cambodia? When had he decided this? How had he made this decision? He just discovered he had a teenager…

"I want this more than I've ever wanted anything. I've researched everything and spent weeks soul searching and making sure this was the right choice—and it is. It makes perfect sense, and I want you with me the way we always planned."

Could she really do that? Could they really do this together? All of this was so sudden and unexpected, yet her gut was telling her that wasn't necessarily a bad thing. Still, she was unsure… "My health is okay now, but there's no guarantee."

"That's why I don't want to wait any longer. On the plane that leaves tomorrow morning is our future together. If you still want it. Want *me*. Otherwise, I'll leave you here with your family and friends, and in time I'll have no other choice than to learn to let you go," Trent said passionately. "But that's not what I want. I want you, Whitney," He slowly, tentatively reached out to touch her trembling hand.

She stared at the plane tickets and the picture of the two-year-old little boy who Trent planned on adopting. It was all so much. But staring at the little boy, feeling Trent's hand on hers, was the first thing to feel truly right in so long.

"Look, I know your world has been shattered and your future feels like a mystery, but what matters is right now and whether you love me enough to trust me and take this leap of faith with me," Trent said.

"Your life has been upended lately, too." What about Eddie? And Angel?

He nodded. "Exactly! That's why I can say with

confidence that life changes—whether you want it to or not. Nothing stays the same, and that's okay. It's how we navigate those ups and downs that matters."

A tear slid down her cheek, and he reached out, wiping it away. "I...uh, I'm not even sure if I'm allowed to fly," she said. Was she really doing this?

All she wanted was to be together with him. Whatever that looked like, sick or healthy, married or not, as parents... She glanced at the picture again and then back at him. It was so hard to believe he was doing this. That *she* was considering doing this.

But maybe the best things weren't planned. Maybe there really was no way to plan for life.

"Is that a yes? You'll come to Cambodia with me? Give us another chance?" Trent asked, looking so hopeful and happy, those damn dimples melting any resolve she tried to have. There was no way she could say no. She didn't want to say no.

She released a deep breath. "Yes...if Dr. Forester says it's okay for me to travel."

He pulled her into his arms and kissed her. "He already did."

"What do you mean?"

"I already cleared it with him before I bought the tickets." He grinned. "By the way, you still have me listed as next of kin."

She smiled through her tears, but his grin faded slightly. "The only thing I regret was not being there for you these last few weeks, and I can't beg your forgiveness enough."

She shook her head. "I needed the space. I wouldn't have let you be there. But don't worry— I'm sure there will be other bad times you get to help me through."

He cupped her face and stared deep into her eyes. "No, sweetheart, all the bad is behind us. There's only good in our future together. I promise you."

She knew life didn't work that way. They'd have their share of troubles along the way, but they'd navigate those waters and bumpy roads together.

"I love you, Whitney," he said, holding her close.

She smiled at her mom, still standing in the window as she hugged Trent tight. She'd missed him so much. Being in his arms made her feel more alive than she had in months. This was where she belonged, and she wasn't ever letting this love go again. "I love you, too," she whispered.

The sound of a horn honking made them turn around.

"What are Sarah and Jess doing here?" she asked, laughing through tears of happiness.

"I wasn't sure I could convince you on my own...with your mom's help, so I called in rein-forcements," Trent said, giving a thumbs-up sign to her two best friends as they walked toward them. "They are your best friends, after all."

"Yeah, they are." Best friends she was forever grateful to have. The only person missing was Lia, but she, Jess, and Sarah had already planned a girls' trip to New York for the following year to visit her. She owed the other woman so much. She owed them all so much.

Whitney thought her world had been flipped upside down that year, and she was right, but the view from here was something she could get used to.

In fact, this new view of the world was a beautiful one.

EPILOGUE

They must have broken some kind of wedding planning record to pull off the day ahead.

As Whitney stood in front of the surfboard-shaped full-length mirror in a room at Dove's Nest B&B, she couldn't believe the reflection staring back at her. And it wasn't the beautiful, antique white, simple, elegant wedding dress or the magnificent pearl jewelry that took her breath away but the look of radiant happiness on her face.

For so long she'd been stressed and tired and unsure and hopeless... So much had changed in two months.

She was feeling better and stronger every day since the bone marrow transplant from Lia. Her doctor's appointments revealed she was healing in the best way. The trip to Cambodia with Trent had been life changing. They'd started the process to adopt a little boy named Kenyo, and Whitney's heart was full just thinking about the possibility of bringing the perfect little boy back to Blue Moon Bay someday real soon. The two weeks away had brought them closer than they'd ever been. Starting a new life together was what they both truly wanted, and this time they were both going in with eyes wide open. No more secrets. Complete trust and honesty.

She loved Trent, and she was finally allowing herself to be loved, with all her flaws, all her past mistakes, all the affection she deserved.

She smiled at her reflection as the door opened and Frankie walked in. "Oh my God, you are stunning," she said. Her hands covered her mouth and tears filled her eyes.

"Do not cry or I'll cry, and this makeup took forever," Whitney said with a strangled-sounding laugh.

There'd been enough tears. Now, she just wanted to see happiness all around her.

Frankie approached and picked up Lydia's veil. "May I?" she asked.

"Absolutely," Whitney said. Her mother was downstairs waiting for the ceremony to begin. She wasn't fully aware of the significance of the day, but she was overjoyed to be attending a wedding. Whitney knew deep down, somewhere, her mother was proud and knew what that day was. Just having her there was a blessing.

Frankie carefully placed the veil headpiece on Whitney's hair, loosely piled on top of her head. "Beautiful," she said as she stood back to take her in.

Whitney hugged her tight. "Thank you, Frankie. For everything," she whispered.

"Of course. I love you, and this day will be perfect."

Together they left the room, and her soon-to-be mother-in-law headed back downstairs as Whitney walked down the hall and knocked on two adjacent room doors.

They opened simultaneously, and her two best friends, looking breathtakingly beautiful in their own wedding gowns, stepped out to join her. Overwhelmed, she knew there would be no saving her makeup after all, as fresh tears cascaded down her cheeks.

"Can you believe we're doing this?" Jess said, her voice so full of emotion as she stood between Whitney and Sarah and linked arms with them both.

"There is no other way I could envision this day," Sarah said.

Whitney beamed at her two best friends. "Well? Should we go get married?"

The others nodded, and the three of them headed down the spiraling staircase of the B&B where three of the most handsome, lucky men waited for their brides.

And just like that, happily-ever-after started for three best friends.

ACKNOWLEDGEMENTS

Thank you to my amazing agent, Jill Marsal, for always championing my work, and to my incredible editors, Lydia Sharp and Stacy Abrams, whose edits made this story so much stronger. This book was the most ambitious storyline I've ever attempted, and I appreciate the support and guidance as I navigated this new challenge. Thank you to the art department for a beautiful cover and the marketing team for the promotion efforts. I'm forever grateful to my family for the encouragement and space and time. And a huge thank you to readers for continuing to support me and my stories.

XO Jen

A Lot Like Forever is an emotional and heartwarming small-town romance with a happy ending. However, the story includes elements that might not be suitable for all readers. Characters with Alzheimer's disease and sickle cell anemia appear in the novel, and the realities of living with those conditions are shown in detail. Additionally, a traumatic car accident is depicted on the page. Readers who may be sensitive to these elements, please take note.

AMARA

an imprint of Entangled Publishing LLC.